For John and Barbara

uk you
or your
Support!

much love
xx

BUTTERFLY
IN THE **BLOOD**

Danielle Carter

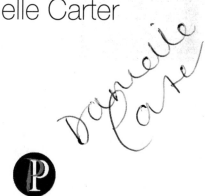

Danielle Carter

Pen Press

First published in Great Britain

All paper used in the printing of this book has been made
from wood grown in managed, sustainable forests.

ISBN13: 978-1-78003-774-5

Printed and bound in the UK
Pen Press is an imprint of
Indepenpress Publishing Limited
25 Eastern Place
Brighton
BN2 1GJ

A catalogue record of this book is available from
the British Library

Cover design by Jacqueline Abromeit

Danielle Carter is 23 years old, and after spending most of her life in Bridport, Dorset, now lives in Bournemouth with her husband and their two pet degus. A freelance writer, published in several local publications, *Butterfly in the Blood* is her first novel. She is a history lover, a comic book nerd and a dedicated tattoo enthusiast. She is currently working on the sequel to *Butterfly in the Blood* as well as her next, as of yet untitled, novel.

Acknowledgements

To my mum and dad for all their strength and belief in me and who I could become.

To my grandparents for filling my childhood with history and make believe, and for encouraging me always.

To Carol Noble and Tracy Willoughby for helping me start this novel, and for helping me see it through to the end.

And lastly, to Matt Swinhoe, as promised, for all the conversations and kicks up the backside when I couldn't do anything but complain.

This is for Sam, for helping me believe I could do this.
Thank you for just being you. I love you.

Those who make peaceful Revolution impossible will make violent Revolution inevitable.

John F. Kennedy

1

August 20th 2075

England

The nubile young woman tugged her dress down, sliding it over her pale skin with the ease that came with experience. There was only a slight tremor in her hands; the faintest hint of nerves. He spied a faint tan line on her wedding finger, where her ring had been removed; abandoned for the evening on her bedside table. He imagined that she would have walked past her husband, both keeping up the pretense that he had no idea where she was sneaking off to, that he wasn't secretly relieved that they would soon have money. It gave him a flutter of pleasure, knowing she had left her family behind to travel here, to him.

She glanced around the office, gawping at the opulent furnishings, the endless wall of books. Her eyes looked out of the expansive window behind him, towards the bridge in the distance. He had chosen this office simply because it had *that* view. He could look out across the city, *his* city; survey his work. It made him feel immortal. Tonight, London looked exceptionally beautiful. The light from the surrounding buildings poured in through the glass, illuminating the young girl. It bathed her in a fluorescent glow, like a spotlight on a prima ballerina.

It reminded him of the first time he had seen his wife, on the stage; back when theatre was something just *anybody* could go to. She had stood before him, the garish lights of the stage swallowing up her delicate beauty. After the show, he had sent her roses. She had not been keen on him, choosing instead to gaze doe-eyed at her leading man. The actor had been taken care of, and after he had bombarded his future wife with gifts, seduced her with diamonds, she had, over time, become his. He tore down her defenses; conquered her.

James Hardwicke leant back against the leather chair, his mind drifting back to the girl that stood before him. She was skinny, with long, wispy blonde hair tucked behind her ears in a childish fashion. She wore too much makeup, but she was pretty, and he liked them to at least be pretty. James smiled to himself before standing to his feet. She was wary of him, uncertain. He stroked her face, admired her smooth skin. She had a flawless complexion, he observed; she reminded him of a china doll, with her sweet little face and fragile body. She didn't move, though he could feel her shoulders tense. She would do nicely, he thought to himself. He tossed a bundle of money at her and chuckled as she scrabbled on the floor, desperately grabbing every note.

"Two hundred, as we agreed. There's no need to count it, I'm a man of my word." She shuddered as his cold eyes swept over her. He checked his watch, and thought of his wife sitting alone in their grand townhouse, in the high-backed chair beside the open fire, waiting for him to come back from his meeting. She knew better than to call him; in the time they'd been married, he'd trained her well. He thought of how she had once been, wild and impulsive; once harbouring delusions of becoming an actress and although he had to admit she had been talented, he had torn her from her daydream and shown her the sort of woman she was born to be. He had watched her, under his tutelage, transform from a boisterous loudmouth, into a discreet, attentive woman - the perfect wife. It was his way, he thought to himself, to take something broken and transform it into something exquisite; like his country.

The hairs on the back of his neck stood on end - there was something about tonight, something that was making him nervous. The rest of the room, with the exception of the circle of light where the girl stood, was shrouded in darkness. Shadows seemed to lurk in the corners, behind the curtains and nestled between the bookcases. He had grown used to this feeling of forever being watched. But tonight, there was something small, something annoying, nagging at him in the darkest depth of his mind. The girl stood in her underwear, shifting from foot to foot. He dragged himself away from his suspicions, from his paranoia. Tonight was his night.

Hardwicke had waited in his office until his colleagues had headed home before calling the whore. This utopia he was working so hard alongside the government to maintain certainly had its benefits. People would do *anything* for money. He laughed out loud and the prostitute leapt to her feet, stuffing the notes into her purse. A picture of a small child fell from it to the floor and she snatched it up, hiding it from him. He stepped towards her and he could see the effort it took her not to move. He shoved her hard to the floor, and she scrambled backwards.

11

"If you want to keep that money, you'll do exactly what I tell you." He tilted her head back and stared into her eyes, those doe-like, damp eyes. He liked to make things beautiful, he thought to himself. He liked to take the mundane or mediocre and watch them grow at his hand. But when something was already too broken to be saved, no matter how beautiful it was, he could not bear it. The girl nibbled at the raspberry flesh of her lips. She was undeniably ravishing but, he reminded himself, just a whore, a slut, who sold her body and threw away her dignity for nothing more than a few pounds. She was no better than any of the others who had wandered into his office, stripping for him with no shame, no hesitation. Hardwicke was loathe to destroy something that was, in his eyes, beautiful; to take these porcelain angels and shatter them. It went against his nature, but he knew, deep down, that they were far beyond saving; that the world for them was forever rotten, corrupt. He would be doing them a kindness, saving them from the world that would strip them down, make them into hollow shells. He had had so many girls before him, of different ages, heights, races, but never had he had such a sweet little thing as this.

He walked around her in a tight circle, his eyes grazing over her delicious body. He returned to her face, gripping it tightly in his hand. She let out a hiss as his wedding ring dug into her cheek. The slut went to speak, her eyes darting around looking anxiously for the exits. He knew she was having second thoughts. They all did, but only when it was too late. He kicked her hard; watching as she rolled over on to her side, groaning. He began to unzip his trousers, feeling his rising excitement.

12

There was one thing Hardwicke enjoyed almost as much as making something wonderful - destroying something ugly, defacing it until it showed no hint of what it had once been. His trousers fell to the floor just as the whore's eyes grew wide and her mouth dropped open. A hand reached out from the darkness, and Hardwicke shook violently as the current from the Taser passed through him.

"Go," Hardwicke's attacker whispered, ordering the woman from the room. She hesitated for a moment, still shaking. The shadowy figure reached into Hardwicke's pocket and removed his money, throwing it at the girl. "You're safe now. Leave, and don't draw attention to yourself."

She nodded and briskly left the room without even a glance at the convulsing Hardwicke.

A foot stamped down onto his throat, pinning him to the floor. His eyes opened painfully, and he gulped as the barrel of a gun was shoved into his face. His attacker held the weapon calm and steady. Their hood was pulled up, and Hardwicke tried to catch a glimpse of their face.

"You should be very careful. Don't you know who I am? Who I work for?" he spluttered, struggling to catch his breath as her foot pressed a little harder on his Adam's apple.

"I know exactly who you are; everyone in the country does." Her teeth showed as she placed a cigarette between her lips.

She was female, he knew that much now.

"What were you planning to do to that woman?"

He shook his head, refusing to cooperate.

She flicked a lighter, bringing it up to her mouth, keeping the gun still in her other hand. "Why play shy now? I know all about how your sick, twisted mind works; I know the things you like to do to women. Women like her, like your wife. How you like to hurt them, listen to them sob and beg you for mercy..." Her foot crushed his windpipe, choking him. "I bet you'd like to hurt me right now, wouldn't you?"

The lighter illuminated her face for a moment. She was beautiful, thought Hardwicke. She was right; he did want to hurt her, to wrap his hands around her neck. "If this is about that slut..." Pain shot through his face as she leant forward and pushed the ember of her cigarette into his cheek. A scream burst from his body.

"You need to learn when to keep your mouth shut. But, no, this has nothing to do with her, although that was deeply unpleasant to watch."

"Is it money you want? Whatever it is you want, you name it, it's yours."

She sneered at him, and straddled him, the gun barely an inch from his face. "You can't buy me, Mr. Hardwicke; I've come for something even your wealth can't buy."

"Oh believe me, I can buy anything I want. I'm sure even a night with you isn't out of my price range."

She struck him hard across the face with her gun, and chuckled as he spat blood onto the carpet. "If you continue to talk about screwing me, I'm going to do a lot worse than hit you. And I'll start by taking away your vital equipment." She pulled back her hood, revealing herself to him.

Hardwicke was taken aback for a moment by her eyes, framed with long lashes. They were breathtaking, but cold and steely, the colour of morning frost. They seemed to look through him as though he were nothing. He felt, all of a sudden, insignificant to her.

"You can't stop the Revolution Mr. Hardwicke. Neither can your prime minister. It's only a matter of time before we win."

His heart stopped; sweat dribbled down his brow. It trailed down his face, resting on the end of his pendulous nose. She transformed from a foolish girl into a threat, and she terrified him. It was the first time Hardwicke had felt anything other than contempt or lust for a woman. She moved the gun a little closer to his face, the cool metal pushing against his skin. To his horror, he felt his crotch become warm and damp. She stood up, a look of disgust etched on her face as she glanced down, to see his shame. "Please," he begged, "I'll do anything, I'll leave the country... just don't hurt me...."

"You're pathetic," she spat. "Can't you at least pretend to be a man of honour?" She cocked her head to one side. "Well, at least you'll be buried like one."

Before James Hardwicke could scream for help, his brain was torn apart by the bullet and splattered across his expensive cream carpet.

2

The air conditioning whirred, blasting cold air down the back of my top; my fingers hammering on the keyboard, marching across the letters, one by one. Another face appeared on the monitor, vanishing at the touch of a button, to be replaced with another. My eyes scanned the screen, absorbing all the information. Every so often I would spot something, a discrepancy or a minor flaw, that was enough for me to hit the print button and send the file down to the lower level - ready to be investigated further.

The room was a massive space, filled with line after line of desks. On the back wall, a gargantuan portrait of our prime minister, John Bowman, watched over us impassively. The sound of constant typing filled the air, almost deafening. I spun in my seat, removing the sheet of paper from the tray of the printer, ignoring the image of the elderly man staring up at me, his eyes wide and frightened. I turned back and found myself staring at an unfamiliar torso.

The man in front of me wore a sharp suit, teamed with a lemon shirt and red tie. His hair was slicked back in a quiff, his chin dotted with a fashionable stubble. His eyes were a glacial blue, his mouth curved in a thin smile. He radiated arrogance, and in my opinion, looked like a complete asshole. I inhaled deeply, twisting the amber ring on my finger. Christina was eyeing him up and down, like a bitch on heat, desperate to be noticed.

"Can I help you?" I held eye contact, trying to force a smile.

"I'm Harry," he began, pausing for a second as though that information should mean something to me. "I'm new here," he continued, waiting again for a response. "They transferred me from a government branch in Birmingham. Since the security here is so lax - too many bastards slipping through the net - they decided they needed me more here." It was a pointed remark, spoken just loud enough for the room to hear.

"I bet they did," I replied bluntly, smiling at him sweetly. The sarcasm that soaked my voice was lost on him and he continued to grin at me inanely as I resumed my typing.

"If you have some free time, I'd love for you to give me the low-down on this place." He leant forward, lowering his voice. "Maybe I could treat you to some dinner afterwards, at my place perhaps? I could definitely swing us a permit, just so you wouldn't have to walk home before curfew."

His voice was grating, setting my teeth on edge.

"Well, seeing as the security in London is so *lax*, I'm guessing I probably won't be getting much free time; I obviously need to do my job better, don't I, Harry?"

He stammered for a moment, his voice trapped in the back of his throat.

"But, seeing as you're so keen to learn more about your new place of work: This is the government's head office, and you are on the level for the Citizen Registration Bureau. My job is to ensure every single person who lives in this country is registered, make sure no one from the Revolution slips through the net, which in your opinion is something you think I am not doing well enough. Is that enough of a *low-down* for you?" His jaw dropped. "And I manage to do it with my clothes on; aren't I a clever girl?"

His colleagues who had gathered in a corner pretending they weren't eavesdropping on our conversation began to roar with laughter. The fattest one hollered over to Harry, raising his mug of coffee, "We told you Harry, Romany's all work and no play. Believe me, we've all tried."

Harry's cheeks began to flush a violent shade of red. His eyes narrowed, and his teeth clamped down on his lip, holding back a hiss of anger. The charming mask had slipped off; he was humiliated. He was clearly not a man who was used to rejection, and he certainly did not appear to appreciate it. He went to speak, but I held up a hand, silencing him.

"You're distracting me, Harry. They hired you to do a job here, not to try and get in my knickers. Get on with it."

Christina scuttled up to seize her opportunity and comfort him, but he ignored her, brushing her off of his shoulder. He stormed past the others, shoving his way into the lift. Etienne, the senior manager of my level, walked over and leaned on the corner of my desk.

"Who knew you could be such a ball-buster, Romany?" He offered me a cigarette, lighting one up for himself. In sharp contrast with all the obnoxious pricks I had to tolerate on a day to day basis, Etienne was a complete gentleman. He glanced around the office at the other workers sat in silence at their desks. Around us, posters covered the walls, urging us to 'Act for our country', and warning that our neighbours 'could be the enemy'. Above them, cameras swung back and forth, moving across each of the desks, one by one. Etienne leant forward, his voice changing into a whisper.

"Have you heard? Somebody murdered James Hardwicke last night. Rumour has it, the Revolution are behind it. Of course they're saying he had a heart attack or some other complete load of…"

"Somebody murdered the P.M's top advisor?" I interrupted.

"Yes, even the P.M has said that he was the real brains behind the changes in Britain. If it wasn't for him, showing the prime minister the way, this country wouldn't be what it is today. The P.M is said to be devastated; he's cancelled all meetings for the day. They say he is inconsolable."

A slender woman, dressed in a grey suit marched by, clutching a pile of papers. I handed her a stack from my desk with a nod, Etienne and I falling into silence until she moved away. We both smiled brightly as she narrowed her eyes, looking at us over her shoulder as she headed to the next desk along.

"Poor man, whatever will he do now?" I whispered.

"Continue with James' work; carry on his legacy." He stubbed out his cigarette, shaking his head. "You might want to double check your list there," he gestured towards my pile of paperwork. "They rounded up a few more gays last night, and a couple of stupid bastards who thought they could get away with hiding books and films from the list. My own fucking neighbour was hiding a load of banned items; reading a little Ginsberg to pass the time. The vans took his family away, so you might as well just take their papers down to lower level. I'll find

19

out the names for you. You'll get a little nod for acting so quick," he smiled.

Any paperwork that came my way for those in breach of the list went straight down to the lower levels of the building, an area where even a respected member of government employment such as me felt nervous visiting.

Douglas McLean, the head of the lower level, was a hard man, with eyes that seemed to bore into your skull the moment you entered his office. McLean was nicknamed 'The Bloodhound', for his ability to sniff out secrets. Just a few weeks ago, a young receptionist called Ellie had entered McLean's office to pass on a message and left in floods of tears, having handed her sister's details over to him. Ellie's sister and her girlfriend were taken by the vans that day. The receptionist herself was gone by the following morning. McLean knew everything and could not be fooled.

I knocked on the door to the lower level and held my I.D up to the camera, bracing myself as the buzzer sounded, announcing my arrival to McLean. I walked past the rows of desks, ignored entirely by their occupants. I headed for the one closest to McLean's office, to hand the papers to his secretary, but as I went to talk to her the door to his office opened, and there McLean stood. The whole lower level fell silent. I glanced behind me, and each of the workers sat with their heads bowed, hoping to be ignored.

McLean gestured for me to join him. He pointed at the empty chair, suggesting that I take a seat, rather than merely hand him the papers and make my escape. The door closed silently behind me, and I carefully maintained eye contact with The Bloodhound. He was a tall man, heavy set with greying hair. Attractive in a distinguished way, his eyes were dark, his lips full. Surprisingly, he didn't wear a wedding ring. I waited patiently for him to speak first, shifting a little as he scrutinized me, sipping whiskey from a tumbler. The clinking ice as he set the glass down shattered the silence and he cleared his throat. I felt sweat trickling a little down the nape of my neck; the air conditioning was broken it seemed, and it was sweltering hot underground. There were no windows, no glimpse of the world outside.

"Good morning Romany. I understand you have some paperwork for me from the latest arrests? Etienne told me you would be coming down." I nodded and placed the papers onto his desk, edging them towards him. His eyes remained fixed on my face. "How are you doing? You seem a little uncomfortable." He popped a slice of spearmint gum into his mouth.

"No, sir," I smiled cheerily. "It's been an extremely busy day, made worse with the terrible news of Mr. Hardwicke. We're working hard to ensure the people are calm in the face of this tragedy."

McLean's lips curled into an amused smile and he nodded, chewing his gum slowly. "Yes, I had heard... such a waste. I was honoured to call James a personal friend and I know that the last thing he would want is for our standards to slip here. The work we do is vital to ensure our government remains in power." It was an accusation, and I steadied myself before my response.

"Yes sir, that is precisely why we are all working so hard. Anything less would be a disgrace and serve to

21

tarnish Mr. Hardwicke's memory. I would personally be more than happy to stay on later to ensure all paperwork is completed."

"I'm afraid that's not my department, but your dedication is admirable. Thank you for the papers; you're free to go." I stood to my feet and headed for the door, pausing as he spoke again. "Romany," I froze. "This is some very good work. If a position in my department should arise, I'll be sure to bear you in mind."

"That would be a great privilege." I kept my bright smile fixed in place as I walked away from the lower level as fast as I possibly could without looking suspicious. As I stepped into the lift I glanced towards the office. McLean's eyes remained on me, as he stroked his chin, deep in thought.

I breathed a sigh of relief as the lift doors opened, welcoming me back onto my floor. Etienne peered up, winking at me. "How was The Bloodhound?" He came towards me, patting me on the back. "Is that a bead of sweat I see upon your brow? Been hiding secrets, pretty girlie?"

I swivelled on my heel, flicking my hair. "Wouldn't you like to know?" I replied with a wink, walking away as Etienne fell about laughing.

Christina peered up from her computer screen and her eyes narrowed. "You know Etienne is far out of your league don't you Romany?"

I paused in my walk, determined not to react to Christina's poisonous statement. But temptation overcame me. "Some of us don't have to lie on our backs to get somewhere Christina."

She giggled, throwing her head back and tossing her hair. Most of the men in the office shot a look in our direction. "Don't be so naïve, sweetheart." Her voice lowered, barely audible over the noise of the office equipment. "In these times, we women have to use whatever we have to get what we need. I just happen to have the ability to make men give me pretty things in exchange for a night with me. And believe you me; I work just as hard as you do, just in different ways."

"Well," I looked over my shoulder at her, and tried not to smile, "some of us have retained our dignity. I personally don't feel the need to prostitute myself to survive. I just seem to benefit from working hard." Her mouth dropped open and I strolled back to my desk before she could think of a retort. But, after five minutes of feeble bleating from Christina's direction, I was satisfied I had emerged victorious.

The rest of the day seemed to pass slowly, as I wondered what had been going through McLean's mind as he had watched me walk away. I'd worked hard to remain off McLean's radar, and now he had taken notice of me.

I was designated to shift through a mountain of files, to establish anyone who was not a British Citizen. When the cleansing of Britain had begun, anyone who had not been born in Britain, or whose parents were not of British birth, was sent back to their countries of origin. This move was supported by many who believed that in order for the country to recover, difficult choices had to be made. And so, regardless of how long you had lived in Great Britain - you could have come here at the age of two, or your parents moved here in their twenties to have you - you were sent back to France, or Tobago, or wherever your family were from. My job for the day was to go through each person's documentation and check for flaws or discrepancies. Nobody enjoyed this particularly tedious task, and so I was often the only one to volunteer.

The afternoon faded into evening, and one by one, the lights began to switch off as my colleagues went home. My wrist watch began to beep, signaling that I had to leave before curfew. As I packed up my handbag, I froze at the sight of a figure stood in the lift. McLean placed a cigarette in his mouth and put his foot in the door, giving me no choice but to go down with him. Hesitantly I walked towards him, taking my place in front of him. Neither of us spoke, but I could feel his eyes burning into the back of my head. As the lift hit the ground floor and the doors opened to let me out, he leant forward, his lips just behind my ear. "Have a good night, Romany."

I struggled to reply, stammering a little. I flashed my I.D at security and closed my eyes as the cold air hit my face. I always felt cooped up in the office, stifled and desperate to be out. I peered back over my shoulder but McLean had disappeared, most likely down to the car park.

"Hurry on, miss," the security guard hissed at me, "it'll be curfew soon." I smiled at him, but he turned back into the building, locking the door behind him.

The sound of my footsteps echoed through the streets, occasionally interrupted by doors being locked, deadbolts being fastened, keys being turned. The security cameras whirred as they followed me, and the tannoy system boomed out its warning: '*All citizens must

24

be in their homes by 9pm. Police will be patrolling to enforce curfew.' As I drew closer to my estate, I passed my identity card to the guard and waited patiently as he scrutinized it. He scratched the back of his thick neck beneath his hat.

"Okay," he handed it back me, "you're free to pass." I nodded my head at him; he gave me a wide smile. "A lady like you shouldn't be walking home alone at night."

"Well I feel perfectly safe, especially when I know there's strong men like you protecting me." I squeezed past his bulky frame and backed away, eager to get home. "But I should get going, don't want to be out and about after curfew."

I scurried off towards my home, squirming as he shouted after me, "One day you'll agree to let me walk you home, you know you can't resist my charms!"

As I rounded the corner, and my home at the end of the cul-de-sac came into view, I finally relaxed. All I wanted was to get home and get into a hot bath.

*

I watched her from the darkness, hidden out of sight from the cameras. She had walked quickly from her work; quicker than normal. She dropped her cigarette to the ground as she approached the guard, fumbling in her purse for her I.D card. He looked at her like a piece of meat, ready to be devoured. My throat grew dry, my heartbeat quickened. As she walked by, his eyes remained glued to her, travelling down her body before resting on her curvy backside. He licked his lips a little and shouted after her. My hand travelled to the gun hidden within my coat. I resisted the urge to blow his face apart and stepped back into the shadows. I had my goal to reach, I couldn't be distracted. I sprinted down the alleyways, avoiding being spotted. I pushed my body against the cold brick wall as a van drove by, its speakers blasting out sharp warnings about the curfew. The vehicle drove on and I quickened my pace, running around the back of her house. Through the window, I could see her eating her pasta. She moved gracefully, like a dancer. I ducked beneath the windowsill as she threw her empty bowl into the sink. I held my breath, and slowly stood back up. With her back to me, she yawned and stretched, the nape of her neck revealed through her hair. I pulled on my gloves, and steeled myself as she walked up the stairs. Beautiful women just weren't safe in this world anymore.

*

I felt the warm water wash over me as I sank into the bath, placing my headphones over my ears. Sometimes, I didn't know what I would do without my personal piece of contraband, my beloved vintage IPod packed full of songs strictly prohibited by the list. Mick Jagger's sexy voice drifted into my mind, and my eyes fluttered shut. All thoughts of McLean and Christina floated away; I finally relaxed. The heat made my head swim. I was so very tired, so ready to climb into my bed, pull the sheets over me and get lost in dreams until the sun began to rise and I had to wake. It was funny how easily I could get absorbed in my own brain; it was my means of escaping when the world outside was crumbling. Suddenly, my reverie was broken by a bang, making me jump up from the water. I grabbed my dressing gown and wrapped it around myself. I shoved my IPod into its plastic bag, stuffing it back into its hiding place behind the sink. I listened carefully, waiting for the sound of footsteps pounding up my stairs. Had McLean sent his goons after me? Had I made some mistake, said something untoward in his office? I frantically tried to remember. I peered out the window, relieved to see an absence of white vans. But then, from the direction of my bedroom, came the sound of shuffling; someone tiptoeing through my property. I walked into my hallway, staring down into my pitch black bedroom. Eerily empty, the silence suddenly seemed deafening. Heart thumping, I headed for my bedroom, ready to face whoever had been so stupid as to break into a government employee's home. I stepped into the room and checked inside my wardrobe, the only hiding place in which an attacker could lurk, only to find it devoid of anything other than clothes.

As I turned around, a figure stepped out from behind my door. His face was covered with a balaclava and he wore all black; he was barely visible in the dark. He stood still for a moment, watching me. I froze, rooted to the spot. My breath quickened. I pulled my dressing gown a little tighter, trying to cover myself. Suddenly, he lunged at me and I dived beneath his arms, kicking his legs out from beneath him. As I tried to run, his hands gripped my ankles, pulling me to the floor. I could hear his heavy breathing as he dragged me towards him, my face burnt by the carpet. I kicked out, catching him hard across his cheek. We grappled with one another, and I felt my body weaken. He was far stronger than me, and

27

despite my speed, he was constantly a step ahead. He pinned me to the carpet and I tried to struggle in vain. I took a swinging punch, aiming blindly, and felt a rush of triumph as he gave a grunt of pain as my fist connected between his legs. He slumped forwards and I rolled from under him and grabbed him, throwing him onto the floor with my full weight. Pulling off his balaclava, I threw it to one side as Beckett's eyes opened slowly, his face screwed up in a grimace.

"I think we'll call that a draw..." he moaned weakly, as he rolled onto his side curled up in the foetal position.

3

I passed Beckett a cup of coffee as he pressed an ice pack between his legs, placing a device on the table to mask our voices to the audio scanners that could be listening in. The object itself was tiny; a circular piece of metal, like a compact mirror, but it transmitted a signal which would block the audio scanners, allowing us to talk without fear of being heard. I had turned up the sound on the television in my sitting room to avoid arousing suspicion. Sometimes, no noise was worse than too much noise in the eyes of the police. Silence meant you were up to something, or not home at all, and breaching curfew was a dangerous game to play, as Beckett knew well.

"That wasn't the politest of ways to announce you were coming to visit."

He peered over his mug and grinned at me. "I was testing you; checking all that sitting at a desk hadn't dulled your reactions." I sat beside him and sipped my own drink. "Congratulations on Hardwicke."

"Thank you, it did go rather smoothly," I acknowledged. "Luckily for me, he'd sent his security away, so he could dabble in his favourite pastime, a spot of sadism." He pushed his curly hair out of his face, deep in thought. "You're certain nobody could've seen you?" I asked, still nervous.

He shook his head and wandered over to the window, drawing the blinds.

"The vans won't be out for another hour, nobody knows I'm here. You know nobody can hide from the cameras like me." He winked at me.

"What did you come to tell me, Beckett? You didn't just come to attack me and have a coffee, did you?"

I had known Beckett since I was but a child; he and I had once been close, and there was even a time when I thought we could have something more than just a friendship, but things were different now. Beckett was the leader of the London branch of our organisation, and I was his dutiful second in command. He had power over me and I was not a woman who was comfortable with being controlled. We were no longer equals in his eyes; I was his second in command, utterly loyal to him, and he trusted me implicitly, like a faithful pet dog. It was a role I was not entirely happy to play. We did not talk intimately as we once had; a divide had fallen between us. And yet, beneath his cavalier swagger, I could see traces of the boy I had adored. I knew the pressures of his position tortured him, and his behaviour towards me was never sincere, he just needed someone to vent to; somebody he could trust. Beckett ran his fingers through his hair and sighed, his eyes glancing around nervously.

"I've decided we need more time before we strike. We are not ready yet."

I slammed my mug down onto the table and stood to my feet. "But the whole point of taking out Hardwicke..."

"I know, Romany," he interrupted, "but I am telling you, we are not ready yet. We're almost there, we just need more time, more intel."

"I'm providing you with everything I know!"

He shook his head and stepped towards me. "I know that, but the information I am talking about is not coming from you." His eyes finally looked up at me and he shrugged. The penny dropped.

"You have somebody else working for us in my patch, another mole…"

He nodded. My stomach flipped. It had been tough obtaining my job in the head office; the tests I'd had to complete, the thorough searches into every aspect of my life; not to mention passing on confidential information to Beckett, and I had done it all believing I was the only one he trusted to do so. It seemed I was wrong. "Can I know who they are?" I asked tentatively.

"No," he answered bluntly. "I'm sorry Romany, but this person's cover cannot be compromised."

I went to argue with him, accuse him of doubting me, but he held up his palms, signaling me to stop. "Please Romany, I wanted to tell you sooner but I had to make a decision. I chose not to tell you. But my informant has told me that now is not the time to strike. It would be far too dangerous and I will not risk losing you…" he paused for a moment "…any of you." His voice broke a little, and his smile warmed. I tried to reply, but he pulled me to him in a hug. "I trust you entirely Romany, but this time you have to trust me."

I pushed him away. "And trust a source I don't know?"

"I trust them; that's all that matters."

"Yes, more than me; that much is clear." Beckett ignored me, and pulled on his jacket and balaclava. "I say we are ready, and you agree. Then this source says we are not, and instantly I am wrong."

31

"I'll be holding a meeting, usual time and place. We will discuss everything then." He snatched up his device and made his way out the back door, disappearing into the dark of the night, leaving me with no answers and too many questions.

*

As I left her home and returned to my own, her disappointed face would not leave my mind. I felt guiltier than she could imagine, and even though I could never doubt her loyalty and passion for our cause, I knew my informant was right. Romany was clever, yes, but she was also too ready for the fight. It consumed her, and if she had her way, she would launch her attack tomorrow. Although it was hard, I had to make the decisions no one else would. I clambered through my window, and crouched silently in the darkness as the vans, those silent hunters, slipping through the night, creeping past each house one by one, drove by, scanning for secrets.

My squat had been declared empty. My informant had helped me no end with that particular dilemma, finding me an empty property out of sight of cameras. It was not easy to find somewhere to hide when you were blacklisted. There was a price on my head, after all. A few months of hard work, soundproofing and finding a generator had made my home almost luxurious. After a moment, the probing van moved on and from the dark, Lexi stepped out.

"Did you see her?" she asked bluntly, her arms folded. I nodded and she shook her head, lighting a cigarette. "Is she as pissed off as I told you she would be?" Another nod. "You put both me and her in so much danger to get to Hardwicke, and now this? You just change your mind… what if they suspected me? Huh? They would have me dragged out of work and bundled me into a torture van." She threw off her wig and scratched her shaved head. "Why have me work as a fucking secretary, dressed up like a tart, for nothing?"

"I don't have to explain myself to you Lexi; I told you and the others why I had made my decision, that's the end of it."

She bit her lip and held back her furious retort. "Fine. But I still think you should've told Romany before the rest of us." She stomped off down the basement stairs, kicking off her heels.

I sank down to the floor, holding my head in my hands and fought the urge to scream. Lexi was right, as fucking usual, but she didn't understand, she *couldn't* understand, all the endless voices shouting in my head, arguing with one another.

*

I hear my mother calling out 'Romany' in her sing-song voice, but I am not ready to go back in. I am only 5 years old and hiding in my field. As I fall backwards onto the ground, I spread my arms out wide. The birds are twittering away, I giggle as the strands of grass tickle my face. The sun is so hot today, and there isn't a cloud in the sky. It is much nicer to be here, in my hideaway behind my house, hidden from view by the tall corn. My parents have been whispering, shouting at night, the games have stopped. My mother doesn't sing while she washes the dishes anymore. My daddy watches the television from the moment he gets home from work. My house is not much fun anymore. I have grass stains on my dress; my mummy will be cross when she sees. She is always cross now.

I am a little girl, boisterous and noisy. I love thinking about the world I live in, that is what I do in my secret hideout. I stand up and look out over the fields, towards the sea. I begged my father to take me to the sea, but he said no. I haven't left our farm in ages. I keep asking him to get us some animals; a farm is supposed to have animals and we don't. At least they would give me something to do, since I'm not allowed to go to school anymore. He shouted at me the last time I asked. He never used to shout.

Everything seems different. The sun is still shining and it is still the nicest summer ever, but everything is changing.

*

Kicking the sheets to the floor, I woke with a start. My arms were damp with sweat, my head pounding. It was still dark; the room seemed too quiet. I pulled the duvet closer around me. My hands were shaking and I suddenly felt sick. I could just make out the sound of the vans outside, creeping past, and I knew they were scanning our road. I couldn't leave the house, even if I wanted to, not whilst they were out there. Tomorrow was my day off from work, I reminded myself, and I had to meet with Beckett and the others. I fell back onto my

34

pillow and stared at my ceiling, blurry dots swimming in my vision.

Eventually, I must have fallen back to sleep because before I knew it my alarm was buzzing and it was five in the morning. I stumbled out of bed and pulled my hair into a messy attempt at a ponytail. My mascara was smeared on my cheeks and refused to wipe off. I could tell it was going to be a bad day.

As I wandered through the streets, the cameras watching over us all, I was careful not to draw attention to myself. The London Eye towered over me, rusting and forlorn. It had been such a long time since it had been filled with tourists. The large bronze statue of our prime minister, solemn and serious, stared down over us imperiously. I pushed my way through the throng of people, all looking at the floor, as desperate to blend in as me.

A small child gripped his mother's hand and peered nervously at the cameras. She tightened her grip and pulled him closer to her. Her face was pale, the skin beneath her eyes the colour of violets and she looked painfully thin, her lips drawn tight together. She flicked her gaze over to me and I smiled at her. She didn't smile back. I followed her into the Underground, and I found myself on the same tube as her. The policemen stood at either end of the train, their eyes fixed on the passengers. Silently, they monitored us. A camera whirred behind my head. We were being watched. We all knew that. The woman sat with her child on her lap, holding him in a vice like grip. A man stood between us, his denim jacket grimy, his eyes bloodshot; the ravages of drink having ruined his once attractive face. He stared blankly at the floor, swaying with the carriage as it moved. As we headed to the next station and pulled to a stop, two officers stood in front of the doors. I could feel my heart beating faster. They had come for someone.

A young woman next to me began to shift, rubbing her arms nervously. I could hear her muttering under her breath, swearing over and over. A strand of her tangled hair found its way to her mouth and she chewed on it anxiously. She glanced over at me, fear making her lip tremble; her eyes wild and darting, like a cornered rabbit, about to be devoured by the hounds. Suddenly, a hand clamped down on her shoulder. She began to scream and tried to make a run for the doors behind us. The mother clamped her hands over her son's ears, burying his face into her, blocking his view of the chaos as it unfolded. Three officers tackled the girl, sneering as she fell to the floor heavily. They pinned her arms behind her back, twisting them painfully. The girl began to cry as they dragged her to the other officers waiting on the platform. "Whatever they told you it isn't true… I didn't do anything wrong."

One of the officers grabbed her face. "So you've not got a pretty little girlfriend waiting for you? And you don't support the Revolution?" Her mouth opened and closed like a fish out of water. "We found the films, at your house… all sorts of things from the list you shouldn't be having…"

The skinny policeman leered at her. "Well, at least your girlfriend will be pleased to see you." She began to cry, begging them not to hurt her girlfriend, to spare her. His fist silenced her quick enough. As the doors closed and the train moved, I watched them drag her past the crowds, all carefully looking away. The mother breathed a sigh of relief and took her hands from her son's ears. A little colour came into her cheeks and I understood her terror; she had thought they were coming for her.

*

I am excited to show my mum the flowers I have picked for her. As I walk back towards my house I can hear my dad shouting. I start to run, faster and faster, dropping my pretty flowers. He is screaming 'Romany', and it scares me. When I reach the back garden, my mother is waiting. She grabs my hand and drags me into the house. I tell her she's walking too fast and she's hurting my hand. She ignores my hiss of pain. Tears are running down her face. My dad is stood with a man I don't know. His face is serious, his hair even messier than usual. He is rubbing his little round glasses on his jacket as he does when he is upset. There is a backpack next to him, and when he sees me, he throws it into the back of the car. My mother kneels in front of me and begins stroking my hair. She passes my favourite teddy, Alfred, to me. She can't speak, she is crying so much. My father kneels beside her and puts his arms round us both; he has started crying too.

"This is my friend Matthew; you are going to stay with him for a little while." I start to shout, refusing to go. My father shakes me a little, and his voice grows louder. "You must listen to me sweetheart, it's only for a short time. It's just that your mummy and I have some business to sort out, then we'll come get you."

"Promise?"

"I promise," they said together, and my father smiled at me. My mother's arms were squeezed tight around me and she kissed me.

"I love you," she repeated over and over. My father began to say the same. We held each other tight for a moment.

My father carried me to the car, and my mother strapped me into the passenger seat. She kissed me once more, her breath tickling my ear as she whispered into it; "Remember Queen Elizabeth, she had to fight for everything in life. Remember you can be as great as her." She smiled sadly as she shut the car door. In that moment, I realised they weren't going to be following us. I was little, but never stupid. Matthew pulled away and I looked back over my shoulder, watching as my parents grew smaller and smaller.

*

Beckett's hideout was an abandoned house, boarded up and, luckily, out of sight of any cameras. If you cut through behind the rows of dilapidated houses you could enter without anyone seeing you, if you knew how to be invisible. I waited on the street for a second, until I knew that no one was looking before slipping down the alleyway. I sprinted down the gap between the houses until I reached the window I had to slip through to enter his home. As I climbed through, a pair of hands dragged me in, pulling me to the floor. Lexi slammed the window shut behind me and pulled down the tattered blind.

"What the fuck, Lexi?" I hissed.

"We can't be too careful, you know that. Besides, it was painful watching you try to squeeze through; I thought you needed a hand."

"Thanks, real complimentary."

She threw her head back and laughed. I couldn't help but admire her.

Lexi was my best friend, and she was one of the most beautiful women I had ever seen. Her skin was the colour of chocolate, and she was tall but muscular, almost Amazonian. With her shaved head she looked tough, but in stark contrast her face was gorgeously sculpted, with high cheekbones and full lips. The first thing I had noticed about Lexi had been her eyes. Unusually, they were an incredible shade of green, and almost feline in shape. When she flicked them over you, you were captivated. They could drive men wild, or make them cower in fear. Most importantly for Lexi, she could use them to cover up her true feelings, hide her darkest secrets.

Men adored Lexi, she looked like a supermodel. I could have named you a dozen who would spend a ridiculous amount of money to spend a night with her, but I knew all the money in the world wouldn't be of any use to them. Lexi liked girls, always had and always would. She whispered to me once in the middle of the night that she couldn't wait for the day to come when she could take a beautiful woman out for an expensive dinner and a moonlit walk through the city without fear of being arrested for doing so.

She offered me her hand and hauled me up off the floor. I brushed myself off and followed her down into the basement. "You're the last one to arrive, he's started without you," she murmured as she led me into the poorly lit room.

Beckett was stood in front of a small group of men and women, talking animatedly. He paused in his speech when he spotted me. I could tell from his shift in attitude that he had been informing them of our change in plans.

"Romany, I'm sorry I was just…"

I held up my hand, interrupting him. "You don't have to explain yourself to me." I knew my tone was sarcastic, and the others could sense it. Their gazes swept back and forth between Beckett and I, waiting to see what would happen next. He merely chuckled and gestured for me to sit.

"As I was saying, I have decided that at present we need just a little more time to prepare ourselves." The group began to murmur, unhappy at his announcement. "I know that you are disappointed, but I will not rush into anything. We have time, god knows it's the one thing we have in abundance. When we hit, we need to be precise, it has to be perfect. There's no room for mistakes."

Beckett was losing his audience, all of whom were becoming more and more agitated. "The government has increased security," the others talked over him, drowning him out. "They have concerns we will strike," he tried to shout. I stood to my feet.

"Beckett is right." He looked at me stunned, and the others stopped, turning to face me. "We will only get one shot at taking them out; if we fuck up that's it. It's over for us. It will take those of us who survive *years* to reach this point again. We all chose Beckett to follow in his father's footsteps; we have to trust him."

Slowly, a ripple of agreement went over the room. Beckett mouthed a 'thank you' at me.

"Besides, for this to work we're going to need the people's help." His eyes narrowed. It wasn't my intention to undermine him but I needed to make him listen to me; he wouldn't argue with me in front of the others. "We need to use the populace, bring them onto our side. At the moment they're too scared to even think about helping us, but the more we publicly undermine the government, the more we will bring them on side. In time, we will have an army of our own."

Elise, sat in the front row, shook her head. "Do you know how risky it will be to bring our cause into the public eye?"

Beckett stepped forward. "Romany is right." It was my turn to be surprised by his support. "Even if we succeed, if we don't have the public on side, we have achieved nothing. But if we have them alongside us when we strike, we will have the advantage. We will have the greater numbers."

We discussed our theories a little longer before it was time for the others to leave. Beckett stood before them all, and placed his hand over his heart. "Let freedom reign." He declared solemnly. We all repeated his words, the motto of the Revolution. It was too unsafe for us to all be in one place for too long; and so our meetings were always kept brief. Lexi gave me an approving wink from the other side of the room, but Beckett turned to me; his face was a picture of annoyance.

"You may be right this time Romany, but don't you ever do that to me again." As he stalked past me, I knew that I had made him nervous. His father had always preferred the idea of me as his predecessor, but the team, and myself, had chosen Beckett. He was Matthew's son after all, it was only right. Lexi had been the only one to vote for me. But it didn't stop Beckett from feeling threatened.

Lexi flung her arms around me. "Nice work babe, you really turned that shit around."

"Yeah, but he is furious with me."

Lexi threw a scowl over her shoulder at Beckett and rolled her eyes. "Fuck him."

The others all disappeared, after shaking Beckett's hand and congratulating me on Hardwicke. Before I knew it the three of us were alone. He chucked me a packet of cigarettes and leant on the back of a chair.

"Do you have any more surprises for me?" His tone was playful, but I could sense the bite of annoyance beneath it.

"Nothing out of the ordinary. The people are restless, but nobody knows what is going to happen next. Bowman is planning another speech to be broadcast to play down the fallout from the riot in Glasgow the other week."

"Why do these people take it on themselves after a few drinks to try and take on the police? With *baseball bats* for fuck sake." Beckett rubbed at his eyes wearisomely. "Twenty-seven people dead. People who could have been saved if they'd come to us; we could have put them to use."

"That's why we need to win them to our cause, Beckett. They want to fight, they want to get their freedom back but they're untrained and clumsy."

He stubbed out his cigarette and looked me in the eye. "I know you're right. I just don't like it when you don't discuss things with me first."

"Well, now you know how I feel." He didn't have a reply to that. Lexi hovered behind me and I could hear her snigger.

"It's going to take time, we can't do it over night," Beckett mused.

"No," I conceded, "but seeing as you've given us more time, we may as well use it properly. There's no use taking out Bowman and his bitches if the people don't trust us. All they have heard is that we are terrorists, out to kill them and their children. They're scared of us."

Beckett flicked on the television and the Government Broadcasting System was in full swing. From 6am until midnight, nothing but government funded and approved television; nothing risqué or 'inappropriate'. Nothing that was against the list, of course. Emilia Raymond's smiling face was beaming at us. Emilia was married to a member of Bowman's government, and as a result, was now the most popular and highly paid newsreader on the television. Her blonde, bubbly personality made her instantly likeable, and importantly to the government, apparently trustworthy. A picture of Hardwicke came onto the screen and Emilia's face became grave. Slowly, Beckett turned up the volume. "I am saddened to announce to you all the death of Deputy Prime Minister James Hardwicke, who sadly passed away after a stroke. The prime minister issued this statement:

'James Hardwicke was not only one of my most valued cabinet members, but my dearest friend. His loss

43

is a tragedy not only to me, but to my country. His legacy will not be forgotten, and we will work tirelessly to ensure his vision is brought to reality. He dreamt of a better Britain, and, even though it saddens me that he will not be here to see it, I will deliver his dream. James was unique and will never be forgotten.'"

Emilia's grief vanished in a second, replaced by her beaming smile as she spouted more pro-government propaganda.

Beckett turned down the volume on her incessant babbling and looked at me approvingly. "Well, this will certainly make the people think for a minute. Nobody is going to believe for one moment that this was a tragic but natural death."

Our discussion was broken by screaming from the street outside.

*

I grabbed Romany's wrist and pulled her to the floor. She pressed herself flat against the wall, and I could hear her suck in a breath as I crawled past her to look up the stairs. There was no sound of my boarded up door being kicked in, or the sound of shouts inside the house. It all seemed to be happening from outside.

I flicked on the computer monitor, showing the images from the security camera that Elise had hacked into. The vans had swarmed around the house on the opposite side of the street. The police had smashed into the house, dragging out a middle aged man who was wearing only a dressing gown. They threw him to the floor and waved books and DVDs in his face, throwing them to the ground. He was pleading with them, scrambling to his feet. His wife, still only in her pyjamas, was brought out. She was limp, her body shaking in fear; she looked utterly defeated. He turned and tried to kiss her, to hold her hand and reassure her. They stopped him with one hit of a riot stick. He fell to the floor as his wife dropped to her knees, cradling his bloody head in her hands. She began to shout at them, telling them how one day the Revolution would win and that they would all burn in hell. They laughed at her and picked her up and threw her into the back of the van followed by her motionless husband. I looked over at Romany and I could see the anger in her eyes as she scraped her fingers through her glossy hair and closed her eyes, trying to calm herself. I nodded at Lexi, silently urging her to keep an eye on our friend. Romany was a brilliant assassin, but also a loose cannon, especially when it came to defending the innocent. Lexi crawled over to her and wrapped her arms around her, ready to stop her if she made a break for our hidden gun collection. I wanted to try and help ease her suffering, the pain she felt at seeing others hurt, but I couldn't. I didn't know how to. I paused for a moment at the look in Lexi's eyes as she rested her chin on the top of Romany's head. The odd feeling in my stomach passed. Lexi was Romany's best friend; the pair of them were like sisters. The police continued to hurl items into the street, shouting at passers-by to move on. Nobody needed telling twice.

Romany threw herself to her feet and punched her fist hard into the brick walls of my basement. A blood stain was left behind, the perfect image of her knuckles. Her scream of fury came from the pit of her belly, as it shook the walls. Lexi looked at me with pleading eyes, as I took hold of her and let her fists pound against me in frustration.

"Shh," I tried to sound calming. "You must be quiet. This place may be soundproofed but you are testing it to the limit." She looked me at me, and suddenly, the fight drained from her.

"Aren't you tired of seeing so much pain in the world...?" Her hands dropped to her side, and she sounded weary. "...I know I am. I just want this to be over, one way or another." Awkwardly, I wrapped my arms around her, and she gently rested her head on my shoulder. I stroked her hair, like a father comforting his child. Lexi watched us with those beautiful eyes; eyes that never betrayed what she was thinking.

As she calmed, Romany stepped away from me, smiling uncomfortably; embarrassed by her outburst.

"I'm sorry. I shouldn't have behaved like that, it goes against everything..."

I held up my hand. "It's not a problem." I really didn't want to hear her apologies for being human for just a moment.

She looked at Lexi, trying to find a way to escape the awkward silence that was becoming increasingly long. "We've got a lot to do." She turned to leave, and I didn't even need to turn to see Lexi ready to follow. "The longer we wait to start, longer it'll take us to win."

"Yes, you're right. We have to decide what our next move will be." I said this, though I knew she probably had this worked out in her mind already. I still, however, had to give the illusion to her that I was the leader, that she actually had to listen to me. She smiled at me over her shoulder, and, if only in that second, I could see the tired, frightened little girl I had once known. But that cold glaze crept back across her face and she was once again Romany, the assassin.

4

"Hello Romany." Harry said, as he lingered at my desk. I tried my best to ignore him, to carry on with my work but he refused to leave. In fact, he seemed to find me amusing.

"What do you want?" I tried to keep my tone light, trying to avoid drawing attention to myself.

"I was just coming to give you some good news," he sneered at me. "Try and guess."

I felt my hand just itching to teach the smug bastard a lesson with the scissors beside me. "Why don't you just tell me, as you're clearly desperate to."

His eyes travelled down to the neckline of my dress. "Well, the prime minister is paying us a visit, in two days; it was supposed to be a big surprise but word got out. McLean was going to throw a small cocktail party in his honour, for senior staff only." He brushed his fingers through his greasy hair. "But since everyone knows, McLean has decided to make it a little more formal. All the staff are invited to attend. The P.M will take a tour of the buildings, then we'll all welcome him with a party to remember." He perched on the edge of my desk, examining his loafers with a critical eye. "And I rather thought that you might attend with me as my guest."

I bit down hard on my tongue, and tried to fight back the replies screaming to be released from my brain. Thankfully, Etienne came to my rescue.

"Actually, Romany has already agreed to accompany me. As the head of this level, I felt it important to ensure I take someone who fully embodies all we do here."

Harry's eyes darkened as Etienne wrapped his arm around my shoulders. "I think Christina may still be available though."

Harry switched his gaze to the buxom Christina, who was practically on the edge of her seat, pushing her formidable cleavage forward. "No thanks," Harry spat, "I'd sooner go alone." He stalked off. I peered up at Etienne, mouthing a 'thank you' to him.

"Does this mean I actually have to go with you?"

He placed his hand over his heart, trying to look heartbroken.

"Of course you do, in fact it's an order."

Etienne was an attractive man, with a tanned complexion and warm eyes. He had a roguish smile, and there wasn't a woman in the building who hadn't tried their luck with him, apart from me, and as a result I was the only one not to be rejected. "Well, I had better try to look my best," I replied. He passed me more files and grinned.

"Well, until then, there's at least a dozen families we believe have tried to dodge being registered. We need to head up a team to get some information; try and find out if we're dealing with deserters or just idiots. If we've got some Revolution members on our hands, that would be just the thing to present the prime minister with. Imagine if we could tell him we'd rounded up a few of those!"

I took the folders from him, and as he left, flicked my gaze over them. The pictures of each person stared up at me, their eyes devoid of anything other than fear. Sometimes, being undercover was a real bitch. I was aware of the cameras, the watchful eyes of my colleagues and I closed the files, picking up the phone to call down to the police department, ready to give them the credentials of the poor unsuspecting people I was sending them after.

*

When I got in, I wasn't surprised to see Lexi sitting at my kitchen table. It didn't make me jump, I was used to her being a regular intruder in my home.

"Looking pretty good princess," she grinned at me. Lexi was always vocal about her disdain with regard to my work outfits. She was stubbing out a cigarette in my crystal ashtray - originally a gift from my office for outstanding performance. I filled up a glass with water, and tried to avoid her eyes. "What is it?" I knocked back the drink, before sitting down at the table.

"Do you know what I did today?" The words caught in my throat. "I sent four families to the vans; I sent the police to arrest them. They took six children today. One of them was six months old." Lexi grabbed my hand, squeezing it tight. Tears began to fall down my cheeks, and I held my head in my hands.

"You know what you do is necessary." She tried to convince me. "One day, the people will thank you for it. The loss of a few…"

"Will be the salvation of many; I know." I could hardly speak, I felt so drained. "There's something else." Lexi looked at me. "I have to go to a party, with my work colleagues, that McLean is throwing." Her eyebrows knitted together, and, even though I didn't want to, I knew I had to continue. "There's going to be a guest of honour." One raised eyebrow, dawning realisation. "The prime minister is coming."

"Shit." She swore, whipping out a packet of fags and putting her feet up on my dining table. "What the hell are you going to do?"

"Well, I'm going to have to go. If I don't it will look suspicious. I'm supposed to be overcome with joy at the prospect of meeting him. Etienne is taking me, so at least that will look good."

Her eyes narrowed a little, and she blew smoke out the corner of her mouth. "Who the fuck is Etienne?"

"He's the guy who I told you about, the one I work with…but that's beside the point Lexi. I mean, I know this is what we're trained for but he's going to be right there, in the same room…"

"No." She dropped her legs to the floor. "It's too risky. Beckett would never let you go if he knew what you were thinking. Just stick to the plan babe." She placed her hand over mine. "I understand, really I do, but it won't work. His bodyguards will take you out in seconds, and then where will we be?" She smiled at me, standing up to pull her wig back on over her head. She tossed her head, flicking her fake hair about. "How do I look?" She pouted.

"Red hot," I replied, completely honest.

She leant forward, kissing me on the cheek. "I'll see you soon. Just be careful."

She headed out my back door, and I locked it behind her. I was yet again alone in my big, empty house.

I stood in front of my mirror, dropping my towel. I examined myself critically, my eyes scanning over my body. Small frame, thin but not skinny and small breasts, but suitable for my build. I wasn't an unattractive woman, on the contrary, I knew I was rather pretty in a doll-like way. I turned slowly, looking over my shoulder. My bare back was a riot of colour. My personal rebellion, I smiled to myself. I had done it when I was made a fully fledged Revolution member, along with Beckett. Across my pale skin, always hidden beneath my clothes, a Phoenix emerged from the ashes. My tattoo, a symbol of what my country would be, what I could become.

I lay down on my bed, wrapping my naked body with the sheets. As I closed my eyes I thought about what my meeting with the man himself would be like. My mind swam. This was a man whose death filled my dreams, and he would be stood just yards from me. Perhaps he would talk to me. Maybe he was a man who could be easily seduced into being alone with me. One way or another, the party would be a challenge.

*

My five year old self was so scared of the faint sound of sirens. Everything was so strange to me. We drove over the hill and Matthew pulled down into a narrow lane where the car couldn't be seen and, grabbing my stuff, he carried me down into the thicket below the hill we were on. He hissed at me to lie down, and we did, hidden amongst the ferns. He had a friendly face, framed with thick brown curls. He reminded me of a prince from a one of my mother's fairy tales, and would have been very handsome, if he wasn't so old. He placed a finger over his lips and smiled, which made me feel a little less frightened. I looked around me and realised I was in the woods above my house, where my father had helped me make my den in the spring. Matthew was looking around, distracted. Once the sirens had passed, he began to clamber to his feet. I suddenly grew brave and escaped from him to run towards my house, to my mum and dad. Matthew chased me. He was fast, but I was smaller, hard to catch. 'Like a rat up a drainpipe.' My dad said. Two gunshots made me stop and when I looked behind, Matthew was stood still too, his mouth open. I kept going, even though I had stitches. When I reached the clearing, Matthew grabbed me and pulled me to the ground, his hand over my mouth. Smoke was beginning to pour from the windows of my house, including my bedroom. The white vans were moving away, heading back towards town. And there, lying in my field below us, were two people, motionless.

*

"What is it?" I had woken to find Lexi stood at the bottom of the bed, her arms folded. I rolled onto my side, shutting my eyes again, desperate to return to what little sleep I could get.

"I spoke to Romany tonight, she had news to tell me."

I opened one eye, waiting for her to speak. "Well? I can see you're dying to tell me."

"They're throwing a party at her workplace, and she's going to have to attend with a man she works with." I sat up, holding back my temper.

"You woke me, from the only sleep I have managed to get in days, just to tell me Romany is going to a party with some bloke?" She smirked at me.

"There's going to be a special guest." I lay back down, my arms over my face.

"You're beginning to bore me Lexi." Her frown made it difficult for me not to smile.

"Bowman." I sat bolt upright, confused.

"The prime minister is attending a party at Romany's offices?"

"Yeah, some guy called McLean is hosting it. All the employees are attending."

I ran my hands through my hair, tugging on it slightly. I placed my feet on the bare floorboards, dragging myself out of bed.

"Woah!" Lexi cried, covering her eyes. "Throw on some jeans boy; I don't need to see that!"

I pulled my tracksuit bottoms over my legs, and Lexi turned back to face me. "We need to think Lexi… What if he senses something isn't right? What if she snaps?"

"She won't." She rubbed the back of her neck. "I can see it in her eyes; she's not going to destroy everything she's worked for."

I stepped closer to my window and peered through the boards. The dark clouds in the sky masked the stars, and gave the moon an eerie appearance. I closed my eyes and listened to the rain hammering the roof. An image flashed across my mind: Romany, dressed in a beautiful scarlet evening gown, twirling in the rain with her arms flung open wide. That scene was quickly replaced with another, as I found myself stood in a dark alleyway, the pouring rain trickling down my neck, dampening my clothes. The alley was lit up by lightning, and at the end of it I could see her lying face down on the floor. Her hair was spread around her, like an angel's halo. I gently pulled it back from her face and rolled her onto her back. Her eyes were wide open, but grey and unseeing. Vicious purple bruising stained the perfect skin on her neck. Romany's life had been choked out of her.

"...I am telling you, she will be fine." Lexi's voice snapped me out of my nightmare and I turned slowly to face her, the image of Romany as a lifeless corpse still haunting my thoughts. "Besides, she likes to do things dramatically; she won't drag him off into some corner and shoot him."

I tried to smile, the taste of vomit burning my throat. "It only takes one mistake, and his police will deal with her." Lexi's smile dropped and she turned her back to me. "I think for both of our sakes, we had better hope that doesn't happen." She walked away from me, and I could hear her leaving. I turned back to the window and tried not to let the thoughts fill my head again. The noise of the vans patrolling the streets echoed through my room and, even hours later, I found myself completely unable to get back to sleep.

*

The day had passed in a blur; the constant sound of Christina's excited babble had driven me close to insanity. We had all been informed that as long as we kept our work passes upon us, we could walk home late after curfew. We were, after all, honoured guests of the prime minister and Douglas McLean. We had all been sent home early to prepare, and as I pulled on my dress, I could feel the adrenaline in my body rising. I gently fed the gossamer fabric through my hands. The dress had been expensive, but Etienne had given me some money towards it, telling me I needed to look 'incredible'. I pulled the gown on, taking care not to tear it. When I looked in the mirror, I found the glamorous woman staring back at me to be a complete stranger. The pale pink fabric glittered in the light, like spider webs in the early morning. Long sleeved, with a plunging neckline and a daring slit up to the thigh, it fitted me like a glove. I slicked on some lipstick and took a deep breath as Etienne knocked on my door. When I pulled it open, ready to show myself off, my heart froze at the sight of McLean stood on my doorstep. He noted my shock and seemed amused by it.

"Apologies Romany, but Etienne is hard at work finishing off the party plans. He was most concerned that he wouldn't be able to meet you, so here I am. And I must say, you look utterly breathtaking." His words were pleasant, but his tone was cold and neutral. Yet even I had to admit that he looked rather dashing in his smart tuxedo. I grabbed my purse and pulled the door shut behind me, desperate for him not to look inside. I wanted McLean to know as little about me as possible. The street was deserted, the silence making my skin prickle. McLean stood beside his black car, with its blacked out windows. I glanced at my neighbour's house, and could see the curtain drop, the elderly woman moving hastily from the window. McLean followed my gaze and smiled at the grimy houses, some of them abandoned; those that weren't, neglected and unloved. "Quite the road you live in." He remarked casually, opening the door for me.

Neither of us spoke on the short journey, I kept my eyes firmly away from him, though I knew his sideways glance was fixed on me. As we arrived, I was relieved to see Etienne waiting patiently for me. He gasped a little as I stepped out of the car, and after staring for just a second too long, remembered McLean's presence.

"The prime minister is just concluding the tour. Everything is ready; he will be waiting for you to escort him in where we can introduce him to the team." McLean nodded curtly at him, before heading into the building to meet his guest.

Etienne offered his arm to me. "You look... I mean, you are..."

I giggled and beamed at him. "Thank you."

He was pink-cheeked, flushing with embarrassment. "Oh!" He reached into his pocket. "I got you something." He pulled out a small, red velvet box. "Close your eyes." He stepped behind me, and draped something cold over my neck, fastening it with fumbling hands. I reached up, and gasped as I felt the large pendant hanging on a silver chain. I looked in the glass windows of the building, and marvelled at the teardrop diamond resting above my cleavage. "Cost me enough, but it's worth it." He smiled at me triumphantly, offering his arm again.

I was lost for words, but as he led me inside I felt an ache spreading across my belly. A man didn't present a girl with a gift like this without expecting something in return. And no matter how much, despite it all, I liked Etienne, he was still a devotee of the government, and my enemy.

I marvelled at the transformation of our largest meeting room. Etienne beamed at his handiwork and led me through the crowd to stand at the back. He passed me a glass of champagne and I carefully sipped at it, determined to drink only a little.

"It's a wonder isn't it?" He whispered in my ear. "All those poor fools out there, in their homes barely after tea time, and we will still be here until midnight, sipping champagne with the prime minister himself."

"Yes," I took another sip, "it is quite something. How much did it all cost?" I questioned, trying to sound interested.

"More than you or I earn in a year," he chuckled. "The food bill alone was obscene - the prime minister has marvellous taste." He took another drink, looking up at the cameras. "And of course, the security bill, that was even more than the food!" He laughed, ushering me across the room to admire the view. Suddenly, the room went quiet as McLean and the prime minister approached. Everywhere I looked stood a dark suited bodyguard scanning the scene vigilantly. As the doors flew open, a loud cheer filled the room and I finally caught my first glimpse of the man responsible for all my misery, my country's misery.

John Bowman was a tall man, with salt and pepper hair and broad shoulders. He had a handsome face, but one which was devoid of any emotion. Cold, dark eyes nestled in tanned skin above high cheekbones and a long, Roman nose. His smile was tight, thin, but it was clear he relished the adoration of those before him. McLean handed him a drink, and we all raised our glasses in a toast to him. I found myself struggling to breathe. I had seen hundreds of pictures of the man- a portrait of him stood above my own mantelpiece - but to see him in the flesh, stood before me, my hatred became almost overwhelming. Bowman's eyes seemed to take in each face, one by one, until eventually they landed on mine. I stared back, unsure whether to look away or keep his gaze. He seemed to scrutinize me, memorizing my features. He was a man who liked to remember faces, just in case they belonged to one of his many enemies. After a moment he moved on, as McLean began to introduce him to other senior staff. Etienne shifted anxiously beside me.

"Oh shit," he whispered to me "what if he comes to talk to me, what the hell will I say?"

I handed him another drink. "Just stay calm," I advised. "I am sure he'll do all the talking for you; you just have to nod and smile in the right places."

He knocked back the champagne, handing his empty glass back to the waiter. Fidgeting with his tie, Etienne began to swear under his breath. McLean was directing Bowman towards us, and as they got closer I could feel my heart pounding so loud I swore the others in the room would be able to hear it. Christina had managed to force her way in front of us, giggling manically and tossing her hair as they paused to allow her an introduction. Wearing a tight red dress, slashed to the navel, Christina did look phenomenally sexy. She leant forward a little as she spoke, pushing her cleavage under Bowman's nose. He eyed her up and down, but looked at her with only disdain. He excused himself, and resumed his way towards Etienne and I. McLean ushered Etienne forward and Bowman shook his hand firmly. I hung back, frozen to the spot, unable to think clearly.

*

They were lying face down, one almost on top of the other. I recognised my mother's red dress, the one Daddy had bought as a birthday present. I slipped from under Matthew's arm and ran. His hands grazed my dress but he still didn't shout, didn't tell me to stop. He came after me, crouching low so he couldn't be seen in the corn. I reached my loving parents, and fell on the floor. A pair of round glasses crunched under my knee. Ignoring the cut, I reached out and touched my mother's hand, shook her a little. It was still warm, but it was heavy, hard to pick up. She didn't hold my hand back. It just fell when I let go of it. I tried to talk to her, to tell her to stop playing. I noticed blood staining my dress. For a second, I thought about how mad mummy was going to be. Then I understood. I crawled backwards and into Matthew's arms. He held me tight, picked me up and carried me back to the car. I sobbed into his shoulder, I couldn't breathe. He'd taken them from me, that mean man, Bowman, I had heard everyone talking about. Matthew placed me gently into the seat, making sure my seatbelt was fastened. As we drove, I looked out the window, watching the trees pass by. I couldn't cry. I couldn't talk. I just wanted to wake up from this horrible dream.

*

"Romany? The prime minister asked you a question." I slowly came back into reality and into the realisation that McLean, Bowman and Etienne were all staring at me. Bowman raised an eyebrow, his lips pursed.

"I'm terribly sorry," I gasped, trying to look in complete awe of this monster. "It's just such an honour to meet you." A smile spread across his face, and McLean looked at him nervously before breaking into merry laughter.

"Romany here is such a dedicated worker to your cause, and even today she didn't let up for a minute. She left here with barely any time to get ready. She's probably exhausted!"

Bowman took my hand and placed a kiss on it, his stubble scratching my skin. "Well, a devotee such as yourself deserves to relax once in a while." Christina looked over furiously, having attached herself like a leech to one of Bowman's party. "And I must say, there isn't a man in the room who isn't watching you right now." His hazel eyes were impenetrable, it was impossible to tell what he was really thinking. "I am the envy of them all," he smiled sardonically.

Etienne laughed raucously while Bowman sipped his drink, still watching me intently.

"Tell me Romany," he watched my hand travelling to my hair, to tuck a strand behind my ear. He was a man who noticed every detail about a person. "What do you think of the work we are doing here?"

"I think," I proceeded carefully, "that in order to put the world to rights, sacrifices must be made and the wicked must be punished." Etienne's jaw dropped but Bowman laughed.

"Very astute of you. I like you Romany - you are the embodiment of everything I strive to have in my people." He spoke like a king, like the ruler of a nation, which in theory he had become. Only, unlike a king, he was not chivalrous or princely, he was a tyrant in a charming disguise. I went to tuck my hair back again, but he leant forward, his hand caressing my cheek as he did it for me. "Perhaps we'll meet again, somewhere a little quieter..." As he turned away from me, led by McLean to another group of drooling admirers, I noticed Harry watching me, his lips curled into a leering smile.

The party seemed to drag on forever, and I spent the time in mindless conversation with people I disliked. Etienne was the perfect companion, never leaving my side. He was witty and charming, barely able to take his eyes from me, and I knew if I had wanted to I could have taken him to one of the empty offices, let him pull up my expensive dress and made love to him. The thought made me a little breathless, the idea of being able to do something reckless and selfish was powerfully erotic. But I knew that becoming physically, let alone emotionally, involved with one of my colleagues held more risks than pleasure. In the corner of the room, I could see Christina rubbing herself against one of Bowman's group like a cat, only to be shoved away with an elbow to her side. She stumbled a little, tipping a little of her champagne to the floor. As I turned back to Etienne, a hand gripped my wrist. Bowman smiled at me, his eyes a little unfocused from the effects of the Jack Daniels he had been knocking back.

"I have to leave now, my work never ends and I have to be up disgustingly early tomorrow." I stepped back a little, dropping my hand to my side. "But it was a pleasure to meet you Romany." He kissed me on the cheek, and I felt my hand shaking. It would take me just a second to use the champagne glass in my fingers to slash open his throat. But as I looked over his shoulder, at least three of his guards were intently watching us. They would easily kill me after, and there was no guarantee there wasn't someone lined up to take his place. His whole government needed to be taken out. It was like a Hydra; remove one head, another would only grow in its place. I gave him a sweet smile as he let me go, and watched him walk away flanked by his bodyguards. I felt nauseous, and the room began to feel unbearably hot. I had to leave, I had to get out, I needed to get home. Etienne was talking to a group of men in the corner, and didn't notice me leave. I would apologise to him when I next worked, he would understand. Blame it on the champagne; say I was frightened about what might have happened. Lying was, after all, one of my greatest talents.

The cold night air hit me, and I pulled my coat over my shoulders. The streets were silent, besides those leaving the party, everyone was locked safely in their houses. The chubby guard on the door frowned at me. "Don't you have someone to walk you home? It's after curfew you know."

"I'll be fine, I have this." I waved my pass at him. He shook his head at me, closing the door behind him as he went back into the building.

"Silly girl," he muttered under his breath.

As I made my way down the streets, past the locked public gardens that were eerily silent, I listened out for footsteps. All I could hear was the sound of the leaves being tossed by the wind. I looked back over my shoulder before I rounded the corner, heading past rows of shops and houses. My heels made noises that echoed through the streets and as a van drove past, it pulled over alongside me. The officer driving had a bulbous nose, and suspicious, squinted eyes. "It's after curfew." I flashed my workers pass at him and he nodded, looking unimpressed. "Ah I see, been hobnobbing with the P.M have you? Very well, just get yourself home quickly; this is no place for a lady at night." He wound-up his window and sped off.

The wind blew rubbish along the street, skittering along the pavement, dancing through the air. As I walked a little further, closer to Beckett's house, a noise made me stop. It was so quiet I wasn't sure I had heard it. But there it was again, a tiny pathetic whimpering. It could have been an animal, but there was something about it, something that set my instincts off. The police van had disappeared, but I should keep walking, I shouldn't draw any more attention to myself than I already had. But there was something about that noise that compelled me to investigate further.

I followed the sound down an alleyway, hiding in the shadows. A large figure crouched over a smaller person lying motionless on the floor. I could hear the man grunting, and the woman on the floor sobbing. He stood to his feet and dropped his trousers to the floor. I crouched low and peered from behind the bins. A light came on in the building beside us and the man froze, waiting for someone to come out. The alley was flooded with light and I caught a glimpse of red fabric beneath his shoes. As he stepped back, the woman on the floor was visible to me. Blonde hair, her large breasts spilling out of her top, it was Christina, dazed and terrified. The man looked over his shoulder, and I darted back into the shadows, steadying myself. The light went out, and nobody came out, leaving him free to carry on with his depraved activity. Christina began to struggle, kicking out at him; but he was too strong for her. As he pinned her to the ground, I knew I had to stop him. As much as I couldn't stand her, Christina didn't deserve this, and I couldn't just stand by and listen to it happen. I searched around me, until my fingers came across a plastic bag. They clasped around it, and I held it tight. I had to be quick, there could be no mistakes. The cameras at the end of the alley were pointing out into the street; they would have seen him making his way down here. They would have seen me. I would have to remove the evidence before the police turned up. My brain tried to focus; count to three, concentrate on the enemy, before you make a move, I reminded myself.

I darted out of the shadows and grabbed the man from behind, pulling the bag over his head. He was strong, and I was hardly dressed for such an activity. He thrashed about and I pushed him hard to the floor, pinning his arms to the ground with my knees. I tried not to look at his face, straining against the bag. After what seemed like an eternity, his body finally stopped twitching, and I was able to relax. I reached into his pocket, my hand covered with the bag, pulling out his wallet and an I.D badge. The man was a fucking policeman. This made things a whole lot more complicated. I turned to Christina, whose drunken eyes were wide with fear, and placed my finger over my lips. "Help me." I mouthed at her, pointing to the body and the gate behind us. She scrambled unsteadily to her feet. There was only one place we could carry the body, the closest and the safest to reach. However, I was more concerned about would happen when we arrived, than of the journey itself.

5

Romany stood with her head in her hands as I tried not to lose all sense of control.

"Let me get this straight. You killed a fucking policeman, to help some woman you work with, and then, your next brilliant idea was to bring her and the body here?!" I was shaking with rage; it was almost unbearable to look at her. My first thoughts when she had arrived, looking beautiful in that incredible dress was that maybe, she'd wanted me; that she'd come here all dolled up, for me. Then I'd seen the other girl, and the body they pulled through behind them. The other girl looked awful. Her dress was torn, barely covering up her sizeable tits, and her face was stained with streaks of makeup. The body was even worse. And once Romany showed me the I.D she'd taken from it, so was the situation. "I knew you going to this party was a bad idea, that you couldn't control yourself."

"I know Beckett, I know it was..."

"Reckless? Dangerous? A goddamn disaster?" My fist came down on the table, and the blonde woman shrunk backwards, almost in tears. Romany, however, just stared at me, completely unfazed. "You're lucky Elise can sort out the security tape of you all wandering down that fucking alleyway!"

"I was helping a defenseless woman, Beckett; what if that had been me? Would you want someone to walk away from me?"

I couldn't reply for a moment, as the idea of her being attacked made me stagger. I steadied myself. "That is not the point Romany, you have risked everything!" She sighed wearily and it suddenly felt difficult to stay angry at her, but my bitter disappointment remained. "And what if she speaks up?"

"I won't." The blonde woman was stood in the doorway, trying to cover herself up with Romany's jacket. She turned around and lifted her dress, revealing the line of a banned poem tattooed on the inside of her creamy thigh. "I know who you are..." She wiped away the black mess under her eyes and sniffed, "...because I'm one of you." Romany flicked her eyes over to me, as shocked as I was. "I'd sooner die than betray you. I just thought Romany was another government whore, that's why I've behaved so appallingly towards her."

"If that's real Christina," Romany pointed to her leg, referring to her tattoo, "then how have none of the men you've been with noticed?"

"Oh I don't sleep with them," Christina smiled ruefully, "I just let them think I will. Gets you just as far without having to get your hands dirty. Let men think you'll do anything to get to the top, they'll give you anything you want until they get bored then you can just move on to the next sucker." She looked at her hands and began to cry.

"Why were you so desperate to get close to the prime minister?" Romany pushed again, still doubtful.

"I hoped that maybe I could get him alone, like the other men wanted, and that maybe I could deal with him myself. You know, kill him. Nothing is more vulnerable than a man thinking with that part of his body." She looked at her hands, and I knew she was disgusted with herself.

"What happened?" I tried not to sound interrogatory, and offered her a chair. "Nobody can hear us here; you don't need to be scared."

"I felt so drunk, and I just wanted to get home. I'm sure someone slipped something into my drink. That asshole was outside, he offered to walk me some of the way to make sure I was safe. But he just pulled me down that disgusting alley, and pulled up my dress... when he saw my tattoo he went crazy, and I just couldn't fight him off. That's when Romany came and helped me."

"Yeah, she's a regular hero." I replied spitefully. Romany flashed me a look that would have driven another man to terror, but I was too angry to care. "But we still have a corpse to deal with, and the police will probably be out looking for him. If we get caught we are fucked." Romany was gnawing her lip so hard it began to bleed a little.

"Unless you use it to your advantage." Christina leant over the table, taking one of my cigarettes from its packet. "Put it somewhere where the public will see it." Romany nodded in agreement, turning to me.

"The Revolution have never made a public show of defiance. Unless you do, you will never convince them that you mean business. The vans will go back soon, and you'll have a half hour gap before curfew is lifted and the police come out. But the problem is how you'll get the body through the streets. We're not exactly dressed for it."

"Lexi will help," I replied. "This is definitely her thing, and she can bring you some clothes." I added pointedly, "If the public see this, if we make it clear it was an act of the Revolution, they will see that we are not afraid." I began to feel fear grip me, wrapping itself around my belly.

"We have been working in the shadows Beckett, killing quietly." Romany reached out to me. "They haven't been able to see what we are doing to help them." I tried to feel confident, to see that Romany was right. It was too fast for my liking, especially so soon after I had told them that we weren't ready. "But if we show them," the thought ticked through my head "then they will know that the day is coming when we will strike. They might just be even more frightened, we don't want them to turn to the prime minister."

"They won't," Christina blew out smoke, leaning back on the chair. "You're not just assassins anymore, you have to be salesmen too. You've got to sell yourself to the public." Romany was smiling, her desire for us to act falling into place. There was just one thing no one but me had considered.

"So we have to sit here with a rotting corpse until curfew is lifted?"

Nobody else seemed to want to answer my question, but that was precisely what we did.

*

The sun rose over the city, and the announcement went out that curfew had now ended. The people began to leave their houses, including myself. The rain had lifted for a day, the black clouds vanished; it was a beautiful day. I closed my eyes as I walked, listening to the sound of birds. Two children walked past me, holding hands, and only their sombre little faces brought the idyllic scene back to reality. I walked into my glass prison, beaming at the guard who only replied with a sneer. I pressed the button for my floor, but a foot stuck in the lift doors. Etienne stepped in beside me. He didn't speak for a second, waiting until the doors had closed to turn on me.

"Where did you go last night? I looked everywhere for you." He looked genuinely hurt, and I felt a small rush of pity for him.

"I'm so sorry Etienne, I think I had a little too much to drink, I just wanted to get home. You looked like you were having such a good time, I didn't want you to feel you had to walk me home, it would have spoiled your night." His eyes grew warm and I saw what I had been dreading; expectation. He pressed the stop button, leaving me suspended in midair, trapped in a metal box with him.

"I know this is really out of order of me, but we have been working together for a while now, and after last night... well, I would like to see more of you." I didn't know what to say. There was nothing I could say to him. He knew nothing about me, and anything he did know was a lie. He was able to live his life normally, in his privileged position, he had nothing to fear. He assumed, naturally that neither did I. But, he was a sweet man, and I could tell he was the kind of man who would take good care of a girl. Had I not been living a lie, had I not been a killer, a member of the Revolution, I would have gladly been his girl. There was no way that could happen, but I just couldn't find it in me to hurt him. Luckily for me, in that moment, a voice broke the uncomfortable silence.

'All employees are to head to their levels immediately.' The words repeated over and over, but Etienne still waited for a reply from me. I wanted to make him better, what was one more lie? But looking into his earnest face, I found I couldn't. Besides that, he was everything I despised, living off the misfortune of others and making a profit in their pain.

"I can't answer that right now Etienne, things are complicated." He assumed I meant that I was with someone, and his face dropped. I leant forward and pressed the button, ignoring his sigh of disappointment. We walked together awkwardly, and as I passed Christina, also making her way to where everyone was gathering, she glanced over at me and gave me a quick smile; so swift it was unnoticed by everyone else.

We gathered around McLean who was pacing up and down, his face dark with rage. He threw down a set of photographs on the table, staring into each of our faces with intense scrutiny, looking for our reactions. His eyes landed on me and narrowed, as though he were trying to stare into the depths of my soul.

"Last night, a police officer was murdered and his body was hung in one of London's busiest areas." He held up one of the pictures, and we all gasped in horror. The policeman's body was hanging from a lamppost, the words 'Let Freedom Reign' scrawled across his forehead in lipstick. "As you can all clearly see, this is the work of the Revolution." He tossed the grotesque image back onto the desk and seemed to snarl at us. "Copies of these photos were found with the body, as well as being sent to us, to the television offices and to the prime minister himself. I want us to go back over every file we have, work out who the hell did this." He stormed away, leaving his audience in disbelief. The muttering around me began as soon as he was out of sight, theories and rumours.

Etienne took hold of my hand. "This is the start of something big, it always starts like this, a few killings and then the riots start again..." He squeezed it a little tighter. "They've never done anything like this before." The cameras whirred behind us, and he stepped away from me, shaking his head. Christina, admirably, had managed to break down into tears, saying how awful it all was. Harry was just stood, staring at me, as though he could read what I was really thinking. The corner of his mouth twitched and as he turned away, I began to feel fear for the first time. We had set the ball rolling and there was no telling where it would end.

*

Matthew shook me gently, waking me up. I must have slept for ages.

"You need to keep quiet now." His voice was gentle, but I knew he was being serious. "If they ask, you need to tell them I'm your daddy, OK?" I wanted to scream at him that, no, I wouldn't tell them. My daddy was dead. But his face made me stop. He was treating me like a grown up; trusting me with something important. I nodded and he wound down the window at the checkpoint, handing the man in uniform some papers. The policeman had a gun, and as he flicked his eyes over me, my lap suddenly felt warm. The seat was damp. My cheeks were very hot, as I knew I had wet myself. I

hadn't done that since I was very little. Matthew didn't look at me, or tell me off, he kept watching the officer.

"Pretty little girl." The police officer nodded at me. "Romany is a very unusual name…" He handed Matthew back the papers.

"It's after her grandmother,." Matthew smiled. I held on tight to my seat, thinking that the policeman was certain to know he was lying.

"You need to go careful driving through the city." The policeman leant through the window and winked at me. "There's been a few problems, but we're taking care of it."

Matthew thanked him, and wound up his window, driving us away slowly. I wondered when he would notice my seat was damp, but he didn't say a word. I had never been to a city before, it was all grey. The buildings were grey, the sky, the road, all grey. There were cameras everywhere, scanning the roads. People walked past us quickly. There was so much barbed wire, so many policemen everywhere. It wasn't at all what I had imagined. But I knew one place that wouldn't have changed.

"I want to go to Buckingham Palace, please?" Matthew kept his eyes on the road, he didn't answer. "Or the Tower of London, my mummy went there when she was a little girl…"

"We can't go there," Matthew interrupted. I didn't want to ask why. I folded my arms and leant against the window, feeling even more miserable. We had to keep stopping to give papers to policemen, over and over. He kept telling me not to look sad, or they would start to ask questions. At the last stop, the policeman looked at my snotty nose and dirty face and frowned. He had a mean face, with a squished up nose. "What's the matter with her?"

Matthew flashed me a look and then shrugged. "You know what kids are like."

The policeman laughed, his fat tummy wobbling. "I know what you mean mate."

We drove along the road, until we pulled up outside some big houses. Some of them had boarded up windows and untidy gardens. But one was beautiful, with lots of flowers outside. A small boy peered down at me from the top window, but he left too quickly for me to see him properly. Matthew was smiling at the house, and he winked at me. I knew that this was going to be my new home.

Matthew flung open his front door, and grabbed a beautiful blonde woman in a big hug. She wore a lovely purple dress, with matching shoes. I followed Matthew, worried about my muddy shoes and damp dress. The lady looked at me, and clamped her hand over her mouth in shock.

"She looks just like her mother," she whispered. She came towards me, and knelt on the floor, her hands on top of mine. "Hello darling, my name is Rose - I'm Matthew's wife."

"I wet myself." I began to cry, feeling very tired all of a sudden. "And my mummy and daddy are dead." She lifted me up and hugged me very hard, and buried my face in her hair. She smelt lovely, like the flowers in my mummy's garden. My mummy loves her garden.

"Well, I'm sure we can sort that out."

Rose took me upstairs, and put me in a huge bath, filled to the brim with bubbles. She washed my hair, and sang to me as she did so. Afterwards, she wrapped me in a warm towel and carried me to a beautiful bedroom. It had a large bed in the middle, with a quilt covered in little roses.

"Did you know I was coming?" I asked as she pulled a white nightie over my head. She looked very sad.

"No my sweetheart. This room used to belong to my little girl." She wiped a tear from her cheek and bit her lip.

"Doesn't she live here?"

"No." She picked up a brush and began to pull it through my hair. "That is why I wanted you to come and stay with us."

*

Beckett was waiting for me when I arrived home, his arms folded. "Everyone is talking about the policeman. I have to say, this is garnering more publicity than Hardwicke; the government can't cover this up so easily." He tossed a piece of paper onto my dining table, and stood back proudly. I inspected his handiwork.

"For England, For Freedom, For YOU. Join the Revolution," I read out quietly. "A leaflet? This is what you couldn't wait until the next meeting to show me?"

"Last night was just the beginning; we have to make everyone pay attention to us. These leaflets will do that. We'll post them through letterboxes, litter them through the streets; bombard people with them until they can't ignore us." He looked so thrilled with his plan, I didn't want to be the one to point out the obvious.

"That's wonderful, but how are we going to print enough of these and not be noticed."

He smiled at me roguishly. "I have friends working in the printing business. They print off the government's promotional material, so nobody is going to suspect them. I have it all arranged." He leant against the door frame, full of arrogant satisfaction.

"So you planned all of this today?" It was almost too much to believe.

"Well, I've been planning this for some time, but it never seemed the right moment. But, after today, we need to strike, while this is fresh in people's minds."

I held back my smile, and watched him shift uncomfortably.

"So, I've been right all along..." He walked to my window.

"I wouldn't say that." As I turned, I caught the smile on his face. "But I suppose, you brutally murdering that police officer wasn't the worst thing you've ever done."

I stepped closer to him, resisting the urge to place my hand on his.

"I know that, after Hardwicke, your source advised you not to strike the prime minister." I proceeded carefully, choosing my words with caution. "I think that was the right decision now, without the people on our side we would have achieved nothing other than to pave the way for another to take his place."

He turned to me, and his gaze softened. "Thank you." In those two words, he said everything he needed to. The pressures of his position were many, I knew that, and sometimes I did not give him credit for that. The responsibility weighed heavy on his shoulders. As he headed for the back door, ready to leave before curfew he paused and smiled at me over his shoulder. Like a jolt, that spark was there again. He stepped out into the dark, leaving me stood alone in my empty house.

6

Rose walked me back downstairs and into the kitchen. Matthew was stood in front of the stove, and whatever he was cooking smelt delicious. My tummy growled. He turned to look at me and grinned.

"Well don't you look beautiful?" He put a plate of eggy bread in front of me and I ate it as quickly as I could, barely chewing each delicious mouthful. Footsteps behind me made me turn in my seat. A boy stood in the doorway. He had dark hair, and a serious face. His eyes were a bright blue, the colour of the sea I used to look at from my bedroom window. They stared at my face and didn't blink. It made my tummy feel a little funny. Rose walked over and ruffled his hair and it made him smile. It made him look much nicer.

"This is our son, Beckett."

*

We had set it all into motion, and as I inspected the piles of pamphlets at my feet, my mind became tangled in a web of decisions. I would begin by having the leaflets distributed door-to-door, hidden in newspapers by our supporters. But that wouldn't be enough, they would simply destroy them; terrified of being caught with them. We needed to think bigger.

The public had to trust us, they had to see us an embodiment of their true selves. In order to do that, we needed to put a face to our cause. A figurehead, a representation of the Revolution. I looked at myself in the mirror, and tried out a charming smile. My face remained dark, barely cracked by the insincere grin. No, I was not going to work. A man would always be seen as a fighter, hard and aggressive. But if we were to use a woman, she would symbolize all manner of things. A warrior, a mother, a sister or a lover, in the public's eyes she could be untouchable, fierce and yet vulnerable. But whoever I chose would be in huge danger. I relayed the candidates through my brain, weighing up my options. There was Elise, my computer wizard. She was pretty in an obvious way, with her blonde curls. But in my opinion she had a stuck-up little nose and overly high cheekbones, giving her a pinched appearance. But she wasn't really much of a field girl, she preferred to work behind a screen, hidden away from the world. Next was Lexi, with her shaven head and Amazonian figure, she would make a strong impression on the people. But she was impulsive, and hard. There was no getting away from that. Although it would make people take notice, it could also scare them away. My final option, and the one I least wanted to opt for, was of course, Romany. But unfortunately for me, she was the best choice. Intelligent, beautiful and deadly, she would be ideal. She was everything I needed her to be. But could I risk losing her? If I placed her for the people to see, I would also be exposing her to the government. They had such advanced technology, voice recognition, a complex database to access. If I was going to use Romany, and push her out onto their radar, I would need to ensure her safety.

Deep down, I had always known that out of the two of us, Romany should have been the leader of the Revolution.

*

Burning, that is the only way I can describe the look in his eyes, as they glanced at me. This meeting had been called in a hurry, it was unlike Beckett. He was a little edgy though, almost nervous. He clapped his hands, silencing the room.

"I have made a decision on our next plan of action. As you all know, I am distributing leaflets to every home in London, though I hope eventually it will be every city in the country." He paced back and forth. "But this will not be enough. We need to begin our assault with something, spectacular." Locking onto me, he stood to his full height, drawing our full attention to him. Everyone was leaning forward a little, hanging on his every word. "I feel that it is time to start gaining the trust of the ordinary citizens." He rubbed his elbow absentmindedly, losing focus for a brief moment. "I feel that in order to do that, we need to put a face to the Revolution." A ripple went through his audience. "I know that for my candidate, it will be risky. Keeping their identity a secret won't be easy." Everyone was on the edge of their seats, desperate to know who he had entrusted with this most dangerous of assignments. "I have decided, as leader of the London section, to hand the position to Romany."

My heart stopped. The room spun. Every set of eyes were now on me, each filled with different emotions:

envy, curiosity, pride and fear. Lexi turned her face away from me. They were waiting for me to make a reply, to thank Beckett for this extraordinary show of faith. But, instead, I stumbled out of the room, holding onto the walls for support.

His hands came down on my shoulders, and he gently turned me to face him.

"I'm sorry to throw this on you, but there's no one I trust more. After all, getting the people on side was your idea."

"So you want to parade me around, expose me to them? They'll tear me apart." I forced him to look me in the eye. "I work for the *government* Beckett; do you really think they won't figure out who I am?"

"Are you telling me you can't do this?" It was a challenge.

"I'm the best you have; I'm the only one who can do it." I began to walk away from him and his triumphant smirk. "I'm just saying I can't, and you shouldn't expect me to."

"You said you would do anything for the Revolution."

I turned and pushed him forcefully away from me. "So that includes suicide does it? Because when they work out who I am, they'll take me in the vans and torture me until I give you up, then they'll kill me, and this will all be for nothing."

He looked horrified, his eyebrows puckered in the middle. "That won't happen."

I got close to his face, so close I could have bitten him. "You had better hope not, or I swear I'll walk them to your front door myself."

Beckett raised an eyebrow. "So you'll do it."

I looked at the floor, shifting back into my cold self. "As I said, I'm the only one who can." As I headed back to the meeting, he spoke.

"I wouldn't let them take you. We can't think of ourselves or each other if we want to win, but *I* swear to *you* I'll die before they take you." He spoke so quietly I wondered if I'd heard right. When I turned, he had closed the kitchen door, hiding himself from me.

"So you're going to go through with it?" Elise piped up as I closed the basement door. I nodded and she clapped her hands gleefully, followed by the others. With the glaring exception of Lexi.

"Are you fucking stupid?" she spat, from the furthest corner of the room. "You may as well go upstairs and slit your wrists, it'll be quicker than what they'll do to you."

Stunned, the others began to awkwardly make their excuses, heading up the stairs to discuss the plans further with Beckett. Lexi went to storm past me, but I grabbed her arm, forcing her to stand still.

"This isn't about me, this is about the Revolution Lexi, and Beckett is right, we need to bring the people to us. It makes sense to have someone representing us to them, or we just seem like some sinister vigilante group."

"That's what we are, and it's worked fine for us so far." She pouted petulantly.

"Grow up Lexi." I released my grip on her and her eyes went dark, as they always did when she was furious.

"I need to grow up? You're only agreeing to this shit because you want to fuck Beckett."

Before I could control myself, my hand flew out, slapping her hard across the face. "He is our leader," I hissed, "and you should respect him, like I do. Once you calm down, you'll see this makes sense." Instantly, I wanted to reach out and apologise, to hold her, but I had to support Beckett's decision, to keep us together. "This isn't personal Lexi, its necessary."

She gently touched the spot I'd hit her, and her unrelenting gaze forced me to look away. She turned away from me, leaving the basement. I pulled on my hair, fighting the urge to scream. We had never been more successful, but I felt as though I was falling apart. There was a small fluttering in my stomach; something I hadn't felt before that was showing its ugly face. I was scared. Scared I was going to fail and destroy our plans. I sank to the floor, burying my face in my hands.

*

I am a teenager. Beckett is lying beside me on his bed, we are smoking cigarettes, seeing who can blow smoke rings first. Rose would go crazy if she saw us. Not that there's any chance she will.

It is a beautiful summer's day and the room is flooded with sunlight. Faded posters of cars and supermodels surround us. Beckett and I have had this 'thing' going on for months now. His parents sent him away for a while and when he came back...well suddenly he seemed a lot less like a brother to me. And since we are hardly ever allowed out the house, we are the only company for each other. Things have become harder lately. Matthew has upped our training, from once a day to almost three times a day. I am constantly exhausted, and I find myself looking more and more to my fag breaks with Beckett. He is worried about his mum, though he will not admit it; Rose hasn't left her room in weeks. His beautiful, radiant mother is bedridden, and just stares at the ceiling, a corpse with a heartbeat. Shortly before he went away, the police came to every house on the street that still had families living in them. They took away our computers, our IPods, our books...everything that violated the list, the list that was now stuck on the fridge. When they had come, Beckett had held my hand to stop it shaking; we were certain they had come for us. Matthew has become more and more irritable, all his energies are focused on the Revolution, in training us to become members. I'm sure he is worried about Rose, but he can't bring himself to face it. His eyes have deep violet beneath them, he hardly sleeps.

When Beckett was sent away, Matthew barely spoke to me, he just worked me harder than usual. I hated being away from Beckett. There were rumours that the police were going to be forcing every male adult over the age of sixteen to join, and Matthew couldn't bear to let Beckett be one of them. This time, the rumour had turned out to be false, but it was enough to make Matthew even more desperate to get us ready to lead the Revolution.

*

I was woken by a gentle kick to my shin. Beckett stared down at me, his head tipped to one side.

"Wake up sleeping beauty." For a second, it was as though we were back in the old house, and he was waking me up, ready for another sunny day. There hadn't been sunshine like it since. Or maybe life was so miserable it just seemed that way.

"What is it?" I mumbled. He reached out a hand and pulled me up to my feet. I stumbled a little, and fell against him. He held me still for a moment, the full length of his body pressed against mine.

"I wanted to say thank you." I looked up at him, at the dark curls hanging in his eyes.

"I'm not doing it for you, I'm doing it for the Revolution." It sounded a little unconvincing, even to me.

"You're not doing it for me?" His lips were close to my ear, his breath moving the wisps of hair that hung there. I could barely breathe, and a desperate need for him rushed through my body. I closed my eyes, and felt his warmth, felt his hand brush my cheek. When I opened my eyes, he had left the room.

*

I can remember watching Beckett drive away that night. I'd gone into his room before he'd left, and he was stuffing his things into a bag. He had to disappear before the vans came out. I tried to speak to him, tell him to stay but all that came out was his name, a tiny whisper. He didn't say anything to me, but I could tell he had been crying. He just grabbed me in a hug, and kissed my neck tenderly. It was so light I could have imagined it. We both knew there was a chance they'd catch him trying to leave, or that he wouldn't make it home. I didn't want to think about that. I couldn't imagine my life without Beckett. As he walked away, I grabbed his hand.

"I'll miss you." I said as loudly as I dared. He didn't look back, and I knew it was killing him. I could see it in the way his shoulders tensed. As he closed his bedroom door behind him, I heard his tiny reply.

"I'll miss you more."

As the car drove away, I could hear Rose's cries from her room.

"They've stolen my other baby from me…" she moaned. I had fallen to my knees, and sobbed silently into my pillow.

*

We could just run away you know…" I whispered, sat in the basement, waiting for Matthew to come down for training. Beckett had only been back a few days, after the all clear had been given - the truth teased away from the rumour. "…We could just go somewhere. Plenty of people manage it and don't get caught."

He peered up at me, shaking his head. "We have a duty Romany, to fight for those who can't. For Eloise, for your parents… never forget that. If we ran away, they would have all died for nothing. We have to win for them."

"You're just saying what he tells you to."

"No." His tone made me stop. "It's what I believe. Some things are bigger than us, this is one of them."

7

I made my way up the stairs, my mind swimming in a fog of the past. I had been foolish, standing there waiting for something to happen. In the end, he had walked away, as he always did. He squeezed my hand, then dropped it, as though my touch burned him. I passed Beckett's room, and looked in to find Lexi perched on the window sill; blowing smoke rings out into the air. The sun filled the room with light, casting shadows as she ran her hand over her shaved head. The floor creaked beneath my feet and she looked over her shoulder, her lips curling into a half-hearted smile. But her eyes were weary of me, and I could still see an angry mark on her cheek where I had slapped her. She flicked her cigarette away and closed the window, pulling the blind down with a fierce tug. Her eyes were shadowed with violet bags, heavy with fatigue.

"You haven't slept?" I asked, and she shrugged, crossing one slender leg over the other. "Look Lexi, I'm sorry for what happened." She threw me her pack of cigarettes, and leapt down from the window, landing heavily on her scuffed Dr Martin boots.

"Don't worry about it. I'd forgotten about it already. Besides, this is obviously something you've just got to do." She looked weary, not like the Amazonian warrior I knew. Her muscles flexed as she lifted the weights Beckett had left out, grunting as she worked out.

"Come on Lexi," I sat down on the bed, "this isn't like you; you know that we have to do these things in order to win..."

She slammed the weights down and stormed up to me, her face close to mine. "How the fuck do you know who I am?" She flung her arms open and stepped back. "You think this is me, just the black lesbian with a pair of nice tits? Typical Lexi, scared of nothing, is that what you think?" She collapsed on to the floor, her head in her hands. "That's what I thought. Some of us aren't completely soulless like you; some of us actually are frightened by all of this."

Though her comments stung, I calmly lit a cigarette and patiently waited for the storm to blow over, but instead was horrified to see tears rolling down her face.

"You don't know what I am Romany, I'm a murderer." She hugged her legs to her body, rocking gently back and forth. "I killed her Romany... I killed her..." She wiped her hands on her arm and looked up at me, childlike in her despair. "When I was a little girl, we lived by the sea, I can't remember where exactly, but I dream about it every night. The smell of the sea, the sound of the gulls, every damn night. My mother was Nigerian, she moved here when she was a baby, and my father was a reverend, from Kenya originally. When all this began, he told me that he would help this country through the darkness by doing God's work." Her eyes glazed over, as the ghosts of her past began to take hold over her. I held my breath, not wanting to break the moment. "My father loved my mother so much, he called her his princess. She was so beautiful, I thought he was telling the truth. I used to ask him why we didn't live in a castle." She smiled and wiped her nose on her arm. "Even in the darkest days, he always made my mother smile. But my mother hated what our home had become, and not long after it formed, she joined the Revolution." She stood to her feet, her hands behind her head. "My father was furious; it's the only time I ever heard him raise his voice. But he knew he couldn't stop her, he knew this was what she wanted. So he said that they would work together, his God and her strength combined. They told me to keep it secret, that it was an important secret I must never tell anyone. My mother worked hard for the Revolution, and when they started rounding people up and taking them to the cities, she was actually excited because she knew it would mean moving closer to a Revolution base. She thought she could do more to help if we were in the city." She began to sob again and her body shook. "They put me into a new school, and told me all the lies I had to tell... Nobody could know where my parents were from, or we'd be sent back there." She scraped her nails over the smooth curve of her head and wiped hard at the tears on her face.

"I was just a kid Romany, just a dumb kid. My friends were talking about whose parents were the coolest. This one girl, some stuck up blonde bitch began saying how her dad worked for the government and how amazing he was and... Fuck it Romany, I just wanted to fit in so..."

"...You told them what your mum was doing." She nodded and her face broke, tears rolling down her face. I ran forward and grabbed her in a fierce hug, holding her close as her body trembled.

"That bitch couldn't keep her mouth shut. They came for her, when my dad was at church. She tried to fight back, but this one guy hit her. He hit my fucking mum.

So I ran and kicked him as hard as I could. He told me he was going to teach me a lesson. So he made my mum watch while he..." She trailed off and fell to the floor, and I fell with her, still holding her close to me. A feeling of nausea swept over me and I struggled to breathe. "...I was just a *child* Romany; I was just trying to defend my mum. When he was done, he laughed in my mum's face and dragged her out the door by her hair. She just kept telling me she loved me, that I was going to be okay. I couldn't move, I just lay there, unable to cry, unable to speak. My dad came home hours later, grabbed what we could carry and took us to the city. It wasn't until we made it to his friend's house that he finally spoke. When he did, it was only to tell them to take good care of me. He locked himself in his room, and didn't come out again. He had managed to keep his faith throughout everything and they destroyed him. He couldn't bear to live one day without her; he couldn't bear to see what they had done to me. He'd just run out of strength."

I took her in my arms and I rocked her gently, desperate to protect her from the nightmares of her past. "That bastard took *everything* from me; I can't let them take you too."

"They won't Lexi, I promise I won't let them..." I began to sing softly, the same song my father used to sing to my mother and me. "...*I feel wonderful because I see the love light in your eyes. And the wonder of it all is that you just don't realize how much I love you...*" Her muscular body nestled into mine, and we curled up together on the floor, as we began to truly realise what had been taken from us.

*

Beckett rolled over onto his side, leaning over me to put his cigarette in the ashtray. He lingered for a second, his face just above mine. My heart pounded for a moment, but as he leant closer, Matthew's voice boomed downstairs, breaking the tension. Beckett lay on his back, sighing loudly.

"You know what Romany, I wish we had been born in a different time." My mind was transported for a second, back to the farmhouse, sitting before the fire listening to my father reading my mother tales of an England from long ago. "Then we could just be two people, lying on a bed, with nothing to fight for except our own lives." He lit up another cigarette. "I never told you about Eloise did I?" I froze; did Beckett have a new girlfriend? "She was my sister." Although I was relieved that Beckett didn't have a girl, I also felt uncomfortable. Nobody had mentioned the lost little girl in this house, not since my first day. Her room had become my room, and all memory of her had vanished. "We were so close. Eloise wasn't frightened of anything. She never backed down from a dare, not even the bad ones. My mum used to sing to her, and even when she told her off, she couldn't stop herself from smiling." He closed his eyes, and smiled. I could tell he was picturing her. His smile disappeared. "When all this shit got serious, Eloise was always happy. Even when Mum was crying and Dad was getting angry, she always cheered us up." He reached into the drawer beside his bed, and passed me a photograph. A pretty little girl with tangled blonde hair and her hands on her hips smiled up at me. The picture was taken in a wood,

92

and her dress was covered in mud. She looked like a fairy. "She used to stick up for me at school; she was really tough you know? Of course, then we stopped going to school."

"What happened?" I breathed, still lost in the photograph.

"We got bored, stuck in the house all day. The police vans started driving by and Eloise said we should sneak out, see how long we could stay out before they bought us home." He rolled back onto his side, but he couldn't look me in the eye. "When my parents went to bed we broke curfew. We were just naughty kids you know? We were walking back, feeling pleased with ourselves. There was this house, and the police were dragging out the family... the kids were screaming, the mum was crying. Eloise, well, she just couldn't stand there and watch. She shouted at them, told them to stop." My heart was thudding so loud I was certain he could hear. "One of the policemen...he laughed at her. Eloise spat at him. He didn't like that, not one bit, being humiliated by a child. He grabbed his gun and..." He closed his eyes and began to sob. I wrapped my arms around him. "I ran, as fast as I could home. When I told my mum what happened she just fell to the floor, screaming. My dad didn't even look at me, he just got his coat and went to find her. He carried her home, through the streets. But nobody even came out to help, they were all too scared."

He held me close and leant his head on my chest. "After the funeral, my dad barely said two words, my mum never stopped crying. My father stopped speaking to me about anything, other than how I was one day *going to lead the Revolution, and about training. It has been that way ever since."*

*

Tea, in my opinion, has a calming effect; as soon as I picked up the warm, steaming cup and felt it wash down my throat, I felt calm. And, as my shaking hands picked up the chipped china to take another sip, I was glad of it. Beckett paced back and forth, and it began to irritate me.

"You wanted to tell me the plan Beckett, so get on with it." He glanced at me, and I hoped my voice hadn't sounded as shaky to him as it did to me. I had lain awake all night, thoughts of what he would ask from me running through my head. I had tried not to seem distracted at work, though Christina had been quick to hiss at me if I seemed to be on another planet for even a moment. But as I had made my way through the night, slipping past the torture vans and cameras, for the briefest of moments I had almost turned back and headed home. I silently moved amongst the houses, moving like a shadow through the night. But, one of the many windows I passed had made me stop, captivated like a rabbit in headlights.

The rain had trickled down the back of my neck as I stepped closer to the window, forcing me to wrap my arms around myself to keep warm. The curtains were pulled apart, allowing me a perfect viewpoint into the living room. A little boy sat on the floor in front of me, smearing paint on the page on his lap. As he peered up at me I froze, expecting him to yell for his parents who were sat behind him, placing my finger over my lips to try and calm him. But instead, he grinned up at me, also putting his little hand over his mouth. I felt myself smiling back, and as he giggled behind his hand, I stuck out my tongue. The man sat with his back to us leant forward, picking up the remote from the coffee table in order to switch off the television, before pulling the woman beside him closer. He whispered into her ear, and she threw her head back, laughing. The sight seemed almost alien to me, the world we lived in had so little for anyone to be happy about anymore. She stretched her legs across the sofa and closed her eyes as he placed a kiss on her forehead. The boy turned his attentions back to his art. The lady sat up and called her little boy to her, laughing as he sprinted over, his messy hands outstretched. She grabbed his little wrists, throwing him onto the sofa, tickling him under his armpits.

My mind began to wander, and it was as though I had stepped through the walls into the scene. I was stood looking out the window, and, at the sound of a little boy's laughter, I turned around. The blonde boy was running towards me, and as I swept him up in my arms I could smell his warm scent mingled with undertones of paint and mud. He buried his face into my neck, sighing gently. I stroked his curls with my free hand and swept them back out of his face, revealing the paint streaks across his forehead. I tutted at him and let him down, gripping hold of his electric blue hands as I led him over to the kitchen sink. I scrubbed his nails, and wiped off his dirty face. He screamed as I chased him across the room, laughing as he leapt on to the sofa. I clambered up beside him and pulled him into my arms, resting his tiny head against me. I could hear someone making their way down the corridor towards us. I looked over to the door, expecting the handsome man of the house to come in. But the silhouette of the figure walking towards us was too familiar to me, and it caused butterflies in my stomach.

The boy jumped to his feet and ran towards the man, his little feet skidding a little beneath him. He swept the child up in his strong arms before stepping from the shadows into the cosy room. Beckett's eyes had a warmth in them I had never seen before, and as he kissed the boy's forehead his gaze never left mine, making my heart race. As he swung the boy through the air a wedding ring glittered on his finger.

A downpour of water from the gutter snapped me from my reverie, and as I looked down I realised my hand had absentmindedly wandered down my damp clothing to my belly. I looked back through the curtains but the family was still sat, cuddled up on the sofa, the parents reading a book to the boy. The knot in my belly tightened. I had never considered what might lay ahead if we won. Obviously the work was needed to put the country back together, but then what? Was I going to spend my whole life dedicated to the cause, or could there be another path for me? Perhaps I could pass the baton to another and truly be able to live. Perhaps I would experience a marriage, maybe even motherhood.

I looked back at the family, unable to leave. I wanted to knock on the door, to ask to join them. But they didn't know me, or what I was doing every day to give them a future. I had spent my childhood training in a dingy basement, making sacrifices no child should have to make, for people like them. Why couldn't it be the other way round? Why couldn't I be the one curled up in front of a burning fire with my soul mate, watching my children playing, oblivious to the work of the Revolution but reaping the benefits?

I pulled a cigarette from my wet jeans pocket, and thankfully, it was dry. My hands were shaking as I lifted it to my mouth and I scolded myself, thinking how stupid it was to think about what my life could have been. It was what it was, I couldn't change it. The little boy looked over his shoulder at me, smiling his cheeky grin. It wasn't over yet, I reminded myself, but when it was, if I was still here, maybe then it could be possible to put all I had done behind me. If we won, anything would be possible. He nudged his father, trying to get him to turn and see me. But by the time they came to the window I had already vanished back into the night.

"Romany?" Beckett's voice broke my daydream and I snapped back into the present. This was my life, my reality. I wasn't a mother, or a wife, I was an assassin, part of the key to helping people like that family live without fear or persecution. I closed the door tight on my feelings and smiled up at Beckett, screaming inside. "I have spent, hours and hours trying to think of a way we can expose you to the people without putting you at risk." He looked towards the door and Elise walked in to join us. Elise was without a doubt, sexy as hell. Blonde hair in tight ringlets, framing baby blues nestled in creamy peach skin. She looked like an angel, but was without a doubt one of the most ruthless women I knew. Her father had been Matthew's closest friend, a computer analyst before the government took control. Once Bowman grew in power, her father's work was declared 'dangerous' and he was taken, but not before he could nourish little Elise's own talent for all things electrical. She was a genius, and her butter-wouldn't-melt face was the perfect mask. She sat at the table, flashing her perfect white teeth in a smile.

"So my darling," Elise leant closer to me, and I could smell peppermint on her breath, "how do you fancy being a movie star for a day?" Beckett flashed her a less than forgiving glance, and she leant back, unflustered.

"What Elise is trying to say, is that we don't feel that having you present our cause to the nation in person is safe." A bead of sweat appeared above his left eyebrow. "Unfortunately, the police are just as highly trained as we are. Instead, Elise is going to make you appear on every television across the country, by infiltrating the government broadcasting system." My jaw must have dropped, as Elise placed her hands up, smiling triumphantly.

"I know a guy." She glanced over at Beckett and whispered behind her hand, "That is, I was sleeping with a guy." He rolled his eyes at her.

"And he's helping us?" I asked.

"No, he just likes to talk after a drink or twelve. Told me everything I need to know about their systems." I stood to my feet, suddenly feeling hot and sweaty. "We'll send out a transmission that will interrupt the government's own. Every family in the country will be watching you."

I tried to take on board her words. But no matter how hard I tried, to feel better about it, I couldn't. I was a killer, and a damn good one, but I was not a fucking television presenter. "They'll just trace the signal, they'll find you Elise."

She threw back her head, letting out a deep, guttural laugh. "Please, how long have you known me Romany? As if I'd let them do that. Besides, I have a plan..." She tried to disguise the look between her and Beckett.

"We're going to film the broadcast in advance..."

"Now," Elise interrupted, earning her another scathing glare from Beckett.

"...and we are going to use Elise's skills to ensure that they cannot recognise this house, or you."

"How are you going to ensure they don't recognise me?" I responded. "Fuck your house Beckett, you can move; if they recognise me, that's it." He stumbled, his brain barely able to string together a sentence. "We may have Elise, but the government has advanced capabilities. Facial recognition software, vocal scrambler deciphers..."

Elise stood up, leaning across the table to place her hand on my shoulder. "You have to trust me Romany. They are not going to recognise you, and whatever technology they have, I can handle it. They don't think we have the capacity for this level of tech, they'll be too busy searching for the woman you're about to become to realise it's all bullshit. It will take them *months* to figure it out, if they do at all. By then, we'll have already won."

I calmed a little, my heart rate returning to normal. Elise was right; she wouldn't send me out across every television in Britain unprotected.

The stranger staring back at me on the screen left me searching for words. She spoke with conviction and courage, and she was inspiring. What shocked me more was that the gorgeous, inspiring woman was me. Elise had done an amazing job, nobody in a million years would be able to decipher her work and know who this girl was. But her words, her belief in her cause, was entirely mine. Truthfully, I felt like a coward, hiding behind a disguise, but I knew it was necessary. I was too deep in the government network. Elise was beaming, like a mother watching her child walk through the school gates, marvelling at her own brilliance.

"This is going to work," Beckett murmured to himself. "This is actually going to work." The colour began to slowly return to his face, and his hands were no longer gripping the chair for dear life. I realised that he had been frightened, for the Revolution's success and for my safety. "They'll never track her down from this Elise, you're a genius!" He picked her up and whirled her around, smiling broadly. It made my head thump a little, watching the pair of them, though I knew it was a foolish thought. He put her down and turned to me, his arms open. He lingered for a second, placing them back down to his sides, standing awkwardly. "You're happy about this right?"

I looked at my feet, fixing a smile on my face that I was certain was showing too many of my teeth. I stared him carefully in the eye, still grinning maniacally.

"Of course. For the Revolution." This may not have been the reply he was expecting or the one I wanted to give but it was what I chose. I wanted to tell him I was a little scared of what would happen once we followed through on this grand plan. I wanted to embrace him and reassure us both that this could only be another step to victory. Instead, I wrapped myself in the safety of my assassin's guise and was careful to reveal nothing. "And besides, Lexi will be pleased to know I'm not in any danger."

He glanced away, shrugging. "Yeah, I'm sure she will be." His voice held a note of contempt, and he withdrew from our conversation, chatting to Elise in hushed tones. It was clear that I was not to be a part of their chat. Elise glanced at me, apologetic, but Beckett was the leader, and if he demanded her attention that's what he got. I was the 'face' of the Revolution, but it was obvious to me who was in charge. Once again, our relationship had shifted, from something meaningful, to strictly business. I was never sure where I stood with Beckett, and it was beginning to tire me. I suppose as I walked away from Beckett, my mind began to whisper to me, whisper to me that perhaps it wasn't the government that was making him so bitter, so consumed with hatred. Perhaps it wasn't the loss of Eloise or of Rose. Perhaps, above all things, the one thing that hounded Beckett; the reason he and I could never be together, was the Revolution itself. He was obsessed, and it was an addiction that had been drilled into him ever since he was a child. Matthew had ensured that his son would never be distracted by love or lust. I glanced back at Beckett, who was still animatedly talking to Elise, his hands gesturing enthusiastically, discussing me like I was not even in the room. The government had technology far superior to ours, it was not impossible that they could work out who I really was. But it didn't matter to Beckett; all that mattered was that I was the next step to victory. Perhaps he was incapable of loving someone. I left the basement, trying to push these thoughts from my brain. I was part of the

Revolution; I had killed for it, and would kill for it again in order for it to succeed. But my mind flitted back to that family I had watched, as I wondered what would become of me once we did succeed. Would I ever be able to escape what I had become, and would Beckett ever be capable of leaving it behind?

8

My dream that night was not of my childhood, but something entirely new. I was stood atop a roof, a dizzying height from the streets below. The world seemed strange and unfamiliar, like a scene from one of the banned comic books Lexi and I used to steal. Indeed, much like the crime fighting superheroes from those prohibited graphic novels, I was dressed in a tight red one-piece, my legs bare with the exception of my high black boots. A cape fluttered around my shoulders.

I stared up into the black sky. The moon delicately wrapped in wisps of cloud, and stars peered out from the misty veil. Below me, a crowd was gathering. They stared up at me, some pointing, some cheering, others jeering. My sight was a little blurred, and as I touched my face, my fingers brushed against the mask over my eyes. The wind was bitter, and I suddenly realised with horror that my tight leotard was backless. I stepped back away from the edge when I saw the limousine pulling up. He stepped out, dressed impeccably in a charcoal suit, staring up at me. My eyes locked on to Bowman, and I no longer felt afraid. I felt only anger, and an overwhelming need to attack. I reached for my gun, but there was nothing, only an empty holster. I was unarmed. The crowd was parting, letting him pass, until he was stood directly below me. All eyes were on me. I recognised the two figures who came to stand beside him, dressed in black, militant uniforms. Beckett and Lexi sneered at me, laughing along with Bowman. Hardwicke stepped out of the limo, his skin drained of colour, deathly pale. I looked down at my hands, and stared in disgust as a small spot of blood in the centre of my palm began to spread, staining both hands. I was a killer. I would always be a killer. I reached to my face, tearing off my mask, closing my eyes at the gasps below. I was a member of the Revolution, and they could all see me now. Everyone was watching me now.

The ground began to shake, and from the heavens came a downpour of Revolution pamphlets. The building I stood on was in flames, licking at my feet. I felt no pain, only relief. The windows exploded, and with a deafening bang, more leaflets shot out of the building, raining down on now full streets below.

Bowman was looking around in horror and began to scream as Lexi and Beckett's hands came down on his shoulders. Hardwicke scrambled back into the limo, and Bowman watched in horror as he sped away. I felt the breeze again and looked down, to find myself stood in nothing but my underwear, completely exposed. The blood vanished from my hands and I was no longer a murderer, no longer a superhero, just a woman. Lexi and Beckett pushed Bowman's lifeless body to the floor, a rose of blood blooming around him. The crowd was baying like dogs, the scent of the slaughter driving them wild. They were staring at me, screaming for me. More, they begged, we want more. Beckett and Lexi gripped one another, panting with adrenaline and triumph. I shrank back, disgusted with them, and with myself. I wanted revenge, I needed freedom but in this twisted fantasy neither pleased me. I needed to be free. The ledge was high, and the wind howled, the babble of the crowd making my ears hurt. I stepped backwards, one, two, three steps, before taking a run up to the edge, spreading my arms and soaring through the air. The crowd below went silent, stood motionless in the drifts of leaflets. Like the phoenix on my back I flew, and closed my eyes, waiting for the fall.

*

Every morning, for as long as I can remember, the world has seemed grey. I don't just mean the clouds, or the dirty, unloved buildings, but the world itself. Like the colour has just been sucked from it. I never stopped to look outside when I woke. And yet, on this morning, after I had woken sweaty and screaming, the first thing I had noticed was the stream of sunlight pouring through my window. I peered out, and admired the frost that had transformed the garden. The world was still grey, but the sun broke through the clouds, making the frost glisten. It looked as though each gatepost, each tree, each burnt out car was covered in a layer of glitter. For a moment, I caught a glimpse of the world I remembered from my childhood. But then a white van passed, creeping past my gate, breaking my peacefulness. The dish on top turned in a slow circle, and I knew they could see me by my window. I released the curtain, letting it gently fall into place. I pulled on my grey trouser suit, and instead of opting for a black shirt, I added a splash of colour with a fuchsia camisole, as well as a pair of leather heels that pinched my feet. I knew that part of my success at the office was my appearance, as shallow as it sounded. As I stepped outside, I pulled my thick duffle coat tighter around myself, stunned a little by the bitter morning air. I had heard nothing from Beckett since I left his home, not even with regards to the broadcast. I was completely in the dark.

I sighed with frustration as the guard held out his hand for my papers, leering at me.

"Well hello beautiful." He chewed the skin on his lip, raking his eyes over my papers. He went to hand them back, pulling them away from me at the last second. "Now I could give these back to you, but in exchange for something." There was a scab on his chin, and he picked at it absentmindedly. "How about a little kiss?"

My body went rigid as he stepped towards me, hands on hips. His breath had the sour scent of alcohol, despite the gum he spat at my feet. I wanted to kill him. He leant forward, eyes shut and at the last second the radio in his van crackled. His eyes snapped open and he smirked at me. "Sorry babe, duty calls. But next time, I'll get you, don't you worry about that."

As he grabbed his radio and I strode quickly away, I could hear his voice growing louder and more agitated. I didn't turn back, I kept walking, my pace quicker than before. I burst into the foyer of the office, and the guard raised an eyebrow at me, suspicious.

"Sorry," I flashed him a smile, smoothing down the front of my suit, "running late."

He scowled at my feeble excuse and pointed at me. "You need to get your ass to your level now; something's going on up there."

I hurried into the lift, apologising as I shoved past those waiting. I tried to listen to their whispers as we travelled up each floor.

"...haven't released a statement..."

"I don't know what to think Julian, honestly..."

One mindless observation after another, but nothing that would reveal to me what was happening. The doors opened on my floor, and I pushed past those stood in front of me, grateful to see Christina stood in the doorway. I went to speak to her, and remembered myself and where I was.

"Christina," I nodded curtly. "What is it?"

Her pout was fixed into place as she flicked her hair back. "Etienne says to get to his office immediately."

I ran past her, and as I looked back she was leaning over her desk, answering the flashing phones. They were ringing off the hook.

Etienne was in his office, staring at the television screen on the wall. As I walked in, he turned up the volume. He spoke not a word, his face white as the papers spread out in front of him. Instead, he gestured for me to sit. A large 'R' swirled on the screen, the words scrolling beneath informing the viewer of an 'impending broadcast from the British Revolution Movement'. The taste of bile rose in my throat. Beckett had waited until I was in work, ensuring I would see my broadcast, but also placing me at complete risk if I was by any chance recognised. Not even I could escape from this building. I was glad Etienne looked so mortified, I wasn't arousing his attention with my own pallid complexion.

The screen went black for a second and I had to force myself to remain in my seat. Had Elise failed? Would they even now be heading to the source of the broadcast to drag her and Beckett into the vans? Would they have found the original footage and be on their way to arrest me? Then, as I contemplated using Etienne as a hostage in the event I should need to escape, an image came on the screen. A beautiful blonde woman with tanned skin filled the screen, smiling confidently. No one could have recognised me, though I slid a sideways glance at Etienne, just in case. Elise's subtle changes had altered my face almost completely. My facial structure had become a little longer, slightly more angular. My eyes were now dark hazel in colour, offsetting my blonde hair perfectly. I was a bombshell. It was hard to see anything of myself in this woman, but Elise had made me seem soft, warm, and yet serious. I loved it.

Etienne was on the edge of his chair, gripping it tight. "It's on every channel..." he whispered in a mixture of shock and awe.

"People of Britain," my voice was a little higher, sweeter perhaps. "I urge you not to turn off your television sets, but to listen to me for a moment. You needn't live in fear any longer. Your so-called government have abused their power for too long. Mr. Bowman has brought you to your lowest and I invite you to fight your way back up, alongside me and my comrades. The government wish for you to believe that we are a danger to you, that somehow they are protecting you from us. That is a lie. It is *us* who are trying to rescue you from *them*. We want to see Britain returned to glory, to see you, its people, no longer afraid of your own shadows. All you need do is believe in us, and support us. For those willing and able, there are many ways to contact us, and I am sure, whether you wish to admit it or not, you know what some of those are.

"For those of you who have too much to risk to fight, then all you need do is be at our sides when the time comes, when we drag the dictator from his throne and throw him into the fire. We will destroy them. We will win. Bowman knows this, and I bet you he is sitting in his townhouse now, cowering like a child. And I promise you that you will be able to wake up free again, that our children will not live as you have, and that our grandchildren will recall these atrocities as a distant memory of days long gone.

"The time is coming, not far from now, when we will strike. From the Revolution, I thank you all. Let freedom reign."

The passion in my words, my conviction to our cause was such that it sent a shiver through my body. Etienne's face was a picture, his jaw hanging open ridiculously. He clamped his hand over it, and was unsure if he was furious or hiding a smile.

"Fuck me," he breathed, "what the hell are they going to do now?" He turned to me, urgent and confused. "Holy shit Romany, the Revolution have never done this before, nobody has ever done this before..."

Out in the corridor, I could see McLean storming across the office in our direction.

"Etienne, you have to shut up now OK? McLean is coming." His eyes grew large, into watery blue spheres, and he looked like a frightened child. I placed a hand over his, trying to hold it still as it shook. "Just try to be calm, don't show him you're panicking."

Watching Etienne trying to pull himself together was fascinating, the way he closed his eyes and began to count under his breath, inhaling and exhaling precisely and slowly. McLean was storming towards the office door and as he threw it open, Etienne stood to attention, scraping his fingers through his hair and adjusting his tie. It was poetry in motion, like an actor getting into character.

"Did you fucking see that?" McLean exploded, spitting out his words.

"Yes sir, I did." I marvelled at Etienne's calm response.

"Well?" McLean tapped his feet impatiently. Etienne paused, unsure of what McLean wanted from him. "What the hell are we going to do about it man? I have every senior member of staff rushing up here, scared witless." He looked at me, and I could see the suspicion in his eyes.

"If I may, sir," I edged forward, trying to come to Etienne's aid, "it was only a broadcast. If the prime minister issues a statement immediately, then I wholeheartedly believe the people will not listen to such nonsense."

"How can we even be sure it was the Revolution, and not impostors?" I despaired at Etienne's naive comment, knowing it was only going to infuriate McLean further.

"They hacked the government broadcast, you half brained idiot! It wasn't going to be fucking schoolchildren was it?" He turned his back on us, marching over to the window. "But, that may not be a bad thing to tell the people..." he trailed off, thinking hard. He stormed out the office, causing a picture to fall from the wall as the door crashed shut. Glass shattered, spraying across the floor, and Etienne pulled me backwards away from it. He collapsed onto the sofa, burying his head in his hands.

Outside the office, I could see the senior members of staff encouraging the workers to continue on, to ignore the ridiculous broadcasts. But I could see on many of their faces more than just fear or concern, but deep thought. If we had reached the thoughts of so many people in just one office, a *government* office at that, what had we done to the rest of the country?

Etienne looked up, his face lined with worry. "Fucking hell Romany, this is bad. The Revolution must be far more organised than we thought if they were able to pull off something like this. First that murder, now this; their planning something, I can feel it."

I sat down beside him, aware of the whirring camera zooming in on us. I wanted to comfort him, to reassure him that he didn't need to be frightened. Instead, carefully not looking at the camera, I gently tipped his chin up, leaning forward to look at him. "Well, we had better catch the bastards then."

The look of horror in his eyes was fleeting, so quick I could have imagined it. But in that moment I knew, that despite his commitment to the government, Etienne was a supporter of our cause, if only half-heartedly. He stood to his feet, and pointed at the smashed picture frame.

"Get Christina in here, she can clean that up." He pulled himself to his full height, puffing out his chest a little. He glanced back at me, and he looked disappointed in me. He truly believed that I was so enthralled with our government, that I wanted the Revolution to lose. At least, I thought to myself as he walked out to speak to the staff, I had played my part well.

I had sprinted my way to the station, having been sent home at lunch. Hunting down innocent families was taking second place to hunting us down, and as a result, I had nothing to do. Etienne, sweetly, told me that I should be with my friends and family, to reassure them that everything would be alright. Some of my colleagues had stayed behind, many had left the building as quickly as if it had been on fire. There was extra security at the tube station, herding people like cattle onto the trains; checking papers over and over, asking people where they were going. I could hear whispers about my broadcast, but nobody was looking at me, I went completely unnoticed. It wasn't safe for me to try travelling this way, I would have to walk. I thought miserably about how painful my feet would be, but I knew I had no choice. Even as a government employee, I was not exempt from scrutiny.

Beckett's house seemed miles away as my heels scraped and pinched my feet. I smiled at the guards I passed, all of whom scowled at me, snatching my papers and scouring them before letting me proceed. The cameras buzzed and whirred and I wondered how on earth I would be able to slip into the alley to sneak into Beckett's home. I slowed my pace, and leant against the entrance to the alley, removing my shoe and rubbing my blisters. A van drove by at a speed, and as the pedestrians scattered, trying to avoid its notice, I darted around the corner, running barefoot until I was safely hidden.

Beckett's house was silent, apart from muffled voices from the basement. He wasn't alone. I wandered down, my steps light as I carried my heels. I froze as he wrapped his arms around Elise, hugging her hard. "You clever thing," he gushed. "You're amazing."

I coughed lightly and the pair of them leapt apart, weapons drawn and trained on me. I stepped into the light of the basement and Beckett swore, putting the gun back into its hiding place. "You scared the shit out of us."

"I noticed." I snapped, my tone more petulant than I had intended. I looked over at Elise, biting down hard on my tongue. My scowl did not go unnoticed as she shifted uncomfortably.

"Well," She stuttered. "What did you think?"

"It went well, I suppose, although I appreciate the heads up, you know, that I was going to be stood in a government office when it went out." My comment was aimed at Beckett, though my eyes stayed on Elise.

"We needed you to see their reactions." I forced myself to look at him. "And they're going to be assuming it's live, so no one can suspect you, you have the perfect alibi."

I lit a cigarette, not offering either of them one. "Well it would be nice to be let in on things just occasionally."

Beckett's eyebrows knitted together, and he touched Elise gently on the shoulder. "I think you need to get back now Elise, or people will start to talk. Make sure plenty of people see you."

She smiled at him, and kept her head down as she walked past me. I didn't receive a goodbye, and I knew I didn't deserve one. I don't know what was happening to me, but I felt sick to my stomach with anger.

"Well that was incredibly rude of you, considering what Elise has just done for us."

"What else has she been doing for you Beckett?" I replied cattily.

He ignored me, but folded his arms. "You're behaving like a child Romany, and it really doesn't become you."

I leant past him to stub out my cigarette and squared up to him. "Well, maybe Beckett, I'm entitled to behave like a child, seeing as I never got to be one. You and your father saw to that." I injected my words with as much venom as I could, and was rewarded with his evident shock.

He gently pushed me away from him, and stepped away, turning his back to me. "Is that what this is all about Romany?" It was easier for me to say yes, than admit why I was really angry. He turned on his heel, marched up to me. His hands gripped me and he shook me a little as he shouted, "Well, you know what, my father didn't just take away your childhood, unless you haven't noticed I wasn't exactly playing with toy soldiers and play dough was I?" He shoved me away, and I felt again that urge to crack the ashtray across the back of his head. "We may not have chosen this, but we have a responsibility to uphold. We owe it to those poor fuckers out there to behave like the people we are."

"We're not people Beckett, we're murderers, and liars. But we pretend to be heroes, all in the name of the Revolution."

He threw his head back and laughed. "So now you have a conscience? It wasn't that long ago you were bragging of being the best killer we have. How dedicated you were to the Revolution."

"Well, you know I'm an excellent liar. I should be, after all, I was trained by the best."

114

He raised his hand, and I didn't flinch. It stayed in midair for a moment, before he dropped it to his side. "Yes my father was a liar. But you seemed to have forgotten, you ungrateful bitch, that he took you in when anyone else would have thrown you into the street. Whatever he became, whatever he did, at least he never forgot what mattered." He stormed away from me.

"He only took me in to use me for the good of the Revolution." I could contain my anger no longer. "He was abusive Beckett, he watched as we *beat* each other and called it 'training'. He encouraged us, and shouted at us if we cried..."

"I don't want to talk about my father!" he hollered in my face. He turned away, punching his fist into the wall hard. He tore at his hair, and screamed.

I wanted to stop him, to help him, but we had gone too far. He turned back to me, and his face was screwed up in rage and pain. "Yes, you are a murderer. Yes, you are a liar. You can never escape that. You have killed people, people's sons and daughters, brothers and sisters, and you did it for the Revolution. You are in too deep to back out now. If you walk away, you'll regret it forever and I will never forgive you. If you leave, you are as good as dead to me."

I stumbled backwards, an agonizing pain in my chest.

"You have spent the last while blowing hot and cold, one minute itching to leave, the next killing policemen and filming a fucking nationwide broadcast. So you decide, stay or go." His face was twisted, ugly. There was not a trace of the Beckett I had spent my teenage years yearning for, that I had spent my first years of adulthood trying to make proud of me.

"I'll stay," I conceded, backing away from him. "But once this is over, I make my own choices. I will walk away and start a new life. Maybe you should think about what you want to do once this is done, what this is all going to be for. You want to take a look at yourself Beckett. There's a fine line between dedication and obsession, and maybe I am not the only one in too deep."

He dropped his hands to his sides in defeat, looking away from me. "Just go." He sighed. As I did so, he stopped me with his hand. "You are to see me tomorrow. I have someone I want you to meet."

It was like Beckett and I had swapped roles. There was a time not long ago when I had been desperate to kill Bowman, to do anything for the Revolution to win. I had been merciless in my killing, conscienceless. Beckett had not been a natural leader, indecisive and weak, and there had been a call for him to hand the reins over to me. But after killing Hardwicke, something had changed in me. I had never dreamt about my parents until that first time. Looking back, when Beckett had told me he was postponing the hit on Bowman, I had felt more than a little relieved. I was tired of fighting, I realised. I didn't know if there could be such a thing as retirement for assassins, but I wished there was. There was a war being waged within me. Part of me couldn't wait to kill Bowman, to finally avenge my parents. The other half wanted it over so I could run away to some little cottage somewhere, to live out my later years trying to forgive myself for some of the things I had done. I had sent families to their deaths; I had worked for the government doing terrible things, all for the greater good. But I knew I would have to be present when

116

Bowman was taken out, whether, at this point, I wanted to be or not.

I sank down into my bath and stared at the ceiling, my eyes drawn to a small patch of mould. It wasn't just about Beckett, I had pretty much resigned myself to the fact that even if I were to walk into his house stark naked, he would still be too engrossed in the Revolution to notice. Like myself, there had been a change wrought in him. Now things seemed to be happening at a quicker pace, he was steelier, more determined than before. In fact, he was the perfect leader. I just preferred him flawed. I knew nothing had happened with Elise, or at least, I hoped not. But that shouldn't have even mattered. I should be focused on my job, on the Revolution. Instead I was behaving like a sullen teenager. Perhaps after years of training and regulations, I was rebelling.

I chuckled to myself and slid under the water, turning the hot tap with my foot. I missed Lexi. Perhaps after everything, she had been right about Beckett. She had always said that he wasn't the one for me, that I deserved to be treated like an equal. It was a pity Lexi wasn't a man, I smiled to myself at the thought. She managed, most of the time, to make things seem normal. I wished I could call her, invite her round. But as the tannoy outside boomed out the curfew warning, I was reminded that wasn't a possibility. That was why it was important to win. Just so I could be normal, if I ever could. I certainly wasn't going to get the opportunity to try unless we did.

I pulled on my old t-shirt, and checked my gun, hidden underneath a loose floorboard. I headed downstairs and pulled down the blinds, double-checking the locks on the doors. The clock in the kitchen told me it was eleven at night; the torture vans would be beginning their patrols. I wondered who Beckett wanted me to meet. Whoever it was, he felt it important enough to ask me to leave my home with him in the daytime.

I picked up the leaflet that that fallen through my front door that morning, and tossed it onto my kitchen table. 'COLLECT YOUR RATION BOOK TODAY', it screamed out at me. Beneath the bold title was my name, and beside that 'Government Employee. Ration Status: Premier'. We had been forewarned about this. Not only were the government controlling our movements, our speech, but now they were going to control how much we could eat, what we could buy. It had only been a matter of time, I supposed. Due to my privileged position, I was allowed a better quality of food, larger quantities. I was allowed foreign cigarettes and even a bottle of wine a month. I threw the leaflet on the table, disgusted. A smaller, folded piece of paper fell out of it, fluttering to the floor. I unfolded it carefully and found myself smiling.

It was Beckett's leaflet, tucked within the pages of the government's own pamphlet. I wondered how he had managed it. You clever little bastard, I thought to myself, careful not to speak out loud.

The leaflet was passionate, heartfelt and pure genius. I was a little jealous not to have thought of it myself. After reading it a couple more times, I sat at my table, flicked my lighter and watched as the flames consumed it.

9

He was waiting for me just around the corner from my home, as I ran up to him, panting slightly. Since the broadcast, police activity was heightened and I had spent much longer having my papers examined. We walked casually through the streets, taking only the quietest alleyways and paths until we reached a house almost perfectly placed between mine and Beckett's homes. It had once been painted white, which had now turned to a murky grey, chipped and stained. The window boxes were filled with crumbling, decaying plants and the windows were impossible to see through, they were so dirty. The only thing that remained to give a hint of what this house had once been was the deep purple front door, with its now faded gold knocker. Beckett led me around the back of the building, and we scrambled down through a window that led into the house's basement.

The smell of damp hit me as we clambered into the room. Beckett's grip on my elbow was tight, and pinched my skin. "If you need a reminder of why we're doing this, here it is." The room was filthy, every surface covered with a fine coating of dust. Dead flies lay curled up, legs stuck up in the air, scattered across the book case. An elderly woman stood uncomfortably in the corner, clearly embarrassed by the state of her home. She looked nervous, and I could tell she was terrified at the prospect of us being caught in her home. Her skin was thin, like parchment paper; her lips pressed in a thin line. She poured us each a cup of tea with shaky hands, apologising profusely for the chipped china. I could tell that the china had once been things of beauty, with delicate gilded edges and dusky roses printed upon them, now they were relics of a better time.

"This is Elizabeth," Beckett introduced. "She was a friend of my mother's. I've brought you here so she could tell you her story; the early days, the ones you and I can't remember. I hope that once you hear this, it will remind you of why it is so important for us to win this."

Elizabeth looked quizzically at Beckett and realising our conversation was private, began to pick pieces of fluff from her patched red skirt. She stood in patient silence, waiting for one of us to speak to her. Her long grey hair was swept up on the top of her head in a tight bun, and the lines on her face made her look far older than I suspected she was. She did not look like a woman who had lived an easy life.

"Please Elizabeth," I invited her to join our conversation, "tell me about yourself." The woman took a seat.

"There isn't a lot to tell you about myself these days, I'm rather uninteresting now I'm afraid. But, a long time ago, I was a philosophy lecturer at the university in Brighton, married to a journalist. Things had been unsettled in Britain for a long time. The crime rate was worse than I had ever remembered it. Every single day there was another murder, another poor child missing. It wasn't just this country, America, Canada, Australia, India, everywhere seemed to be tearing itself down from the inside. After the war with Russia, we had no money left, no resources left to help any of our allies. My husband's work began to dry up, although there was so much happening overseas, nobody would allow travellers into their countries. Especially not journalists, and no one was allowed to fly out of the UK. Before we knew it China was attacking the US with chemical weapons; Spain and Portugal were tearing lumps out of one another. Tokyo was a ghost town after their war with China. The only country that seemed to be staying out of it was Britain, and that's only because we were too busy fighting amongst ourselves." She began to fiddle with her skirt, looking nervous.

"These people, just ordinary folks like you or I..." She checked herself for a moment. "Well, like me, they began to form these groups. Reckoned they were trying to prevent crime, but the problem was, they were attacking people left right and centre with no evidence. We knew something had to give." She picked at a mole on her face with her index finger, scratching away as her eyes glazed over, lost in painful memories. "Then, the attacks began. Bio-chemical attacks, they called them; said it was terrorists from overseas trying to break us. They used words that were too fancy for us all to understand, but I knew that it was bad. The water systems were polluted, hospitals were hit, whole schools of children died after drinking water out of their fountains. I was petrified it would be my students next."

I resisted the urge to put my hand over hers, as she choked back her tears.

"The whole country descended into chaos and the government members fled the country one by one, terrified that they would be next. And, in the midst of it all, one man stepped forward ready to help us. John Bowman, the only remaining member of the government. He said he had the police and army on side, that he knew the key to saving us all. We were desperate and scared. If he said he could help us, then what did we have to lose? He was young, smart and brave. He was voted in as prime minister not long after. The government disbanded, replaced by his friends and colleagues. Prisons all over the country were soon filled with criminals, and we began to feel a little safer at night." She eyed my device nervously.

"It's okay," I reassured her. "They can't hear us."

"For a couple of years, it all seemed to be better. But my husband kept saying, over and over, that something just wasn't right. But I didn't care, just so long as we were okay. Slowly, the cameras began to appear, and the check points. People were being urged to move into the cities to keep them safe. The Royal Family were all ushered up into Scotland for their 'protection' and weren't seen or heard of again. Newspapers became unavailable, and the television stations were being lost. But people didn't seem to mind the changes, they just didn't want things to go back to how they were. Then, a year later, the vans appeared. If anyone dared to speak up against the government, they were herded into the back of the vans and just like that, they vanished. You couldn't even chat in the street without the government knowing what you were saying. My neighbours were taken, the day before my husband's birthday." Her hands shook. "My husband, God bless him, just couldn't take anymore. He began to work late into the night, barely making it back in time for curfew.

"One night, after the leaflets came telling us about the list, he told me what he had been doing. He had information, about the government. He kept saying it was enough to bring them down. I kept telling him to be quiet, that the vans could be outside, but he didn't listen. He said that Bowman had been responsible for the bio-chemical attacks. That Bowman had been selling his chemical weapons to countries across the globe, and the millions he gained from doing so were used as bribes to win the army and police on side, and even more money having anyone against him assassinated to put his supporters in their place. He had proof, he said, that Bowman had criminals placed in labs, using them to test the chemical weapons on. Like fucking guinea pigs." She spat out the words before calming herself.

"Two days after he told me all this, my husband didn't come home from work. The vans came to my house, just to tell me I was lucky that I wasn't going with my husband, that they'd be keeping watch over me." She closed her eyes, and began to cry. "All it took was a few more years, a few thousand people disappearing and a couple more attacks on hospitals and schools to convince us all that the terrorists would keep reappearing, to get Bowman to where he is now - controlling us all, with a nice batch of chemical weapons hidden away, just in case we get out of hand." She smiled at me through the tears. "I didn't give up on my husband's research or on his memory, I just became so frightened. You taught us all not to be afraid anymore."

There was a silence, that lasted so long that Elizabeth began to fidget, scratching at her arms.

"Thank you." I placed my hand over hers and she flinched a little. She was frightened of me, although after a moment I could see her relax, as she cupped my cheek gently. The smile she gave me was genuine and warm, and reached her eyes. She was a woman with amazing strength, and she made me feel ashamed of how I had behaved.

"I didn't tell you because I wanted you to feel sorry for me, or to upset you, I just want you to know what you're saving us all from." A cough rattled through her, shaking her fragile body. She wiped her mouth, and the smile vanished.

Beckett rose to his feet and plucked a blanket from the back of his chair, wrapping it gently around Elizabeth's shoulders.

"Thank you sweetheart." She patted his cheek, and Beckett glanced over at me, his cheeks turning red. "Would you help me upstairs, I feel rather tired."

I took hold of her right side, and together Beckett and I helped her up to her living room. Elizabeth's large open plan living room, with its once fancy kitchen, had also become her bedroom. Beckett lowered her gently into the double bed, tucking her in. The living room was less bleak than the basement, but still had the air of despair about it. The photographs on the walls had yellowed, the quilts on her bed stained.

"You can stay if you like." Elizabeth attempted to smile as Beckett switched on the television. "My dear nephew keeps my cupboards stocked, so you're welcome to help yourself to something if you're hungry." She leant back against the pillows. She looked like a queen entertaining her guests, I thought to myself. A faded elegance clung to her, with her immaculately applied makeup which only emphasised the lines etched in her skin. She was not a woman who was going down without a fight. Beckett's face was full of admiration and love for the little lady, as he folded his arms, smiling upon her like a proud father. But I could sense sadness too. It seemed to be in every corner of this house, watching over us like an old friend. "Yes, Etienne is a real darling, makes sure I never go without."

Beckett carefully didn't look over, and I bit my tongue as I went to tell Elizabeth that I worked with Etienne and yes, he was a darling. It would not have gone down well with either party. But I smiled inside, thinking of Etienne using his generous government ration points to help a lady in need.

Elizabeth's eyes fluttered closed, and Beckett gently touched my elbow. He led me upstairs, through a door at the end of the corridor, which he shut quietly behind him.

"She's a wonderful woman," I conceded. "Thank you for bringing me here."

The room we stood in was full of boxes, stacked everywhere, paintings and framed photographs stacked haphazardly against them. He walked over to the dressing table, and plucked a photograph that stood amongst the dusty perfume bottles and dried up make up. He touched it gently, and didn't seem to mind as I looked over his shoulder. A younger, beaming Elizabeth grinned up at us, holding up a glass of wine in a toast. Beside her, arms wrapped around her, was Rose.

"My mother adored Elizabeth. They were such good friends, and when Elizabeth lost George my mum did everything she could to help her. When my father became so fixated with the Revolution, my mother hardly saw him, and it destroyed her. She too lost the love of her life, just in a different way. And so, Elizabeth became my mother's support. When my mum died, I think it was just too much for Liz, she just shut herself in this house, surrounded by memories and she hasn't left since."

"Why haven't the government taken her?"

"Why would they?" He carefully replaced the picture. "This is how they would have us all, shut indoors, hidden away. Easier to deal with." He chewed his lip. "I have visited Elizabeth as much as I can, although it has not always been often enough. She has always just seemed like an empty shell, a zombie. Just going through the motions but not really living. The only time she came alive was when I told her our plans." He sat down on the torn stool. "And then one day, Elizabeth told me that story and told me that she was done hiding away. She didn't care if they came for her, she wanted to help us win. Bless her, she even told me that once we won she was going to take a holiday, she didn't care where, as long as it was beautiful."

He stood to his feet and wiped the dirt off a picture hanging from the wall. Elizabeth stood, dazzling in a white gown, showered by confetti. She smiled at the camera, but the tall man in a smart suit beside her was looking down on his petite bride, his eyes wet with tears. It was a beautiful image, one which made a lump grow in my throat. "Elizabeth is dying." I spun around, Beckett was hugging himself and his voice was weak. "Those fucking bastards have turned off her heating. All she's got is her oven and a fucking little fire her neighbour bought. They've left her here to die, like a dog. And the woman has cancer."

He began to cry and instinctively I grabbed him to me, hugging him tight. "She had everything Romany; a happy marriage, a lovely house, a great job and they tore that all down around her. You know she was pregnant when they took George... she lost the baby."

I let him go, and watched him as he walked over to a box marked 'George'. "She kept everything he had ever touched, and she refused to leave this house. They beat everything from her, even her courage and now, when she finally gets that back, it's too late for her." He stroked the box with a finger. "She's going to die in this house, and then they're going to take it from her. And they'll probably destroy all of this and there is nothing I can do about it." He took a deep breath and when he turned back to me his face was calm again, tears vanished. "I won't let her down Romany. There are thousands of people like her and it may be too late for Elizabeth but we can save them."

Elizabeth coughed downstairs, crying out in pain. He left to help her, leaving me stood in this heartbreaking room, filled with a dying woman's happy memories.

*

I sat at my desk the following day feeling numb as I tried to process my stack of forms. Face after face stared up at me from the crisp pages, desolate and desperate. Children, women; the elderly, the disabled. I wondered how many of them were living like Elizabeth; how many were living in poverty. I was thankful that so far there were no forms to be sent down the chute to McLean's department, to be rounded up in the vans.

I glanced over at Etienne's office, where he had been ensconced for the entire morning. He was on his phone, talking animatedly, running hands through his already messy hair. I thought of what he had been doing for Elizabeth. In the back of my mind lingered the thought that perhaps Etienne was Beckett's other mole in the office. It would certainly make things a whole lot easier if he was. I watched as he slammed down his phone, and stood to his feet, pacing back and forth. I heard footsteps as someone made their way towards me and as I turned to greet them, Harry's leering face brought a new level of anger into me.

"What do you want?" I made no attempt to be polite, choosing to continue with my mindless typing. It was actually preferable to talking to Harry.

"Checking out the boss were we? Maybe hoping for a little seeing to in his office after hours? I'm sure he could manage before curfew, just." I clamped my hand down hard on the computer mouse, gritting my teeth. But he wouldn't let up. "You know, from what I heard, Etienne isn't even interested in women if you catch my drift..."

"Listen to me you vile little man," my voice came out in a hiss, which seemed to be louder than I anticipated as the majority of the office glanced over. "Maybe if you stopped thinking with that useless piece of gristle in your trousers and used that peanut sized brain of yours you would realise that accusing your boss of being gay is not exactly clever. I mean, I'm assuming you don't want to pay McLean a visit." His eyes darkened, fixed on me. His upper lip twitched, a sign I assumed showed he was angry. He tried to fix on his charming smile, faltering a little. "I didn't think so. And I promise you, I would sooner fuck Etienne, or any other man in this office, than look twice at someone as pigheaded and disgusting as you. Now get out of my sight."

I hadn't noticed Etienne stepping out of his office, until he shouted at Harry to get back to work. Harry lingered for a second, scowling at me. Etienne yelled at him again and finally, he stalked away. Etienne nodded towards me. "Romany may I speak with you please?" His voice was tense, his eyes cold as he stood holding open his office door for me to enter, closing it behind me with a bang and drawing the blinds.

"McLean wants to speak to you." He flicked open a device on his table, and my heart began to pound. Whatever he had to say about McLean he didn't want it heard. "Before you go down there, I want you to know that he will be speaking to all of us, even the senior members of staff." He sighed. "That Revolution broadcast the other day has made the government nervous. There have been rumours of people, in the streets, trying to fight against the police. Arrests in other cities have skyrocketed. It's only a matter of time before it reaches London, and McLean knows this. We don't know what the Revolution will do next, but if one broadcast can cause this level of activity, what could they do next?" He rubbed at his temples, closing his eyes.

I leant forward, whispering. "What does this mean?"

"It's a fucking nightmare. The government weren't prepared for this shit. I mean, they've always felt threatened by the Revolution but they had no idea what they were capable of. And now McLean is talking to everyone, trying to reassure people, or trip them up, I don't bloody know." His hand shot out and gripped mine. "There's something about you Romany. There's something in your eyes that I just can't put my finger on. Sometimes I see so much in you, something I can't explain. Then the next time I look at you, it's like you're on lockdown. I don't know if you have anything to hide, or if it's just me being ridiculous, but I'd like to know you better. I'd like to know what it is your hiding behind those eyes." His thumb caressed my hand. "Just be careful down there is all I am saying, you're a smart girl and you make an impression. Just don't make the wrong one." He leant a little closer and, hesitating for a moment, placed his mouth on mine tenderly. His lips barely brushed against mine. Again he paused, before kissing me again, harder. Desire swelled within me, and I kissed him back, our tongues meeting, entangling. He pulled away, leaning against the back of his chair. He was breathing deeply, unable to look at me. "Now go," he panted. I stood to my feet, flustered. I looked back at him as I headed for the door, but he had spun his chair around, his phone glued to his ear again.

Nobody seemed to have noticed our kiss, as I passed my colleagues' desks to make my way to the lift. I pressed the button for McLean's level. My brain was buzzing, a million thoughts rushing through it at the speed of light. Not so long ago everything had been simple, I was a member of the Revolution. End of story. I found my colleagues reprehensible, I despised my double life. Now, suddenly my double life seemed like the easier option. I had long accepted that Beckett and I would never be together, and then everything became complicated. There seemed to be a fine line between love and hate, judging by Beckett's behaviour. One minute he seemed to want to tear my clothes off, then he wanted to humiliate me. Now I had Etienne, with his pleading eyes and handsome face, who actually *wanted* to be with me. I shook my head. No, not with me, this wasn't really who I was. He was falling for Romany, the government worker, not the real me. Not a murderer. I imagined telling Etienne about me, and how long it would take before the vans arrived. I felt trapped, between a rock and a hard place. Either way, I felt as though I was living a lie. Which in theory, I was. I counted down the levels, bracing myself. I couldn't be distracted, especially not when facing McLean. The doors opened. The blinds of his office were shut, and I knew McLean didn't have cameras in his office. If shit hit the fan, I would have to take him out and find a way out the building. I fixed on my brightest smile, and tried my best to sashay my way towards his office. I was buzzed in straight away, he was expecting me.

He stared at me hard as I entered, taking a seat before I was asked. I crossed one leg over the other, making sure to show a little thigh as I did so; after all, it couldn't hurt. McLean took a look, but his eyes lingered for barely a second before honing back in on my face.

"How much do you know about this broadcast?" Direct and straight to the point, no room for idle chat.

"I saw it; I was talking with Etienne in his office when it came on."

"You and Etienne are close?" He sipped a glass of water. The insinuation was clear.

"He's my boss. I enjoy my job and I like to make sure I am on good terms with my colleagues. Makes life easier for us all." Smiling politely, playing it a little dumb. "Is that an issue?"

"No, just an observation..." Another sip of water. Time to think. "...I want you to know that I will be calling every member of staff in for a talk. I want to reassure you that you have nothing to worry about."

"I know," I interrupted. "I have every faith in our government, and as far as I am concerned, the Revolution haven't even the courage to show their faces. This broadcast was a desperate attempt to gain attention. So, I am definitely not worried."

Those glacial eyes swept my face again and I worried it was overkill. "Well, I am glad you believe that." He licked the corner of his mouth. "You know, I wish everyone shared your belief. You have probably heard about these 'riots', if you can even call them that."

"I have."

"Some people just can't see that what we're doing is for their own good. If we abandoned the government, these rules, we'd be at the mercy of Russia or America - these rules are in place to protect us. Some people, like the Revolution, just can't see that. The prime minister rescued this country, and it may not be back to the glory days but one day everyone will see that this was for the best, like you and I do."

He was trying to provoke me, I could feel it. I tried to keep on smiling, keep on looking merry. "I don't know a lot about you Romany, outside of work. Your papers aren't very detailed." Shit, I thought wildly, he'd been reading up on me. So much for staying under his radar.

"There's not a whole lot to know, sir. My work is my life. I work, I go home, I eat and I sleep."

"Days off?"

"Wishing I was working. Or cleaning up my house. Either way, nothing interesting."

He chuckled, and looked in the file on his desk, my file. "You're unmarried."

"Yes I am, but I'm only young."

He conceded that fact. "And you're an only child, parents deceased." He was talking about my fake parents, I reminded myself, the ones from my elaborately crafted past. "I too lost my parents young; it changes you, don't you think?" Again, the hint of accusation.

"Yes it did change me, but I was blessed that I had time with them." The lies left my mouth easily, flowing off my tongue like honey.

McLean nodded, emotionless. "You don't have friends?" he smirked.

"Haven't you heard what they say about me around here? All work and no play."

"Precisely the type of worker we need. It's people like you who keep this government, and our country alive." He was serious. "Well, I hope that after this little talk you will see that this silly broadcast means nothing; we continue on with our great work. I am sorry for dragging you down here, for something so trivial. But, it is our procedure to talk to all staff, just to be on the safe side." So he *was* checking if any of us were involved, we were all under suspicion.

"Of course, needs must." I stood to my feet, desperate to leave the office.

"You know something Romany, you are quite something." The water reached his lips again. "I am going to be keeping my eye on you, there's something very interesting about you. I'd like to see you go far."

My heart sank.

10

I pulled on my grey sweatshirt and checked my watch; I had more than enough time to make it to Beckett's and back before curfew.

I was relieved to see a different guard on the checkpoint, one who wanted to move me on as quickly as he could. I didn't think I could keep my temper if my admirer had been there instead. I hurried to Beckett's, eyeing up the looming black clouds, threatening a downpour. Stood by his alleyway was a small child, wide eyed and hollow-cheeked. He stood in shorts and a t-shirt, shivering. He looked around, left and right, sobbing. A police officer walked past, ignoring the child and me. The little boy was alone. It shouldn't have mattered, I should have walked past him, to Beckett's. But I couldn't leave him. If he was still out here after curfew they'd take him, regardless of his age.

"Are you okay?" He flinched from me, ready to run. "Hey, it's alright, I'm not going to hurt you." I knelt down, and took off my jacket, wrapping it around his shoulders. "You look cold," I explained. He smiled shyly. "Where are your parents?"

"My mother went into the shop, to try and get some food, but she's been ages. The man in the shop told me to wait outside. I went to try and get her but the door was locked," he said sadly.

"Do you live near here?" I asked. He nodded in reply. "Well, couldn't you walk home and wait for her?" He shook his head. I didn't ask anymore, I didn't need an explanation. Perhaps all this boy had left was his mother. he wasn't going to leave her.

"My dad doesn't live with us anymore," he offered, trying to explain himself.

I squeezed his hand. "I understand."

Across the road, the shop door opened and a skinny woman with dirty blonde hair, tangled and messy, stepped outside. She clutched a bag of shopping to her, holding onto it tightly. The man stepped out behind her and slapped her hard on the backside, leering.

"See you next time sweetheart," he called after her. She shuddered a little, and tried to keep a hold of her shopping as she tugged down her ragged dress. It was a red scrap of cloth, barely covering her thighs. She'd gone to the shop dressed in what had once been her best dress, ready to do anything to feed her child. And she'd done it too. She spotted me stood with the boy and ran over.

"What is this?" She snatched hold of his hand. "Who the hell are you?"

"I promise, I meant no harm; I just saw your son here and wanted to check he was all right."

Her face relaxed a little but she maintained her grip on her son. "I didn't just abandon him," she said. "I was..." she trailed off, not wanting to say anymore in front of her son.

"Choosing the very best for your strapping young man," I offered, trying to stop her discomfort.

"Yes." She could barely manage a smile at the boy as he looked up at her. "I wanted you to have lots of goodies, and I had to spend our coupons wisely." She mouthed a thank you at me, gripping hold of her son's hand as she led him down the road. She didn't return my jacket, and I didn't want it back.

I could hear muffled voices from the basement, several in fact. I had expected Beckett to be alone. As I wandered down the steps they went silent, and as Beckett and his guests came into view their eyes were fixed on me. Four people stood with him, each staring at me, on edge. On Beckett's right stood a tall blonde man, with a chiselled chin, glacial eyes and wide shoulders. Like Beckett, he wore a tight fitting leather jacket that seemed to struggle to stretch across his broad expanse. He wrapped an arm around the woman beside him, one who was far taller than me, yet still dwarfed by her massive partner. Her black hair hung in long tendrils over her face, masking her from me. As she flung her head back, her eyes remained fixed on me; dark pools of brown, filled with anger. She stared down her nose at me and she oozed a powerful sexuality, such that even I found it hard to tear my gaze from her. She was not the prettiest woman in the room, but she was striking and there was a certain mystery about her.

To Beckett's left, a shorter, almost squat man folded his arms. He had a pugnacious, squashed little face, with a turned up nose and squinted eyes. Next to him was a statuesque blonde, curvaceous and leggy. I suspected she was older than she looked, but with her youthful skin and pouting lips, she was still stunning.

Beckett stepped forward, a huge grin fixed to his face. "Romany, I'm so glad you're here!" He rushed forward at me, leading me to his gathered friends. "Let me introduce you to Eve," He gestured to the blonde, "Philip," the short stocky one, who it transpired ran the

Exeter branch, "and Erin and Peter. Peter is the head of the Manchester section." The blonde smiled at me, but Erin continued to stare at me through her hair, still wary. "This is Romany, my second in command." He said it with pride, and I noticed I had once again been promoted to his right hand woman. Erin's face relaxed and she held out her hand. It was missing its little finger. I took it in a firm handshake and she smiled at me. "You're the one who took out Hardwicke." I nodded. Beckett's smile broadened.

"These are just a few of our new members Romany, they're going to be helping us to recruit more people from the other cities. I have been explaining to them everything we have done so far." He was beaming, his chest puffed out.

"I bet you're wondering how you can trust us." Erin lifted her shirt, and revealed a quote, tattooed just below her breast. She flashed it so quick I could not read it, and I didn't feel it would be proper to ask her for an explanation.

"And how can I be sure that's real?" I asked, keeping my tone light. Beckett looked mortified but Erin threw back her head in laughter.

"You know what, that's exactly the same thing I'd ask you." She looked up at Peter, glancing back and forth between Beckett and I. "I think it's time we left, Pete; we don't want to get back after curfew. We don't need that shit." She shook Beckett's hand. "We'll meet again, and don't you worry, you're going to be getting plenty more members, we'll see to it." She placed her hand over her heart. "The Revolution has begun, Let freedom reign."

Beckett and I repeated the gesture. The odd little man flashed me a smile, one which seemed to transform his whole face. Eve reached back to him."Come on darling, let's go." She gazed at him lovingly, and I felt myself feeling a little envious. She was clearly besotted with him, and I was curious as to how the two of them had ended up together. As the group bustled out, escorted by the charming Beckett, I was left stood alone in the basement. I waited for Beckett's footsteps and he rushed towards me, insisting I sit with him.

"So much has been happening..." he gushed. "Our broadcast has changed everything. We've had more people wanting to join than ever before and not just here, but in all the major cities. Peter and Eve were based in Manchester, leading the Revolution up there, and moved here to help us prepare, and their contacts there say that they've had *hundreds* joining." His eyes were a little glazed with excitement. "The tables are finally turning Romany, we're stronger than ever. When we strike, the government won't know what hit them!" He grabbed me in a fierce hug, his strong arms wrapped around me. I breathed in his musky, peppery scent and a warm feeling spread in my belly.

He suddenly leapt to his feet. "I never realised before, how close we are to victory. I know now what I have to do to win, Romany; and I've realised that I am no longer afraid." He knelt before me, clutching my hands. There was a crazed look in his eyes, his hair wildly sticking up in all directions. "I should never have questioned your loyalty to me. Everything you have done has led us here. The Revolution is becoming a force to be reckoned with."

"And here you are, its dutiful leader." My tone was flat, and I could see it stung him. He stood to his feet, staring down at me.

"You may not like it, and I can hear the envy in your voice, but I am the leader Romany. And I was weak before, frightened. I was everything my father said I was, pathetic." I went to argue with him but he held out his hand, like a sultan commanding his harem. "You won't argue with me anymore Romany. I love you deeply, you're like a sister to me." The reference stung. "But you are under my command, and you will do as I say. I am done playing games with you. We can't stop now; we must strike again, harder than before."

"What exactly do you have planned?" I didn't recognise the proud, dominating man in front of me, looking at me with power and perhaps a little contempt. Beckett was threatened by me. I was a far better killer, smarter than him, and everyone knew the only reason Matthew hadn't insisted that I should lead was out of loyalty to his son. I was the better choice to lead; and he knew it. Now, he was showing his authority.

"I will tell you all when we next meet." So no letting me in on his plans, again. He may say he loved me like a sister, but I was just one of his flock at the moment.

"Fine." I stood to my feet. "I'm assuming I will be involved somehow."

"Don't you worry about that." He lit a cigarette, inhaling deeply. "I'm putting you right in the midst of the action. You are, after all, my very best assassin." It made me feel sick, hearing him talk about me like his property. I had always wanted to be his; his lover, his girlfriend, his friend, but certainly not his 'very best assassin'.

140

"Right." I turned away, ready to leave. The air had grown heavy, and I was in no mood to listen to Beckett anymore. I had come here to congratulate him, *us,* and try to maybe reconcile our differences. Beckett clearly was not interested in that. He was managing just fine, in fact he was flourishing. I looked over my shoulder at him, but his face was still dark, brooding. "Who *are* you?" I asked, my voice a squeaky whisper. Damn it, I sounded like a child, a little girl. I had wanted to sound full of hatred.

He looked away for a moment, taking another deep drag on his cigarette. "I'm being the person I need to be to win." His face softened, he smiled at me a little. "And one day Romany, you'll thank me for that." He turned his back on me. The conversation was over.

*

"What did your father do, before all of this?" I am nursing yet another bleeding cut on my arm. It is part of the territory, Matthew keeps telling us. Sometimes, I'd like to take his gun and...
Beckett shrugged, breaking my thoughts.

"He won't tell me. All he says is that it has helped shape who he is today. I think it must have been something to do with the army, something big. I mean, look at everything he knows. He knows how to kill a man, how to use guns... he wasn't a fucking accountant."

I hesitated for a moment, unsure of whether to ask the next question. Beckett rubbed the side of his face and I could see the deep red stain of blood on his fingers.

141

"Is that why you let him talk to you like that?"

"Like what?" he said.

"When he calls you stupid, says I'm better than you, that he wishes I was his child and not you..."

"He doesn't mean it, he's trying to push me, get me to do better." He tried to sound blasé, but I could see the hurt in his face.

"You already are better. You kick ass at every training session and it still isn't enough." His gorgeous eyes stared into mine, and my palms felt itchy, getting sweaty.

"He's my dad Romany." he said, as though that was enough to excuse him. That bastard was poisoning Beckett's mind, his soul, and in that moment, I hated Matthew more than ever.

*

I ignored the guard's usual disgusting remarks as I made my way home. I thought about what had just happened. The change in Beckett had happened without me even noticing. Like alchemy, he had been turned from tin to gold. He was strong, fearless and maybe a little heartless. He was slowly realising what was needed of him, in order to win. I would always be better than him at making a man's heart stop beating, but I would never be prepared to make the choices Beckett would.

I tossed my keys into the bowl after I locked my front door. My watch told me I had plenty of time until curfew, it had after all, been a short visit. My phone flashed at me. I had one message. None of the members of the Revolution would use phones to contact each other, it was well known they were all bugged. I picked it up tentatively, waiting for it to speak.

"Romany, its Etienne. Look, I know I was out of order, doing that earlier. But I want you to know, this isn't a game for me. I don't want some office fling. I know we can't talk in the office, but maybe one night this week we can meet? I know you like me too, or you wouldn't have kissed me. I know the work we do is hard, I know it takes up our time, but does that mean we can't... I don't know, be happy together? Well, anyway, I need to get back home before curfew. So, I guess I'll see you tomorrow." His voice cut out, and I threw my phone across my living room in frustration. I flung myself down on my sofa, and looked around my living room. The crappy old TV in the corner was covered in dust, as was my bare coffee table. An old Tiffany lamp stood in the corner, and was the only light I used. Since the cost of electricity had skyrocketed at the government's hands, I liked to use as little as possible. But my bare, hardly furnished living room made me feel even worse. I earned a healthy wage, unlike the other poor sods in the country, but I resented owning anything luxurious; my life was enough of a lie as it was. My house was eerily silent, and I debated switching on the television, but I knew I wouldn't be able to stomach another night of pro-government TV. I couldn't move, my body felt drained. I lay my head down on my battered cushions, and dragged a blanket over myself. I closed my eyes, and drifted off into a deep sleep.

*

I woke on my sofa, my eyes still glued together with sleep and make-up. Someone stroked my hair and, dreamily, I pulled them closer to me. Their lips met mine, and I kissed them deep, as though I were taking a gulp of an icy drink on a summer's day. I heard their groan of satisfaction, their hands tangling in my hair, stroking the nape of my neck. My eyes fluttered open and Etienne smiled down at me.

"Well good morning my darling."

I sat up, confused. My living room was not how I had left it. It was filled with beautiful furniture, with an expensive and audaciously large television mounted on the wall. I scrambled to my feet and looked out of my window. There was no guard or checkpoints in the street, only expensive cars and perfectly manicured lawns.

"What's the matter?" Etienne's arms wrapped around my waist, and he rested his chin on my shoulder, staring out of the window with me. He smelt good, sprayed with an expensive cologne. He gently manoeuvred me round to face him.

"Where do we work?" I shook him a little.

"What?" he laughed.

I asked again.

His eyebrows knitted together and he stroked back my hair. "Oh dear, maybe you did have a little bit too much to drink at the Swanson's last night," he smiled. "I'm a lawyer sweetheart, and you work at the school, teaching drama. Remember now?" he said jokingly. He lifted my left hand, and a huge diamond glittered on my wedding finger. "And we're getting married next year - or did you forget that too?"

Married? I thought over and over, as he nuzzled my neck, which I had to admit was fairly distracting. My eyes snapped open, snatching me from the intimate moment as my mind flitted to Beckett. Etienne looked at me quizzically, looking a little hurt.

"How about, I pop out and buy us some breakfast?" I backed away slowly, smiling so hard it made my face ache.

"That sounds like a wonderful idea." He pulled me to him, and kissed me again.

As I pulled on my jacket, I heard the television flicker to life. "And labour has won by a landslide..." I peered around the corner of the door, and watched as a handsome man in a smart suit waved for the cameras. "And there he is, our new prime minister..." It was not Bowman. This was all getting too strange for me. I sprinted out the front door, and began the trek to Beckett's.

The house was beautifully painted, with flowers blooming in the window boxes. A tall woman in jeans and a t-shirt opened the front door, and I could hear the squeals of young children playing behind her.

"Excuse me," a lump caught in my throat, "is Beckett in?"

She stared at me for a second, confused. "Nobody by that name lives here. Sorry."

She went to close the door, but I stopped it with my foot. "Has anyone by that name ever lived here?" I was a little out of breath from my long walk, and it made my voice husky.

"No, not that I know of. Now please leave my property or I will be calling the police." She slammed the door in my face, leaving me stood out in the cold. Thoughts raced through my brain. Where the hell was he? And then it came to me, there was only one other place he could possibly be.

The house looked the same as the day I had arrived, down to the flowers in the window boxes. I tapped the knocker hard, my stomach churning. I wanted him to be there, more than anything. Slowly the door opened, and to my relief, Beckett stood there. He was dressed in a smart jacket and jeans, a crisp white shirt open at the collar. Even his curls looked tidy for a change.

"Romany?" He looked over my shoulder into the street. "Is everything OK? It's very early."

"I needed to know you were okay..." I puffed. "...What the hell is going on?" I asked, and he frowned, looking about nervously. Another glance over my shoulder and he opened the door for me.

"Come in Romany, don't just stand there in the cold."

He led me through the house, and to my amazement, it was exactly how we had left it. How it was in my memories. We stepped into the kitchen, my heels tapping on the slate tiles. He poured me a cup of coffee and handed it to me. He gave me a polite kiss on the cheek as he did so, and a little squeeze on the shoulder before taking a seat opposite me. "Now, what on earth is the matter?"

"What is going on Beckett? Why is everything suddenly so different?" I asked frantically.

"Different? What are you talking about?"

"Bowman? The curfew?" He stared at me, uncomprehending. "What about the cameras? The

146

Revolution?" He shook his head in confusion. "Okay, so how about your parents? Eloise?"

He looked down at his own cup of coffee, his eyes prickling with tears. "Did you have to bring that up Ro?" He had never called me 'Ro' before in his life, but I seemed to be getting somewhere. "You know I don't like to discuss Eloise's accident."

"It wasn't an accident Beckett, they killed her!"

"That guy was drunk, and definitely shouldn't have been driving, but it was still an accident."

"Drunk driver? What the..."

"I know Mum falling ill like she did just pushed Dad too far, but he wasn't a well man. I don't understand why we need to drag up all this old shit, it was a long time ago..."

Footsteps came from behind me, but I was too focused on Beckett to pay attention."Beckett please, I don't know what's going on here..."

He grinned broadly over my shoulder and stood to his feet. "Morning sweetheart!"

I turned around and to my horror Elise entered, tying up her dressing gown, but not before giving me a glimpse of her creamy flesh."Romany, what a surprise!" She enveloped me in a hug and I was too stunned to respond. My head was pounding at the temples. "Is everything alright?" She glanced at Beckett nervously.

"I think Romany had a bad night last night. Her and Etienne were out, remember?"

"Oh dear, did you party a little hard?" Elise laughed. "You do look a little pale." Above us came the thundering noise of someone running across the floor. "Oh no, he's awake." Elise kissed Beckett on the cheek.

Bile rose in my throat. He wrapped his arm around her waist and buried his nose in her hair. A little boy ran down the hallway towards us, his arms flung open.

"Auntie Romany!" he screamed, leaping up at me, wrapping his arms around my neck. I held him tight, frightened to drop this little boy in his blue pyjamas. I let him down and he hurried to Beckett, who threw him up in the air, dangling him by his legs.

"Go careful!" chided Elise. "Poor little Matthew's going to be sick otherwise."

Beckett's son, named after his father, who apparently had not been the same man I had known. Which left me with one question. "Um, where are my mum and dad?" I asked.

Elise and Beckett glanced at each other in horror.

"Romany," Beckett let Matthew down and ushered him out into the sitting room and Elise followed, seemingly glad to leave the kitchen. "I don't know how to say this; your parents died when you were a child, in a house fire. That's when you came to live with us. Don't you remember?"

I leapt to my feet and grabbed him by the shoulders. I grabbed his face and kissed him hard. He gently pushed me away, his hands gripping me firmly. "Please Beckett, please remember..."

"Ro, I don't know what's gotten into you, but you can't behave like this. What if Elise or Matthew had seen that?"

"But, it's always been you and me..."

"No," he said firmly. "It's always been you and *Etienne*. You're like my sister Ro, and I love you, but this just isn't like you." I stumbled backwards, gripping

148

the table for support. "I don't know if you're still a little pissed but you can't just go kissing your friends." I was going to be sick. "You love Etienne, I know that, and I know whatever the hell that was, it was a massive mistake. I think you need to go home to your fiancé, we need to get Matthew ready for school..."

I sank to my knees, my head spinning. A loud ringing began, drowning out Beckett's shouts. Nothing was right; nothing was how I remembered it. The ring carried on, getting louder and louder.

Then, I woke up.

I tumbled off the sofa, the phone ringing beside me, still lying on the floor where I had thrown it. I checked my watch, it wasn't time to get ready for work yet, curfew was only just about to be lifted. I sprinted over to the window and peered through the curtain. The checkpoint was there and the guard. A van crawled slowly past on its final patrol of our estate and I let the curtain fall. I grabbed the phone and answered it.

"Yes?"

"Fucking hell I thought you were never going to answer!" Etienne's voice called out, exasperated. "Listen, I'm sorry I'm calling so early. The prime minister is going to be coming in again today, to give us all some reassurance about this broadcast nonsense. I only just found out from McLean. So I want you to be in early, so we can all listen to the brief on what's going to happen and you need to look your absolute best. Though, you always look nice," he said shyly before hanging up.

I tossed the phone onto my sofa and rubbed my eyes, leaving black smears across the back of my hand. So I was yet again going to come face to face with Bowman.

149

I looked back outside, as the van disappeared out of my cul-de-sac. I wandered up to my silent bedroom and pulled out my clothes for the day. I clicked on my bathroom light, and stared at myself numbly in the mirror. My eyes were cupped by deep bags, and my lips were cracked and sore. I looked dreadful. I tried to smear on some make up. My body was weary and exhausted, and I could take no pleasure in deciding what to wear. I wanted to crawl back into bed and pull the sheets over my head. I pulled out a silk shift dress in a deep amethyst shade. I tugged on my black blazer over the top and pulled back my hair from my face. I looked presentable I supposed. I hated spending money on clothes, it made me feel rotten inside when I thought of all these people struggling to pay for food and heating. But Beckett had always reassured me that it was necessary; part of my disguise.

The gentle thud of post falling through my door made me come to, out of my musing. I walked downstairs, and picked up the pile of pro-government leaflets. I went to toss them into the bin, when a small sliver of paper fluttered out of it to the floor.

'Meeting. Two night's time.'

It was time to find out what his plan was.

*

Etienne was waiting for me in the foyer, his brow dotted with tiny beads of sweat. He frowned at me, concerned. "You look exhausted, is everything alright?"

I rubbed my forehead, holding back a yawn. "I didn't sleep so well last night." I explained. "Just couldn't

150

relax." I forced myself to look him in the eye, and tried to smile. For a moment, I thought of how he had kissed me in the dream, and my gaze slid down a little to his lips.

"You know, I could have definitely helped you to relax," he whispered as the lift doors shut. His tone was provocative, playful; he wanted me to know exactly what he meant. I stumbled my words, and to my horror, I could feel my cheeks getting warmer. The warmth spread through my body, and the image of Etienne, slowly undressing me, flashed through my mind. He turned to me quickly, watching with amusement as I pressed myself against the walls of the lift, leaning away from him. He leant close to me, his breath warm on my face. "I could come round tonight; I could show you how to get some of that tension relieved... As the lift came to a stop, he leapt away from me; the slightest hint of a grin on his face.

The doors opened revealing the imposing figure of McLean. He glared at Etienne and swiftly transferred his eyes to me, and for a very brief moment something other than contempt or suspicion passed through them. Disappointment perhaps? Whatever it was, it unnerved me.

"Get your asses out of the lift, he's due up here any minute." A little swirling began in the depths of my stomach, and I scuttled behind Etienne and McLean, past the others who were gathering for the prime minister's arrival. It had taken every inch of my inner strength not to slice the P.M's head from his shoulders with a champagne glass last time we had met, and I wasn't sure how; in my exhausted and irritable state, I could cope with it.

"At least she looks nice," McLean muttered. "He took a shine to her at the party."

We stood in our group and, hidden by the others, Etienne gently stroked my wrist. The lift doors opened and there he was, immaculately dressed in a navy blue suit, his hair scraped back. It seemed to be streaked more with grey than the last time I had seen him, perhaps the result of my little broadcast? Those around me broke into excited applause and I joined in. He glanced back and forth between us, taking in each of our faces. When he reached me, his lips curled into a smile, and it made the hairs stand to attention on the back of my neck. Bowman held up a hand, and the clapping died out.

"I know this is somewhat of an impromptu visit, but I know that many of you saw the broadcast from the so-called 'Revolution'. I have come to urge you all to dismiss this foolishness; it is little more than a publicity stunt. The Revolution are cowards, who hide away in the shadows and can only reveal themselves through a television screen." Those around me roared their approval, like hounds baying for blood. "And I will not let these miscreants destroy my government, or tarnish the hard work you all do here. I know my means are tough, but I hope you can all see now that they must be. I cannot be weakened by them, and with your help I will purge this country of the scum." Another collective shout. Etienne clapped his hands, but his face was grave. It was impossible to tell what he was thinking. The speech ended, and the PM made his rounds, allowing my

152

colleagues to fawn over him. Bowman stared intently at me as he drew closer to me.

"I remember you, from our little cocktail hour." I went to reply, but the words choked in my throat. He stepped back, opening his arms wide. Like a preacher to his devoted flock. "It is for the good of the next generation, people like this sweet and hard working young lady, that I am here. I want you all to fight alongside me."

"How can we do that?" a voice from behind me shouted passionately. "We could burn them out of their homes, the traitorous bastards!" it yelled.

"No no," Bowman laughed charmingly. "Just continue with your efforts towards our cause as you have been doing every day."

A hulking beast of a man stepped forward and leant carefully over Bowman's shoulder, whispering in his ear. Bowman batted him away, as I would perhaps swat away a wasp. Fucking big wasp though, I thought to myself with a chuckle. The huge man stepped back, rejoining Bowman's other three bodyguards. Bowman turned slowly to McLean, as though he could hardly be bothered to do so. "I'm afraid I have to leave, but I do. Would you have an office I could use to make a phone call? Perhaps you could take my men here and offer them some refreshments while they wait for me." He turned to his cronies. "McIntyre, you come with me."

The giant followed him to the lift and McLean ushered the other three, who did not look happy about being separated from Bowman, down to the cafeteria. I watched the numbers of the lift count down. He was on the second floor. I turned to Etienne.

153

"Would you excuse me for a moment? I need to go use the 'little girls' room'."

"Fine." he shrugged. Christina glanced over at me. I could sense the urgency in her eyes, and an unspoken message passed between us. She was going to cover me; we had to know what the PM was up to. All of a sudden, she fell to the floor, in a beautiful faint. A crowd rushed around her, and as I slipped out of one of the doors, ignored by the cameras that were honing in on Christina, I could hear her whimpering; "I am so sorry, I have just felt so under the weather lately."

I sprinted down the stairs, and slipped out onto the second floor. Bowman and his crony slipped into the office ahead of me. I gazed around. One camera ahead, focused on the corridor. The office was just out of its range. But it would still be able to hear me if I made a sound. I slid down under the window of the office Bowman was stood in. I could hear his raised voice.

"What the fuck is it McIntyre?"

"Sir, I thought you would want to know that..."

"I don't pay you to think, I pay you to take a bullet for me, to make sure nobody can get close to me. Not to think!"

McIntyre didn't answer. I peered over the top of the window. Bowman and McIntyre were facing away from me, Bowman looking out the window and McIntyre staring at his back. There was a security camera on my side of the room, fixed on them.

"Sir, I just think we should leave here now, the security risk on this building is high. We have intelligence that..."

Bowman flung himself around, hitting McIntyre hard across the face with the back of his hand.

"I told you that I don't care what you think!" he hollered, spittle spraying McIntyre's face. McIntyre could have strangled Bowman with one hand, but instead he cowered. Bowman tugged on the bottom of his suit, slicking down his hair with a hand. A thick band of silver winked on his thumb. I noticed that McIntyre wore a similar one. Perhaps a way to distinguish Bowman and his bitches, to spot them from the common people. I stored that thought away and watched as Bowman gripped McIntyre by his lapel, almost nose to nose with him.

"Now, I don't want to hear you challenge my choices again, or I'll make sure the vans show up at your house. You don't want your wife to watch you being dragged away. Maybe I'll tell her about your little perks of the job?" McIntyre shook his head, quivering a little. "Good, now let's get the others and go."

I hurried back into the stairwell, sprinting up to my floor. As I slipped through the door, Christina smiled at me wanly. Robert, a rather obese man who was good with computers and very little else, was fawning over her. I wandered to my desk, and steadied myself for a moment. Bowman's carefully constructed facade had dropped for a moment, showing me a little of what was underneath. He was a man like any other, but he was dangerous, and quick to lose his cool. I glanced over at Etienne's office. He was sat at his computer, tapping away at the keys furiously. He looked up at me and I turned away quickly, taking my seat. Another pile of files to go through, another load of people whose futures lay at my fingertips. One click and they'd be sent to McLean and rounded up like dogs.

Again I felt weary. Bowman's visit had been an anticlimax and I had done nothing but stood there, just another of his adoring, stupid worshippers.

I very deliberately avoided Etienne over the rest of the day, and the following one. I expected him to be pushy, to confront me. But he found it almost amusing, how carefully I chose to do things in the longest way possible so I had no free moments for him to wander over to my desk. How I took the longest route to the other floors to avoid his office. He watched me with a small half-smile, and a raised eyebrow. It made me angry, thinking of him, and how he regarded me as nothing more than some girl he worked with and wanted to take home. I had to remind myself, over and over that it wasn't his fault; that was exactly what I had wanted them to think, that I was a nobody. Our workload had nearly doubled since the broadcast, and luckily for me, Etienne had been swamped by paperwork.

I thought about the meeting with Beckett, how he had something big planned for me. It wasn't that long ago that I would relished the opportunity to do whatever it took for Beckett, for the Revolution, but now there was something stuck in my throat, scratching in the back of mind, scrabbling to get out. Doubt. I grabbed my bag and coat and made my way for the lift when Etienne poked out his head.

"Still ignoring me?" he teased.

I pushed past to get into the lift. He shot in behind me, pressing the button before I got a chance, which was just one step too far.

"You're going to have to talk to me sometime Romany. We do work together, after all."

Something in me snapped, and I squared up to him, the smug smile wiped from his face. "Yeah, maybe I do need to talk to you about what happened the other day, but I'll do it when I'm ready. I am getting fucking tired of these lift meetings, I really am. So I am going to get out, go home and I will see you after the weekend. It's my weekend off, and I will not be spending it with *anyone* from work." I stepped out of the lift, leaving him to stare after me, open mouthed.

*

Beckett was alone when I arrived, waiting anxiously for the others to arrive. His face lit as he rushed to greet me.

"I'm so glad you got here first. I need to talk to you." He led me down to the basement. "You didn't tell me about the P.M's little visit..." There it was again, the hint of accusation.

"It wasn't very eventful. He showed up, preached to us about staying true to his cause and left again."

Beckett's eyes narrowed a little, as he tossed three photographs onto the table, Bowman striking McIntyre, Bowman grabbing him by the lapels, another of him close to his face. I snatched them up, shaking them at him. "How the fuck did you get these Beckett?"

He shrugged, pleased with himself. "That's not what matters...this is."

He handed me a flyer with a flourish. The pictures were plastered across it with 'THUG IN A SUIT', and beneath the screaming headline: 'Is this the man you want running your country?'

My hands were shaking as I read it. "I saw this happen," I stammered, "there was no one else there... I don't understand how you got them." He smiled, clearly not willing to tell me anything further. "Are you going to distribute them?"

"Yep. Just like before... only this time, we've got real footage of the P.M ruining his perfect image." He was practically jumping up and down in excitement.

"You can't hand these out Beckett." I said firmly.

He stared at me, his glee turning to anger. "Why the fuck not?" he retorted.

"Because if you do, Bowman is going to know that there is one of us in the building."

"Believe me," he snorted, "you and my other mole can take care of yourselves."

"That's not the point."

"Who are you trying to protect?" he asked softly, dangerously.

"People like me. Like Christina; like any of the poor assholes that McLean could accuse. Bowman is going to be furious when he sees this, he will want arrests."

Beckett paused for a moment, thinking over my words. "So this has nothing to do with Etienne then?" Simple enough question, but I could hear the anger hidden beneath the nonchalance.

"Excuse me?" Then, slowly, it dawned on me.

"You've been having your mole spy on me?"

"Well apparently it's the talk of the office."

"Who the fuck told you that?"

"It doesn't matter who told me," he hissed, his finger in my face. "I expected better of you than to open your legs for some government pig."

I threw back my fist, aiming a punch at him. He grabbed my arm at the last minute. "How dare you!" I struggled to get free, and caught him hard in the stomach with my other hand. I went to run up the stairs but he grabbed me from behind, pinning my arms to my side. "I haven't slept with anybody!" I whirled around, grazing his nose with mine, his hands tight on both my wrists. I stayed there for a second nose to nose. "Do you hear me now? I haven't slept with *anybody.*"

His eyes widened and his grip on me slackened. "Shit Romany..."

He let me go and without hesitation, I slapped him hard. "That's for accusing me of being a slut. And besides, whoever I end up with is none of your business is it, seeing as I'm just like a sister to you?"

He went to speak, stumbling in his speech before stepping backwards, shaking his head. "I won't watch one of mine with one of *theirs.*" Still shaking his head, he gathered up the pictures. "I won't have my second sleeping with the enemy."

I resisted the urge to hit him again.

"That won't be happening," he nodded at me.

"These leaflets will still have to go out." I went to protest. "Romany, we're getting so close..." he pleaded, "...when an opportunity like this comes up, we have to take it."

"What if they accuse me?"

"They won't, you're safe."

"Then who? Some poor sap that you don't know. You know they'll kill him right?" He stared back at me, impassive. "I forgot, just because he works for the government that makes it OK. So who is it Beckett? Who's the fall guy? Maybe he has kids, or a wife..." I protested, ignoring his sighs.

"Sometimes Romany, we can't be saints; we have to make the tough choices."

"We don't get to decide who lives and who dies."

"In this instance I have to."

I placed a hand on his shoulder, trying a different tactic. "We have the public's attention; the broadcast was enough to almost increase those on our side three times over. We don't need to do things this extreme. If you do there'll be an investigation into our department... just give it a little more time." He looked at me, and the rhythm of our breathing began to match in pace. "Please Beckett." It was barely a whisper. Neither of us spoke, staring at one another. My eyes pleading, his full of pity. Footsteps from above broke the moment, and he shook his head, as though clearing me from it.

"My mind is made up Romany. I'm sorry." He walked upstairs and I could hear his voice, full of excitement, as he greeted the other members.

They trotted down, one by one, and Lexi frowned at me, concerned. She glared at the back of Beckett's head, as she came to stand by my side.

"He told you about the leaflet," she said flatly.

"You knew?" I replied incredulously.

"Yeah, I knew. And I also told him that it was a huge mistake and a massive risk to take. He won't listen though, he's made up his mind. I'll give him one thing;

160

that he's actually starting to man up," she said thoughtfully. "I mean, we actually seem to be going somewhere now."

Beckett cracked his knuckles as he stood before us, his select little group. "Two days ago, these images were captured at a government office." He passed around the leaflets stacked behind him. "We are going to distribute these photographs across the country. It will be a direct attack on Bowman, one which will deeply impact on his public image."

"Revealing his true colours!" cried Philip, gleefully.

"Exactly." Beckett nodded. "But, this will not be enough to ruffle his feathers as much as we need. We need him to be unsettled and distracted in our build up to pulling him down from his throne." There was a shout of approval and a fist in the air from those around us. Lexi merely pulled up an eyebrow in interest. "Which is why," Beckett continued. "Romany and Erin are going to take out his head of security." There was a murmur of interest as those around me stared over their shoulders at me.

Lexi raised a hand. "Why the hell are you sending in our best girl, with someone we hardly know?" she asked, falsely polite. I expected Erin to leap to her own defence but she merely inclined her head, conceding Lexi's point.

"Jonathan McIntyre is a man with a large responsibility resting on his shoulders, and sometimes he likes to relax," Beckett explained. "With women." There was a light chuckle from the men in the room, and an air of disgust from the women. "That he has paid for."

"That still doesn't answer my question," Lexi piped up.

"He likes young, Caucasian brunettes. And that is precisely what he is going to get."

So Erin and I were to be McIntyre's girls for the night.

"Erin is highly trained, and more than capable of this assignment. Peter has recommended her for this mission, and I trust his advice. We are going to make Bowman feel vulnerable. It means he will also have to take on a new head of security, someone he is unfamiliar with. It will mean he will become an easier target."

Erin winked at me. But I couldn't muster up any enthusiasm. It was, in Beckett's defence, an excellent idea, but as I closed my eyes, I could see the face of the policeman who had attacked Christina, straining against the plastic bag. Eyes bulbous, mouth gaping like a fish deprived of air. There was blood on my hands, and it was soaking into my soul.

11

I was curled up in my bed, the covers pulled around my chin as the wind howled outside. A crack of lightning lit up the room and I buried myself under the sheets, clutching my teddy. My door creaked open and I shut my eyes tight, trying to be brave. A warm familiar scent made me feel better as my mother climbed into bed beside me.

"Don't be frightened sweetheart, it's only a bit of a storm." I peeped up at her, and I could tell she'd been crying again, even though she was trying to hide it. "How about a story?" I sat up, feeling a little bit better.

"An old one," I decided.

My mummy reached behind her back and pulled out my favourite book, a very old brown one. 'A History of Kings and Queens of Europe.' I couldn't read, but I'd heard my mummy reading it so much I could remember the title.

"So, who do you want to hear about tonight?"

"Queen Isabella!" I cried out, feeling very excited. I'd already heard about Marie Antoinette the night before, and that hadn't had a very happy ending.

"Okay... Isabella was born on April 22, 1451 to John II of Castile and Isabella of Portugal..." I lay back on the pillow and listened as mummy told me all about Queen Isabella. My eyes got heavy and I snuggled under the duvet, feeling very sleepy.

*

Beckett's little band of adoring followers slowly left, one by one, but he held back myself, Erin and Peter to discuss the plan further. Lexi stayed to be petulant. Beckett didn't argue with her. He carefully avoided talking to me directly speaking only about Erin and I as a pair. Erin's eyes glittered with excitement, her tongue flicking over her teeth as she smiled. She turned to me, and I could feel Lexi tense up a little. She wasn't happy about being excluded. Erin beamed at me, radiating pride and happiness.

My stomach tightened in a knot. Beckett wouldn't listen to me about the leaflets, there was definitely no way out of this one. I would have to put my shit to one side, and do my work for the Revolution.

*

Lexi glared at me, her arms folded. Romany had whisked out of the room with Erin and Peter, without so much as a glance at me. She had agreed to my plan, had even seemed a little impressed. I expected Lexi to follow her like a little lapdog, but she remained, her eyes boring holes into me.

"What?" I asked.

"What do you think you're doing?" she asked me politely, nibbling on her lip and examining her nails.

"Lexi..." I warned, "...don't start."

"You do realise you could be putting her at risk, don't you?"

I grasped at my hair in exasperation."It's not my job to worry about Romany's feelings; I have to do what..."

"...Is right for the Revolution. Yeah, I get it." she interrupted. "But you're putting everyone in that office at risk."

"They work for the *government* Lexi, they deserve whatever they get." She recoiled a little from me, disgusted.

"They're still people, Beckett, and they're just doing the same as us, whatever they can to survive." She shook her head. "Romany seems to be the only one of us to understand that."

"It wasn't that long ago she was the one pushing us to do whatever it took."

"She only said that because she knew it's what you wanted her to believe!" she screamed at me, glancing at the staircase, terrified we would be heard. I pushed the basement door shut and turned back to her. She was panting, her muscular shoulders rising and falling with her quick breaths. "And now you want to send her with someone she has never worked with before. With someone she's never even trained with... Do you want her dead?"

The words hit me like a punch to the throat."Of course not."

"But you're not going to change your mind?"

I rubbed my face, the stubble on my chin scratching my palm. "No."

She nodded for a moment, and she could hardly mask her contempt. "Then you've made your choice." She looked triumphant. "You've chosen the Revolution over her."

Before I could speak she strode confidently to the door, flinging it open. "If you get her killed Beckett..."

she paused for a moment. "...I'll destroy you." She walked away confidently, leaving me with a hollow ache in my chest. I had strived since I was a child to be the best leader I could be, and I was there. I was making the shit choices, for the greater good. But there was something bittersweet about it. I sank onto the hard metal chair beside me, and lit a cigarette, inhaling deeply.

*

The inky black dress clung to me, gently sliding over my skin. It sparkled under the dim lights of the street, like a million stars glittering as I walked. The neckline was plunging; my hair was pinned up, making my neck look swanlike and elegant. The guard on the door patted me down, searching me for weapons. His lips were parted and damp. He slid a hand down my leg and I grabbed it. "That'll cost you." I hissed. He sniffed and sneered at me. "More than you could afford I'm guessing." The smile vanished as he let me through the front door of the building.

McIntyre was important indeed; there were no cameras pointing on his beautiful townhouse. I had marvelled as I walked past the guard, handing him the passes Beckett had obtained. I was in the most exclusive area in the city, the one with the privilege of being unmonitored. Mostly as only the truly privileged lived here. The security was high but once we were finished, there'd be no evidence of us being here.

Erin was waiting in the hallway for me and even I found myself catching my breath at the sight of her. Her hair was curled, pinned on one side. The scarlet evening gown slid over her body, enhancing her curves. Her eyes were outlined, with a feline flick and she looked amazing. A sliver of light splashed across the hallway, coming from upstairs.

"Ladies, please come up," a voice echoed in the darkness, and Erin nodded at me grimly. We wandered up the marble staircase, our heels tapping on the floor. All the doors in the corridor were firmly shut, with exception of one. I walked ahead of Erin, and took a deep breath. Like an actress stepping into the bright lights of the stage, I got myself into character.

I walked into the room with my head held high and Erin followed my lead. We stood side by side as McIntyre stepped out of the adjoining bathroom. He was wearing a suit, and he looked even larger to me than when I had last seen him.

"Well," he gasped, licking his lips, "I have to say that old Mickey boy has outdone himself."

Old Mickey Boy was going to be in some deep shit when we were done, I thought to myself. Then I thought of the other women he had sent here, and didn't feel guilty in the slightest. McIntyre rubbed his hands, and I noted the absence of a wedding ring. Erin placed a hand on her hip and leant to one side slightly, whereas I stood stiff backed, a little haughty. His eyes flicked back and forth between us. He stepped closer and I resisted the urge to back away. He pulled Erin towards him, and there was only a very brief tensing of her shoulders as he ran his colossal hands through her hair. He tilted her head back a little, and she averted her eyes coyly. Gently, he shifted her to one side and came towards me. I stood my ground and met his eyes defiantly. He stroked my face and, taking hold of my hand, led me to the bed. Gaudy, with deep red curtains hanging from the golden four-poster frame, it was a display of wealth. Black satin sheets slid beneath his huge bulk. It was a bed made for doing dark deeds. I waited at the foot of the bed as he leant back on the pillows.

"You first," he winked, before glancing at Erin. "Don't worry; you won't be left out sugar. I've had a really hard day, why don't you come here and help me relax." I tried to block out the thought of Etienne telling me how he could help me relax as I crawled across the bed and straddled McIntyre. He leant up to kiss me and I pulled away.

"Not the mouth."

He laughed and pulled me forward, nuzzling my neck with his slobbery lips. I could hear Erin's light steps as she almost silently closed the door, flicking the lock. McIntyre was far to occupied to notice as he began to tug on my dress, running his hands up and down my back. I sat up and stared down at him, slowly moving my hand down to his belt, taking my time to undo it, keeping my eyes on his. I pulled out his belt from the loops with a flourish and held it taut.

"Tie me up..." he leered. Well that would certainly help matters. I tied his hands to the bedpost, taking my time on the knot. He looked confused and tried to struggle a little, the belt offering no purchase.

"My first boyfriend was a sailor..." I explained, trying to sound seductive.

"Oh really?" he smiled. "What else did he teach you, my little pirate."

I glanced at Erin who nodded, a barely noticeable incline of her head. McIntyre closed his eyes in ecstasy as Erin clambered over, wrapping her arms around me.

"Shall we show you?" she said, her voice smooth as honey.

"Oh yes!" he cried gleefully, as I took a firm grip on his tie and Erin used the belt on her dress to tie his feet to the bed. The stupid oaf was too engrossed to find it suspicious. She stepped gracefully off the bed and picked up one of the satin cushions that had fallen to the floor. In a flash, she brought it down on his face as I gripped his tie, pulling it tight. He began to struggle, desperate to take in air. The bed began to rock back and forth with the sheer might of his thrashing. I could see the sweat beading across Erin's forehead and the veins in her arms protruding as she forced the cushion onto his face. She began to moan seductively, trying to mask the sounds. His muffled screams were little more than whimpers as he became slowly weaker. I pulled the tie tighter, and tighter until he stopped moving. After a minute or so, Erin lifted the cushion. I clambered off his massive bulk, and avoided looking at his face, with its bulbous eyes and open mouth.

Suddenly, Erin pulled out her sharp metal hairpin and sliced it neatly across McIntyre's throat, stepping backwards from the blood spilling from the wound.

"What the hell?" I mouthed.

"I'm not taking any chances," she hissed. "I have Peter to think of. This fucker wakes up, he could find us, and find him." I bit back my rage and ran over to her, messing up her hair. She grabbed me and kissed me hard, smearing our lipstick, ruffling my hair. I tore the

169

bottom of my dress, and she ripped the neckline of hers. Before we left, I flicked on the shower in his wet room, my heels sliding on the black marble floor.

"Okay, now we look like girls who have been up to no good." She giggled a little and looked over at McIntyre's body, lying inanimately. "Let's go." We walked down the stairs nonchalantly, and smiled coyly at the guard.

"Jesus girls," he leered, "sounds like you were worth the money. Hope that bed's in one piece."

"Oh yes..." Erin simpered, "he's having a shower."

"Ah," he winked. "I'll leave him be then, he'll be needing a rest."

She smiled as we slinked past, clutching one another as we scurried off down the road as quickly as we could without seeming suspicious. We dashed into the nearest alley, where we had dumped a bin bag of clothes and changed swiftly from our outfits, tying our hair up.

Our expensive dresses went up in flames, as we walked out of the expensive estate, leaving behind nothing but fake names and a dead body.

*

I stood in the shower, letting the water flow over me. I turned up the heat until my skin turned a flushed pink. I relished it as it ran over my back, burning me deliciously. My hands were trembling as I squeezed the lurid green gel onto them, before scrubbing myself with the hard brush, again and again. Erin and I had parted ways, walking fast to make it back before curfew. I wondered if she had succeeded. Every creak and tap in the house made me jump. What if we had made a mistake? What if they'd found our dresses? They could be on their way for me now. I had slept restlessly, still fully clothed. When I had awoken, the first thing I had done was thrown up. That was a first.

The phone rang and I stepped out the stream of scalding water, wrapping a towel around myself. I hurried down the stairs leaving a trail of soggy footprints behind me.

"Romany!" a nervous, anxious voice hollered down the phone. "Oh god, I'm so glad I got through to you."

Etienne. I thought for a moment about hanging up but he sounded desperate. I flopped down onto my battered sofa, tucking my legs under me. "What's up Etienne?"

"Terrible news, things have gotten even worse. Something dreadful has happened. I know it's early, but I need you..." he hesitated for a moment, "...to come in early. Please."

"I've just got out the shower but I'll be as quick as I can."

"You shouldn't tell me things like that while I'm sat in my office alone."

My fleeting pity drained and I hung up. I was in no mood for his games. The post hit my doormat with a thud, and as I walked over, I could see the leaflet, poking out of the top of the government junk mail. I snatched it up off the floor, tearing it into pieces. Beckett had chosen to play the dangerous hand, and now I had to walk into the lion's den, to face McLean, and whoever Beckett had chosen to take the fall.

The atmosphere was stifling as I stepped into the building. The guard shot me a sideways look, checking

171

his watch. I'd gotten ready quicker than normal, rushing to get in. He didn't speak but locked the door behind me.

"Who are you trying to keep out?" I tried to joke.

"I'm keeping you all in," he replied grimly. I stepped into the lift and tried to keep my smile fixed while he stared at me, waiting for the doors to close.

My floor was completely empty, the phones ringing eerily in the silence. Etienne was slumped over his desk, clutching his forehead. I knocked gently on the door, letting myself in anyway when he didn't look up. I stood awkwardly for a minute as he raised his head, his eyes bloodshot, hair untidy. He flicked a device on the table, masking our conversation. He nodded at the camera. "It's off," he explained. "The guard thinks were up to no good in here," he chuckled sadly.

I sat down in front of the desk and he took in a deep breath.

"Jonathan McIntyre was murdered last night; he was the prime minister's head of security." I clutched the table, the sweat beads collecting on my forehead all too real. "They discovered his body this morning, around about the same time these were posted around the city." He tossed one of Beckett's leaflets on to the table and I caught my breath. Perhaps Etienne suspected me; maybe he was Beckett's mole. "I wanted to warn you. It seems these pictures were taken from a security camera in this building?"

"Here?" I gulped.

"Yes," he nodded sternly. "And we know who the person responsible is." I braced myself. What if Beckett hadn't been careful enough? "Kinley."

Rupert Kinley was a security guard on the lower levels, often working in the security office. I had never spoken to him, but I knew he had an unsavoury reputation. He was known for touching up the women, and using the cameras to spy on them. I had, however, met his wife, and she was a timid woman, painfully skinny and shy. She often sported bruises. Despite myself, I didn't feel quite so guilty. Beckett's mole had made the best of a dreadful decision.

"What about his family?"

"McLean is taking care of them," Etienne said dismissively. I gripped the table harder. "He's going to help them financially, ensure that they don't suffer for his wrongdoings. Kinley's already been taken from the building," he explained.

I uncurled my fingers, and slid down in the chair. I was a little taken aback by McLean's kindness towards the sweet Mrs. Kinley. But I knew there had to be an ulterior motive. That man did nothing that wouldn't benefit himself.

Etienne focused on me, his eyes scanning mine. "I want to keep you safe Romany. Don't you understand that? In this world, especially now, everyone needs someone they can rely on."

"I can look after myself," I tried to say jokily.

"No," he shook his head, "nobody can."

He stood to his feet and walked to the window. "I know you don't love me, and I can't say in complete honesty that I love you, but we care about each other don't we?" he asked sincerely. "Right now, the way things are, is that not enough?" He turned back to me, his hands opened, eyes pleading.

I stared at his desk, at the objects that littered it; stapler, fountain pen, diary. "I don't know Etienne," I answered, as honestly as I could. "Maybe it's because of how things are now, that we both need something more than to just settle." He chewed on his lip and I felt a pang of guilt. "I like you." I blurted out. "But at the moment, I have no idea what that means." A little hope glistened in his eyes. "But I don't want you to keep on trying to have these conversations with me. Our department is going to be watched Etienne, so for now, let's just make it through today, and each day after that; and see where tomorrow takes us." I took a deep breath.

"One day," Etienne said, choosing his words carefully, "you're going to want more than this, a family perhaps? I could be the person to give you all that."

I felt an odd mixture of emotions, guilt, a little stab of lust and, overwhelmingly, betrayal. I felt as though I was letting Beckett down in some way, which was crazy, especially as it was so clear he didn't want me. Or, if he did, I came second to his first love, the one he could never keep away from: the Revolution. I leant forward and placed my hand over his. "Let's just call this an understanding, for now, until this craziness blows over. Just wait, please, I'm not ready for any of this yet. I just want to get through every day the best I can for now. But I promise, we can talk about this sometime soon."

He smiled and nodded. It was an empty promise, one which meant almost nothing. But, and it was the smallest of buts, there was a chance that when all this was over, and the Revolution won, that perhaps there was a future for Etienne and I. He wanted a future after all. But, I reminded myself, this was a man who knew nothing about the real me. He was falling for a rouse, an elaborate disguise. But, maybe he was falling for the person I truly was.

Lost in my tangled web of thoughts, I hadn't noticed the stream of others coming into the level. Each of them looked pale and washed out, all of them nervy and on edge. Christina kept glancing our way, and there was a green tinge to her face. Everyone was terrified that they would be the ones accused of leaking the photos. McLean stepped out of the lift and Etienne jumped to his feet.

"Shit, we need to get out there." I scurried out behind him, and felt McLean's sardonic sneer before I actually saw it. Harry stood in the corner, wearing a very similar grin.

"I'm so glad you could manage to tear yourself away."

"I'm sorry sir." Etienne's grovelling apology made me feel ill. It was degrading, watching him lick the boots of someone like McLean.

"Now, I am sure you all received one of these today." McLean held up one of the leaflets. I could hear everyone sucking in their breath, balling their hands into fists to stop them from shaking. "And I hope, for all your sakes you paid no attention and destroyed them as the piece of nonsense bullshit they are." Everyone nodded eagerly. "Of course you did. Now I will not deny that these images were taken within this building, but they have been warped in their content, to the Revolution's advantage." He paced back and forth, taking a long hard look at each of our faces.

"Now, I may as well tell you all that the man in this picture, Jonathan McIntyre, was killed last night. He was the prime minister's head of security." A gasp, so quiet it sounded like a whisper, rose from his enraptured audience. "I want you all to know, that the prime minister is distraught and as you can imagine, devastated that these photos have served only to blight his fond memories of his dear friend." A perfect rendition, clearly rehearsed. "We are certain that this atrocity was committed by the Revolution, in an attempt to break down our prime minister but I am telling you now, it will not work." His voice was thick with emotion, his conviction etched on his face.

"Now..." He paused in his pacing, eyes narrowed. "...I'm guessing you're all anxious to know who the traitor in our ranks is." I could feel my body tensing, and the brush of Etienne's fingers on the back of my hand was calming. McLean stared at me, almost through me, and I kept my face serene, keeping my gaze locked on his. "Well," he stared at me for a second longer before stepping back, arms flung open. I allowed myself to breathe again. "You will all be glad to know we have apprehended the offender and defector. He is a security guard, who had access to the photographs."

"What about his family?" Christina piped up, to my disbelief. "He may be a traitor, but they haven't done anything wrong."

"I have personally seen to it that they will not be involved in any way, and this facility will help his wife and children." I felt my legs weaken as I thought of that frightened, browbeaten woman and her wide-eyed children when they got the news Daddy wasn't coming home, that the vans had taken him. She must have thought she was next, that her children were going to die in some 'institution'.

McLean's mouth was moving, more inspirational crap I suspected, but all I could hear was white noise. He turned to walk away and the room began to spin. How could Beckett do this? How could he do this to someone, to a family? Etienne was talking to me, but I couldn't hear him, he drifted in and out, like a radio losing signal. Harry was watching me, amused. He seemed completely unfazed by the catastrophes. I prayed that he wasn't Beckett's mole; that would be enough to make me completely lose all respect for Beckett. I didn't remember walking to my desk, I did it almost on auto-pilot. But as I came back down to earth, I wondered when life had become so complicated. I had known who I was. An assassin, a devoted member of the Revolution. I had this thing with Beckett, I had my undercover job, working with people I had nothing but derision for and now, everything was becoming worse and worse, and it felt heavy, like stones being pressed upon me. Something had to break; I just didn't know what it would be.

*

I sat at my desk, trying my hardest to focus on the paperwork stacked in front of me. My fingers traced over the words, my brain not taking them in. Suddenly, a deafening boom came from outside in the streets, shaking our entire building like an earthquake. My stack of papers fell to the floor; scattering and I dove under the desk, hands over my ears. Christina was staring at me, mouthing something. My ears were ringing, white noise screaming through them. The smell of burning, acrid and strong, filled my nose, made it hard to breathe. The noise died out, and I crawled out from beneath the desk. Etienne dashed out of his office, hauling me to my feet.

"Are you alright?" He pushed my hair back, checking me for injuries. I gently pushed him away.

"I'm fine." I said shakily. I turned to the window. In the road was a burning police car, surrounded by charred pieces of paper, too far away to decipher. Those around me began to panic, pushing and shoving to get out of the exits. I turned and sprinted to the fire exit, hurrying as fast as I could to reach the street below. Etienne followed, hollering at me to stop, or to slow down, something I couldn't distinguish over the screams and shouts. The stairs seemed endless, as I pushed past others making their way out of the building. The imposing glass atrium was filled with people, all looking terrified. The smell of burning grew stronger. I ran past the guard, shrugging him off as he lurched forward to stop me. "It's not safe!" he screamed after me.

As I shoved open the doors, I could feel the heat of the flames from where I stood, the smoke in the air making me catch my breath. It was stiflingly hot, and I could see Etienne recoil from the heat. The car was ablaze, reduced to its bare bones. Behind me, the foyer was filling up and I could see McLean, at the head of the throng, trying to calm them down. I stepped forward, closer to the fuselage of the ruined car. I carefully picked up one of the smouldering flyers, and felt sick to my stomach as I recognised the photographs spread scandalously across it.

Etienne placed a hand on my shoulder, gently manoeuvring me away from the blaze. "It's not safe here today." Etienne held me close to him as he addressed McLean. "We should let these people return home until we have the situation," he gestured at the inferno "under control." McLean nodded reluctantly, and stared at me with a meaningful edge to his glare. Etienne's grip became a little tighter. "I'm going to walk Romany home."

"I am going to need to talk to *everyone* Etienne, you realise that don't you?"

"Not now," Etienne replied firmly. "Nobody can handle this now Doug." The finality in his voice made me jump a little; I had never heard Etienne sound anything other than gentlemanly. McLean gritted his teeth and turned to the gawping masses gathering behind him.

"You are all free to return to your homes for the day, to assure your loved ones that all is well. No doubt word of this little stunt will spread quickly. But tomorrow, you will all be in here, and I will be talking to each and every one of you."

We were all under suspicion. That was clear. Etienne sprinted back up and grabbed my coat and purse, wrapping it around my shoulders. I could hear the screaming sirens of the police cars approaching, and I felt claustrophobic. I had to get out.

12

I let Etienne walk me down the road in complete silence. I was hardly aware of my feet moving. My mind was skipping over and over the same question, like a song on repeat. When had Beckett become so ruthless? I realised we were heading in the direction of Beckett's house. We turned off, into a pretty little estate with perfectly manicured trees and mowed lawns, a haven from the grey, bleak London streets filled with cameras and propaganda. It reminded me of where McIntyre had lived. The sick feeling returned to me. The guard stared at us, his face pallid.

"I just heard, over me radio, about the car."

Etienne glanced at me awkwardly and nodded gravely. "Yes, it was horrific. But we mustn't pay any attention. If the Revolution wanted to really get some attention, they'd have killed someone."

"What, like that poor policeman? I knew Eddie, he was a good man. Feel terrible for his poor wife."

My head was spinning. Yes, if Beckett really wanted some attention he would have killed someone in that explosion. But instead, he had got exactly what he wanted without such violent means. He had gotten *my* attention.

Etienne led me through his front door and with a tone that told me he wasn't to be argued with, asked me to take a seat. Sinking into the comfy sofa made my body finally uncurl from its tense state and I tipped my head back, closing my eyes.

"I think this calls for a cup of tea." Etienne said with a sigh.

I listened to him banging and crashing in the kitchen. He began to whistle and, despite myself, I found that the domestic air he provided was, if nothing, very nice. My home had always been an empty shell, one which was the roof over my head and very little else. Beckett and Lexi hardly ever visited, and it often felt lonely. As Etienne carried in two cups of tea, placing one on the polished table in front of me, I could feel his eyes on me. He took a seat opposite me and blew across the china mug, his eyes resting steadily on my face. Neither of us spoke for a moment, sipping our teas.

"Are you alright?" He broke the silence first, with a rather mundane question.

"Is that all you could think of?" I replied with a smile.

"Right now, yes." He sighed again and I could see the strain on his face. "Everything's changing Romany." He placed his tea down and clutched his face. "I don't know what to do. After the murder, those photographs...now this! It's all happening too fast, and it's all leading back to our building."

"I don't think anyone is suspecting us Etienne, they have the guy who leaked the pictures." He shook his head, and to my horror, his eyes were looking a little damp. "And besides, the Revolution probably only blew up that car in retaliation for the arrest of Kinley." He shrugged, defeated.

"I know, I know." He pulled out a packet of cigarettes and placed one between his lips. I realised how long it had been since I had smoked one. "But, this isn't going to be the end, I can sense it. Once this has been investigated, once Kinley is dealt with, maybe it will die down; but I know this can't be the end." He chucked the cigarettes to me and, automatically, I lit one. It hit me in an instant, filling my lungs with its toxic smoke, easing my anxiety. "You know, I do realise how lucky I am." He gestured around the room with a flourish. "I've always felt so guilty, living like this, when the rest of the world is struggling to get by. But that's life isn't it? There have always been the rich and the poor, it's just the divide is much clearer these days." His hands were shaking, and he twisted them together, interlocking his fingers. "I'm not a bad person, Romany, really I'm not. I just feel that if judgement day is coming, maybe I have to, I don't know, atone for my sins."

"Etienne, we all do what we can to survive." I tried to sound reassuring.

"We send people to their deaths Romany, and we get paid for it." As soon as the words left his mouth, he pursed his lips together, terrified we'd be overheard. I went and knelt before him. I gently wrapped my hands around his, and he glanced at me, the pulse in his wrist quickening a little.

"Etienne, you have to believe me. You need to do whatever it takes to keep yourself safe. Working for the government is our protection." I absently rubbed his palm with my thumb. "You should never feel guilty, you're only doing the best with the life you have." As I looked up at him to smile, I realised how close his face was to mine. I swallowed hard as his lips parted a little. "Etienne..."

He pulled his hand from mine and placed it on my cheek. It was warm, but in no way unpleasant. "I know," he said desolately. "You're not ready yet." He moved a little closer, and suddenly his lips met mine. He kissed me softly, and then a little harder. I felt my body respond, and he pulled me on to his lap. It felt so good, to have someone want me, to have someone kiss me that I lost my mind. He lay me back on the sofa, his body pressing against mine. I wanted him to undress me, to kiss me all over, to fuck me. I wanted him to do everything Beckett wouldn't. Selfishly, I wanted him to make me feel normal for a moment. But then, he stood up. "You're not ready," he repeated, sighing as his hand let go of mine. He smiled as I clambered to my feet. I rubbed my cheek, and a smudge of ash blackened my fingertips. I pulled on my coat and Etienne frowned.

"You're going home already?" I nodded, tightening the belt of my jacket. "Well please let me walk you." He leapt to his feet, over eager.

"Really Etienne, I'd sooner be alone."

He sat back down, despondent. "Well, I suppose I'll see you tomorrow." He got up and lit another cigarette, and sat back in his chair, staring at the ceiling. I wanted to say something to make him feel a little better, to reassure him that once the Revolution won things would get easier for him. But I knew that like me, Etienne had to live with the things he had done.

As I walked down the road, towards Beckett's house, I knew that Etienne had marked me as the one to help all the nightmares disappear, to love him despite the horrors he had caused. A part of me idealistically thought that maybe Etienne and I could truly be there for one another, love each other despite the awful things in our pasts. But I knew, that was an impossibility and that I was living in a fairytale. The guard took my paperwork, and I reminded myself grimly that in this world, there were no fairytales.

*

I had woken in the middle of the night, to find Beckett stood by my door, his face shrouded by the darkness.

"You need to come with me." His voice was serious, unnerving.

"What is it?" I asked, pulling on my dressing gown. But Beckett had already begun to walk away, leaving me to scurry behind him. We walked down the corridor, feeling our way through the pitch black, careful not to make too much noise. Beckett reached back for my hand, and his was sweaty, squelching on mine as he gripped it tight. We walked downstairs, and I could see the light coming from the basement. Matthew was waiting for us.

*

I could hear someone storming across the floor above my head, the sound of their stomping echoing down to the cellar. I braced myself. Things were about to get ugly. Romany flung open the basement door and stared at me.

"How could you?" Her words tore through me like bullets. I began to stammer, and I realised how stupid I must've looked; cowering and unable to speak. Embarrassed, I turned my back, which riled her even more. "Don't you dare, Beckett." I had never heard her so angry before. She came flying at me, stood as close to

184

me as she could be without our bodies physically touching. "I had to hear all the sad stories about Kinley, you know, the guy you sent to the fucking vans? I had to hide under my *desk* from an explosion. Oh and tomorrow, I get to go into work, be interviewed again and spend the rest of the day shitting myself, waiting to see if they work out who I am!" She took a deep breath and ran her hand through her hair. Her outfit was sleek and elegant, a white tank top tucked into a little red skirt. But her hair was a wild mess, tangled and out of control. Her jacket was hanging open, the tie on it loosened by her constant fidgeting. "All while you sat in your basement like a coward."

I went to argue but she was in a world of her own, relentless. "You know, I am pleased you've finally found your voice Beckett. I'm glad you've learned to make the tough choices. But stop acting all high and mighty, when all you're doing is sending people out to do your dirty work."

"Don't you think if I could go out there and do it I would?" I opened my packet of cigarettes, screwing it up when I discovered it was empty. I kept it nestled in my fist, a little cardboard stress ball.

"No," she replied, brutally honest. "I think you like hiding behind the scenes. Maybe that's why there's no sign of the end."

"We're getting there."

"Are we? Because I can just see this spiralling out of control."

"The time is coming," I said through gritted teeth.

"Bullshit."

That one word was enough. Enough to make the red, pulsing anger in my brain come to the fore. It reared its ugly head, and I was not man enough to stop it. I grabbed her by her shoulders. "So you want to talk about things being terrible, about how I've done something so dreadful... you kill people Romany." Her skin turned puce, and the sight of her face screwed up in pain was like a punch to the chest. But it wasn't enough to stop me. "You take away people's lives, you watch them die. You do it in your office, and you do it outside of there too. So don't you dare stand there and tell me that what I'm doing is wrong. I'm doing what I have to for us to win. Yes, pinning the blame on Kinley is not something I'm proud of, but it was that or I let them find you."

She tried to shrug me off but I was holding her still. "I told you I wouldn't fight with you anymore, and I stand by that. You're a part of this Romany, whether you want to be or not. We have to win, and that means getting our hands covered with blood and shit." She shoved me hard with both hands and I grabbed her by the wrists, ignoring her hiss of pain. "And I mean it, and this is the last time I will say it, I am the leader, and you will follow my instructions. I will not be spoken down to like we're children again." She cowered a little, trying her hardest to maintain her cool facade. She could have broken down in tears, and it would have done nothing to break my fury. "You're going to do *everything* I tell you to, because it is what is needed for us to win. I am done with you." I pushed her to the floor and as she went down with a thud, she stared up at me in disbelief.

"Look at yourself!" she scoffed. "We both know I was always better than you, at everything. Your dad always said so. And now I'm becoming the better person it would seem."

I snapped. My fist went back to strike her, and it was only the shout of someone from the staircase that made me stop.

"Don't you dare!" Lexi stepped out of the shadows, a gun from our stash trained on me. "I'll shoot before I let you hit her."

I lowered my hand, and she put the gun down. Romany was still on the floor, her hand raised in defence. My stomach did somersaults.

"Christ Romany, I'm so sorry." I leant forward to help her up, but she crawled backwards towards Lexi, who crouched next to her, wrapping her arms around her friend protectively. "I've just been so tired lately..."

"Save it," Lexi interrupted. "Why don't you go upstairs, I want to have a chat with Romany."

I stood there for a moment, useless and ashamed. She flicked her thumb towards the door again, and I stumbled over, in a daze, heading up the stairs.

I walked up to my bedroom, and caught sight of my reflection. Red-faced, hair untidy, bloodshot eyes; I looked a state. I sank onto my bed, the battered old mattress sagging under me. I stared at the back of my hands mindlessly. I didn't recognise myself. Romany had always mattered to me more than anything, and I'd hurt her. And I wasn't sure I could finish this without hurting her more.

*

Lexi wrapped her warm arms around me, squeezing me. I nestled against her and let the tears flow. After a few minutes of uncontrollable sobbing, I found it within myself to try and maintain some dignity. Unsteadily, I got to my feet and went to take a seat. Lexi threw me her packet of cigarettes and, taking a seat beside me, lit it for me with her gold lighter.

"You know, he may be the biggest asshole going at the moment, but he really does care about you." She forced the words out begrudgingly.

"Oh yeah, it looked like he really cares. I begged him not to send out those leaflets and then he stages that pathetic stunt..."

"That was my idea," she interrupted, with only a hint of sheepishness.

"Yours?" I asked incredulously.

"Yes, I thought it would be enough to help get some of the heat from your place. You couldn't possibly have done it, you were *in* the building, and we didn't tell you because that way your shock would be entirely real." My mouth must have been hanging open as she finished. "It was Beckett who wanted to tell you, I was the one who stopped him."

I replayed her words in my mind, twice over to be sure I had heard correctly. She rubbed my shoulder and although I wanted to be angry, to smack her hand away and storm out, all my energy had been drained.

"Oh Lexi," I rubbed the back of my neck. "Why didn't he tell me all this a minute ago?"

She shrugged, and rolled her eyes. "I was listening to you, you didn't exactly give Beckett a chance to explain things. You were shooting your mouth off, and the poor guy looked like a bunny in headlights," she sniggered, not unpleasantly, and gave me another squeeze to the shoulder. "Look, I don't like Beckett, and it's not because of the choices he's making now; it's because he has always been a brat, since day one, and that's not going to change. And I don't like seeing the person closest to me getting hurt." She took a long draw on her cigarette, closing her eyes for a moment. "But, he has always tried to protect you, I'll give him that. A real knight in shining armour." This time when she laughed, it was with warmth. She was being only a little sarcastic. She suddenly looked at me seriously, crushing her burnt out cigarette under her boot. "You really have no idea what he's done for you."

"Other than abuse me and belittle me, leave me out of everything when I am supposed to be his 'second' or pet, or whatever I'm meant to be."

"No, I mean before all of this crap between the pair of you." She withdrew yet another cigarette, but I shook my head as she offered me one. "You know that Matthew and Beckett fell out," she began to explain.

"They never really got on."

"You're right there, but things got a whole lot worse after Rose died didn't they?"

I nodded.

"Well, Matthew started to lose the plot big time after that, and he kept saying he had the answer to everyone's prayers; that he was the one to save us all. And he said that there needed to be sacrifices to do it." Her hands twisted, her nails digging into her palms. "Well, he started spouting about how our people should use the fire of their faith." She looked at me pointedly, as though I should know what she meant. I shrugged at her uselessly. Lexi gave a little exasperated sigh. "He wanted to use suicide bombers."

I caught my breath, and found it a little hard to find it again. There had been a time, Matthew told us, when suicide bombings occurred so often, all over the world, that nobody batted an eyelid when they heard about it.

"And first person he wanted to send out, as one of his human explosives, was you..." Her voice drifted out, and my brain swam. She didn't say a word, she let what she had told me sink in. I felt an icy cold chill creep up my spine, tightening around my neck. Matthew, the man who had raised me like a father, had wanted me to blow myself up; in the name of the Revolution.

*

We walked down to the basement and I gripped the banister as my eyes adjusted to the light. There was a man tied to a chair in the middle of the room. His head was covered with a pillowcase. He was a big man, with a round belly which caused his shirt to strain at the buttons. Matthew turned to us, and I was horrified by the wild glaze over his eyes. He was unshaven, his lips crusty and split.

"Shut the door," he barked at Beckett, who scurried up the stairs to do as he ordered.

We stood there in our pyjamas, glancing nervously at one another. Matthew whipped off the pillow case and the man stared around, his eyes squinted.

"Who the hell are you?"

Matthew grabbed his face, yanking it around hard to face him.

"Don't you recognise me?" The man shook his head. "You don't know what you did to me?" Matthew spat. "You took my baby away from me!" he bellowed, punching the man hard in the jaw. "What's your name?" he asked, his voice calm for a moment.

"M-m-martin," the man stammered, blood spraying out of his mouth. "Look, I really don't know what you're talking about..." I stole a glance at Beckett, who was staring at Martin, his eyes narrowed. I had never seen him look so full of anger. Matthew hit Martin again hard, before pulling a photograph from his pocket; waving it in his face.

"Her name was Eloise. She was just a child. And you murdered her, all because she dared to stand up to you." Another punch, this time to the stomach.

Martin shook his head. "I'm not the same person I was... after the things I did; I changed."

Matthew picked up a gun from the nearby table. "People like you never change."

Martin's eyes widened as he saw the gun and he began to sob. "Please, I have a family..."

"You don't deserve them," Matthew sneered. He turned to Beckett and handed him the weapon. "We've waited a long time for this son." His smile should have been tender, fatherly, but there was something far darker piercing through it. "Do it my boy - for Eloise."

With shaking hands, Beckett raised the gun. Martin was shaking, snot and tears running down his chin.

"Please," He shook his head, "I'm a changed man..."

"Oh yes," Matthew cackled. "I heard all about how you want to repent, to join the Revolution and write your wrongs. Well you can't."

Martin's eyes were screwed up tight as he cried. "I swear, I never meant to hurt her, I only wanted to scare her, to make her run home. But she moved and... oh god..."

Beckett hesitated for a moment and Matthew turned on him.

"Do it boy. For once in your sad little life do what is necessary."

I went to speak but Matthew shoved his finger into my face. "You keep your mouth shut or you'll find your ass on the street." He knelt beside his son, helping him to keep the gun steady. "Take a deep breath Beckett. Remember what this man did to your sister."

"But maybe it was an accident..." he mumbled.

"No," Matthew answered, "he just wants you to believe that to save his skin."

Martin opened his eyes and I pitied him. What if he was telling the truth? "My kids are going to be wondering where I am..." he whispered to himself.

Beckett's hands were trembling as Matthew muttered more encouragements to him, more minutes past and Matthew began to lose patience.

"Get on with it!!" he bellowed.

I leapt backwards as the gun went off, the bullet passing through Martin's forehead in a spray of crimson. Beckett dropped the gun and stared at the ground as Matthew hugged him. "That's my boy," he enthused. "That's my boy."

*

"I'd have said no," I whispered, although I wasn't so sure that would've been enough to stop Matthew.

"Matthew didn't get the chance to tell you. He went bragging to his little successor, and Beckett suddenly grew a backbone. He told him that if Matthew so much as mentioned the idea to you, or to anyone, that he would strangle him himself." I was stunned, and more than a little confused. "Matthew died not long after, and Beckett never forgave him."

I leapt to my feet, and couldn't decide if I wanted to walk up to speak to Beckett, or leave the house and get the hell away from all this insanity. Lexi pulled me back down beside her, with a sharp tug to my top.

"Look, you're not to go storming off up there and telling him all about this. When Beckett told me, he made me swear never to tell you."

"So why did you?" I snapped.

"Because even though he is a complete idiot, the one thing you can't accuse him of is not caring about you. He gave up the only shred of a father-son relationship they had left-for you." She crushed yet another cigarette on the concrete. "And I think you need to back off a bit. You mocked him relentlessly for not being the big-shot leader and for not making choices; now he is you're constantly at him for that. And you know what? It pains me to say it, but he's not doing a bad job. Yes, he is completely obsessed at the moment, but maybe we all should be - if we want to win."

I had to admit that she was completely right. Which made me feel a million times worse than I had when I'd first woken up this morning. "Lexi..." I said in a daze. "If Beckett's right and we're getting close to finishing this, what are you planning to do, you know, after it's done?"

"Well," she leant back, and looked deep in thought, "I'm not going to be helping form some new government with Beckett, I can tell you that." My smile must've vanished as she gave me an apologetic smile. "Or you know, he might not do that..." It was a lame attempt to back track. "...But you asked me what I'm going to do." She paused again, smiling to herself. "I'm going to go home. To where I lived with my parents. I'm going to get myself a house by the sea and I'm going to walk on the beach, every day; summer, winter, sunshine or rain. I'm going to be on that damn beach."

I nodded. "That sounds like a pretty good plan. At least you have one."

"You don't?" she asked.

"Nope," I laughed.

"Come with me," she blurted out. She shook her head, clearly embarrassed. "What I mean is, if stuff doesn't work out, quite the way you want," she chose her words carefully, "you could always come with me."

"Maybe," I nodded. "Maybe I'll just do that." She grinned at me and I wrapped my arm around my impenetrable fortress of a friend.

As I left Beckett's I thought about walking up to his room, where I knew he'd be sat brooding. But I knew that I would only go making things worse if I went in there and blurted out everything Lexi had told me in confidence. I pulled on my jacket and walked out into the fresh air, finally able to take a deep breath. I walked like a zombie, one foot after the other, my head thumping with the worst headache I'd ever had. I could barely think on the walk home, and as soon as I got back, I crawled into my bed, the cover pulled tight around me.

13

Matthew has been given permission to take Rose to a doctor. She is sick, all the time, she can't keep food down. We are completely alone in the house, without Matthew or any other Revolution members. Things have been awkward between us. I think Beckett knows how I feel about him, how much I like him, and not in a brother-sister way. We are lying on his bed as usual, smoking cigarettes, but something is different between us. We are carefully not touching, and I can feel goosebumps all over my skin. He stubs out his cigarette very carefully and deliberately and it seems appropriate for me to do likewise. Something big is going to happen; I can feel it in the pit of my stomach. He has the little furrow in between his eyebrows, the one he only gets when he is putting his mind to something, like when his father is showing us how to attach a silencer. He sits up and leans over me, his face very close to mine. He is fucking beautiful. He gently touches my hair and I can hardly breathe, I don't want to in case he stops. Everything has stood still; it feels as though we are the only ones in the world. And then, so lightly I could almost have imagined it, he kisses me. We stare at one another, silent, neither of us sure what to do next.

*

Etienne slid a little black velvet box across my desk, without a word. I stared up at him and raised an eyebrow. "What's this?"

"A birthday present." I glanced around the office and went to protest, but he held up a hand. "You're on file; I know when all my employee's birthdays are. I haven't been researching you."

I went to pick up the little package, pulling my hand away at the last minute. "I don't celebrate my birthday." It was pretty much true. Beckett and Lexi were the only two people who remembered, and we didn't do presents anymore. Hadn't since we were teenagers.

He pushed the box towards me again with his index finger. "Tough. You need a little something to cheer up your day, we all do today. Besides, it'd be rude not to accept it."

I could feel the eyes in the office on me, and Christina was smiling at me behind her hand. I unwillingly picked it up and flicked it open, gasping a little. Simple but stunning diamond studs winked up at me, nestled in black satin. "Oh my god Etienne... I can't accept these." I looked up, but he had already darted back into his office. I shut the box, tucking it into my handbag. As I looked up, Harry leant on the edge of my desk, a sardonic sneer spread across his face.

"I wonder what on Earth you had to do to get that," he said with a sniff. I was in no mood to play his games, and turned to my computer. "You know," he murmured, leaning in closer to me, "I have something I could give you for your birthday..."

I grabbed his face in my hand, and stared him in the eye."I am going to tell you for the last time, you're a disgusting insect of a man, and I wouldn't touch you if my life depended on it." I shoved him away hard and leant back in my chair, smiling with satisfaction.

"But you'll do it with Etienne?" he stammered. "If you're going to go for it, why not share yourself around the whole office."

"That is quite enough, Harry." McLean's hand came down on Harry's shoulder, his voice gentle and dangerous. "Unless you have forgotten, I want to speak to all of you today. Let's not make my opinion of you lessen before you enter my office." Harry scuttled away like a disciplined child, head hanging. "Romany." McLean addressed me. "You're first."

Christina was watching me with concern in her gaze as I followed him. I glanced over my shoulder, and could see Etienne staring after us, as though he would chase after me. Dead man walking. That's what I could see in everyone's eyes as I walked by. Of course, each of them had either had this talking to, or were due it. We were all in the same boat.

I took a seat opposite him and watched with wary eyes as he poured each of us a glass of water. Sliding the glass towards me, he raised his own to his lips, sipping it carefully. The noise of his swallow seemed deafening in the heavy silence. "I hear it's your birthday." He placed the drink back down.

I nodded in reply.

"Well, I hope you have a wonderful day. Once this is over, of course." A swift reminder that it didn't matter what day it was, our work was never done. "I want you to know you are in no way under suspicion." Which plainly meant I was. "But I need to know what everybody saw, to ascertain what happened."

"A car got blown up, Mr. McLean; I really can't tell you much more than that."

"But it happened on the same day as the murder of Mr. McIntyre, and these leaflets being posted through everyone's front doors." He tossed a flyer onto the desk and I carefully kept my face neutral.

"I understand that, but I honestly don't understand what that has to do with anyone who works here."

"We arrested Rupert Kinley for selling those photos to the Revolution," he remarked.

"So surely he's the one who can help you most," I replied.

"Mr. Kinley is maintaining his innocence. And he claims to know nothing about the car bombing." He watched me intently, scanning for anything that could betray my true feelings.

"Well, clearly he's lying," I said, trying to sound convincing.

A smile spread across McLean's face, and he made a small note in his tiny notepad. "Clearly," he replied, in a quiet whisper. He snapped the notepad shut, tucking it into his breast pocket. "Before you go, is there anything you can remember from yesterday? Anybody acting suspiciously, before or after the car blew up?"

"No, sir. Everyone was just scared as hell."

"You weren't." he noted. "You got very close to the fire. In fact, Etienne had to pull you away from it."

"I wanted to check nobody was still inside," I stammered, thrown for a moment.

He leant forward a little closer to me, scanning my face. "How very gallant of you. You're clearly not the little wallflower everyone thinks you are. Office affair, rescuing people from fires..." I bit down hard on my tongue, refraining from flying at him in rage. "...I was right to keep my eye on you."

He dismissed me, and I wandered away from his office in a daze. He was suspicious of me, that much was obvious. But, I didn't know when he would choose to act on his suspicions, or what he would do to prove them. I felt the cold sweat of fear spreading over me, and when I got back to my desk, Christina walked past, on her way to McLean's office. She gave me a little reassuring smile, before fixing on her brightest smile, swaying her hips so every man in the office would look.

She wasn't gone long, and she didn't look as washed out from the experience as I suspected I did. Etienne was next, followed by Harry. Each person in our department went down, some came up looked unfazed like Harry, others ruffled and strained like Etienne. But each of us faced McLean. All in all, my birthday was the longest day I'd had in a long while.

I threw down my keys, chucking my jacket to the floor. I wanted to eat, get in to a hot shower, and get the day finished with. Etienne's present tumbled to the floor from my bag and I picked it up uncertainly. I gasped a little again at its contents and, despite my concerns, placed the studs into my ears. I looked at myself in the mirror, admiring how the diamonds caught the light. A thud came from my kitchen, from the back door. I froze, listening out. Another light thump - the back door being closed. I braced myself, and crept along the hallway to my closed kitchen door. I could hear the culprit, sneaking around. Something being placed gently on the side, the sound of scratching and scraping. Taking in a

200

deep breath, I threw open the door, ready to confront the intruder.

Lexi stared at me, having leapt into the air. "You scared the shit out of me! I thought you weren't going to be back until five."

I shrugged. "Finished early. And I scared you?" I asked incredulously, noticing the CD player on the side for the first time. "What are you doing breaking in? You could've just knocked on the door you know."

She looked a little embarrassed, her eyes all wide and puppy-like. "I wanted to surprise you - on your birthday."

I relaxed a little, feeling a little ashamed at my snappy attitude. "I'm sorry Lexi, had a really bad day."

She handed me a little bundle, wrapped with newspaper and string. I tore it open, and pulled out the scarlet silk scarf tucked inside. "It's not much, I know. But once we're past all of this, I promise I'll buy you the biggest present ever."

I dashed forward, wrapping my arms around her. "No, I love it!" I tied it around my neck, posing with my hands on my hip. "I think it makes me look very glamorous," I said with a chuckle.

"There's something else," Lexi smiled. She pushed my small table across the kitchen floor with a horrendous scraping, turning to the CD player. "A dance for the birthday girl." She held out her arm, pressing play on the stereo. "Nothing illegal, I promise."

I took her hand, grinning inanely as the familiar music began.

*

I walked behind the houses, clutching the package tightly to me. Getting past the cameras in the fading daylight hadn't been too much of a challenge, and besides, it was worth it. I was going to tell her everything. It was an appropriate day to do it; after all it was her birthday. I walked up to the back door and froze as the very faint music drifted out to my ears. It wasn't anything from the list, I knew that much, but it seemed odd to be coming from her house. I stepped to the window and stared through, my nose practically pressed against the glass. Lexi pulled Romany to her, taking hold of her hand and placing it on her own waist. I glanced around me, checking nobody was having a nose. Lexi held Romany tightly, smiling as they swayed to the melody. *Unforgettable...that's what you are, unforgettable...though near or far.* Lexi was singing the words out loud and Romany was chuckling. Romany daintily twirled, with a little sway of her hips. *Like a song of love that clings to me...how the thought of you does things to me. Never before... has someone been more...* Romany threw her head back and laughed as Lexi spun her around with a flourish, flinging her out and spinning her back into her arm. They were a beautiful pair, and the way the setting sun illuminated them was breathtaking. *Unforgettable...in every way, and forever more...that's how you'll stay.* I wished to hell it was me, holding her close to me and moving her to the music. I would scoop her up and plant kisses all over her face. Lexi threw her up into the air, her face showing only a little strain, her eyes glittering with tears. *That's why, darling, it's incredible...that someone so*

unforgettable... thinks that I am...unforgettable, too.
Lexi whispered a 'happy birthday' into Romany's ear, and the smile Romany flashed back to her made my heart pound a little harder. I stood there a moment longer, lost in her happiness.

She never knew how much I loved to see her smile, how much I'd have loved the freedom Lexi had to just love her, without a million other responsibilities stopping her from doing so. Romany *was* Lexi's main responsibility, she came before anything else. A lump caught in my throat and I walked back to the door, ready to knock. But I couldn't force myself to do it. She was so happy, so lost in her little world with Lexi, I didn't want to be the one to break the magic for her. I placed the package carefully on her doorstep, and turned away, heading back out of her garden at a brisk pace. Maybe another time, I told myself, but not now. Now wasn't the time after all.

*

Lexi stepped back with a bow, the music fading out into silence. She turned off the stereo and there we stood, smiling at one another.

"Thank you." I sighed. "That was a really wonderful way to end what had been a terrible birthday."

She lit me up a cigarette and handed it to me. "See," she smiled, "I told you it wouldn't be illegal. Although there were a few songs on the list I could've got you to dance to." She winked. Lexi checked her watch and swore gently under her breath. "I better be heading back before curfew." She stood to her feet and gave me a fierce hug. "Take care of yourself babe. And happy birthday again." She stepped to the back door. "I guess I'll see you at the next meeting. Rumour is, Beckett's got something big up his sleeve."

I didn't reply, I really didn't want to be discussing the Revolution now. She bent down and picked something up off my doorstep. "Hey Romany, this was on your doorstep." Lexi handed me a little box, wrapped in purple. "I wonder who it's from?" she cooed. I put the parcel down and ushered her out the door. "Aw, you're no fun! Tell me what it is okay? I want to know!" I closed the door on her and pulled down the blind.

I inspected the little packet for a moment. Eventually, I snatched it up and tore off the wrapping, staring at the gift inside in shock. The tiny coin sat inside, barely fitted in the palm of my hand. It was old, older than anything I had ever held before. I was almost too afraid to touch it. As I lifted it, it hung from the delicate chain, twirling in the air. On the back, engraved in tiny, barely visible writing were the words 'For in our past, we find our future.' There was nothing offensive about it, nothing which could be construed as illegal, it was just a beautiful and heartfelt gift. I fastened it around my wrist, and vowed never to take it off. It was a reminder, of something long before me, of the world how it had once been. I stared at the memento, and I knew who it was from.

*

I stepped into the basement, and was shocked to see more people packed into it than ever. Beckett was mingling, exuding confidence. He spotted me, and excused himself, rushing towards me. Before we could stand awkwardly, with nothing to say, I pulled him into an embrace. "Thank you so much for the gift, it's beautiful."

"You knew it was from me?" He smiled broadly as I nodded, before noticing the diamonds in my ears. "It's not as beautiful as those. From Etienne?" he asked grimly.

"Yes, I didn't want to keep them, I do have to keep up appearances," I shrugged. It was the right thing to say, a reminder that I was on board. He looked well today, his hair neat and tidy; those dark curls actually trimmed for a change - I imagined Lexi had finally forced him to let her cut them. His eyes bore into me, those dark pools of bronze hard to look away from. "Honestly, yours is so much better."

He blushed, and my heart began the familiar patter that it always did around him. It was funny, how easily I could forget the things he'd said, the things I'd done, when everything was wonderful between us. We broke apart, as we realised most of the eyes in the room were on us.

"This looks important Beckett; there's a lot of people here," I leant forward, whispering into his ear. I had the satisfaction of seeing his shoulders stiffen. So perhaps I hadn't entirely lost my charm.

"Well," he coughed to clear his throat, "it is very important." He rested his hand on the small of my back and led me to the front. He stood a little in front of me as he clapped his hands to address the group. Philip was stood at the foot of the stairs, clutching his gun for dear life. We'd never had an armed guard in place, something big was brewing.

"Okay everyone," Beckett began, standing with a straight back, his chest puffed out. Even I had to admit, he looked like a figure of authority. I glanced over at Lexi, who was waiting with a bored expression, for the next plan of action. Elise was leaning against her, those blonde curls pulled into a dishevelled bun. I scanned the unfamiliar faces and spotted Erin and Peter. My stomach tightened into a little knot as I remembered the last time I had seen Erin. Her hair was in a very tight ponytail, and her mulberry lips were pursed. Eve was stood beside them, staring over at Philip every five seconds. Christina was stood nervously at the back, her eyes darting around the room. "I can't say that I've had much time to prepare for this, but here it goes." He glanced back at me. "Someone very dear to me has made me realise that we have played games for long enough," I froze as he continued. "And that now is the opportune moment to strike. Our numbers are higher than ever before, and Bowman is weak. He no longer has his head of security, and he is struggling to find his replacement." He played with his watch, hands behind his back. "It's time for us to finish." He was rewarded by a shout of approval from his captive audience.

"How?" Lexi heckled.

"Now, I had thought that Romany here might have some ideas." He turned to me, arms folded, smug little smile. I felt the irresistible urge to punch him. But I could see Lexi, her smile spurring me on.

"Well, there's due to be a government meeting at the Houses of Parliament. The first in a long while."

"Bowman hardly ever goes to those," the voice of a short, heavy-set woman, with black cropped hair that didn't suit her round face piped up. She had cold blue eyes that were fixed on me.

"He is this time. His people are urging him to make an appearance. It will help prevent the government from losing face. And besides, he wants to pass a new law." Etienne had told me about the new law with a stony face just yesterday. "He wants every male over the age of 16 to join his police force. And he wants to introduce a compulsory military club for all those under that age, as an 'after school club'." There was a gasp of horror, and a harsh swear word from Lexi.

"We can't let that happen!" Eve called out.

"Exactly," Beckett nodded gravely. "He would be vulnerable there."

"He won't be appearing with a large security retinue, only a few. He wants to appear as 'one of the people'," I interjected. The murmur of excitement made me feel confident. But, there was a stumbling block. "The meeting is only two weeks away." It seemed an impossible timeline and I expected for there to be a sigh of disappointment but I was met by blinking, confused faces.

"And how is that a problem?" Philip piped up from the stairs. "We're the Revolution, we specialise in the impossible!" he roared, followed by a round of applause, a cry of approval and an adoring kiss blown by Eve.

"So it's agreed, two weeks time, we hit Parliament!" Beckett said, with a clenched fist raised in the air.

"We'll need more people!" another voice called out - coming from a tall black man, with the longest dreadlocks I had ever seen. He blew smoke from his lips, I watched as it curled up into the air.

"Then we'll get more. We underestimate our nation; when we make the move, they will follow. We have been shopped to the police have we? They *want* us to win - we just need to give them the courage to join us." Beckett ushered me forward to stand beside him. I felt a little sting of pride; he wanted me with him - his equal.

"Then what?" Peter asked, ignoring Erin's elbow digging into his ribs. "After we win, what do we do then?"

Silence crept over us. Beckett looked at the floor, staring hard at it as though it could provide the answer.

"Well, I suppose that some of us will have to stay behind to help clean up this mess."

A feeling of bitter disappointment swept over me, and I tried not to show it as he looked at me for approval. "And I know that both Romany and I will be seeing this out until the end." I smiled hard, until my face ached. I had been a fool, thinking we'd ride off into the sunset on a white steed once Bowman was dead. Why did I think that the prime minister being six foot under would suddenly mean it would be over? I had heard this a million times and only now did it ring true. I had behaved like a child. I realised that whilst I'd been stood thinking Beckett and the others were staring at me, waiting for my response. "We'll see it to the end," I nodded and Beckett beamed at me, looking more than a little relieved. I wasn't wholly sure I meant it, but I knew that to get us through the next two weeks and beyond, I had to.

14

Etienne smiled at me.

"There's something different about you today," he observed quietly, as those around us headed down to the canteen for lunch, "and I don't just mean the diamonds."

I tried my hardest to smile, but it felt hollow. In the space of a day, whatever it was I'd been feeling for Etienne seemed to have evaporated into nothing more than friendship and pity. But, I had just two weeks to keep up the pretense, I reminded myself. Two weeks was nothing. "I'm just feeling far more positive. And we have work to get on with, so you should stop distracting me." I swatted at him with a folder and he leapt back.

I turned to my computer, and felt that familiar ache as I sorted through person after person, checking them against the database. Two weeks, I thought again, and none of these people will need to worry again. Etienne was still hovering, and he stuffed his hands into the pockets of his suit. "Do you want to join me for lunch?"

I examined the greying sandwich, the curled up ham squashed between two rather thin slices of bread. Etienne bit into his, chewing mechanically. His nose wrinkled up and he tossed the sandwich back onto his tray. "God," he exclaimed, "you'd think with the amount of work we do here, we'd at least get a decent lunch."

"You don't often eat with the common people, do you Etienne?" I said jokingly.

He rolled his eyes and sipped his cup of coffee. "Have you heard about the P.M's visit to Parliament?" He asked, his voice lowered. "A real two fingers up to the Revolution eh?" He took another bite of the sandwich, and as crumbs lingered on his lip, I felt a little disgusted by him. Maybe he was just the government lackey I'd always considered him to be - I'd just been taken in by diamonds and pretty words. But then he smiled at me nervously, and I wondered how much of it was the part he felt he needed to play - if he was in the same position as me; trying to make it through each day.

Harry was sat on the corner table, the ringleader of his group. He lit a cigarette and began to regale them with a story, relishing the gawp of his spellbound audience. He threw back his head in laughter, and the rest of his little gang followed suit; all nudging elbows and winks. Etienne glanced over his shoulder and shook his head.

"I don't know how that little prick managed to get a job here."

"He said he was transferred from Birmingham," I replied.

"Hmm? Well all I know is that Daddy has money - enough for him to start working here, no questions asked." He sipped his coffee again. "Doug can't stand him, and if Doug hasn't got enough clout to have him moved; that tells me something."

I lit up a cigarette, and watched Harry for a moment. He spotted me staring, and sneered at me, whispering to his friends who all stared my way, chuckling. Etienne covered my hand with his. "Ignore them. That lot have barely got the brains to change a light bulb between them. Unlike you, they're only here because they're ruthless; not because they're smart."

I nodded, feeling more than a little guilty. I wasn't here because of my intellectual ability - I was here because Beckett had worked every possible contact to get me here, it was just sheer luck I had been deemed dedicated enough to join this exclusive club. I watched Etienne poking his sorry excuse for lunch with his finger. What side would he take in two weeks time? Life wouldn't be easy for people like him once it was all over, people who had chosen to protect themselves be working for the government. We needed to be forgiving, I thought to myself as I shoved the half-chewed sandwich into the bin. Tolerance and forgiveness, they were the key to restoring this country.

*

"There will be extra security employed that day, and that can be used to our advantage." Beckett scowled at the map, hammering his finger on it.

"So all we need are police vans and a load of uniforms – easy," I remarked, trying not to smile as he stared up at me, unimpressed.

"I can deal with that, it won't be a problem."

We'd been holed up in the basement for the whole of my day off, going over and over our plan to attack parliament.

"What about weapons, ammunition?" I asked.

"My source in your building is helping there," he replied, engrossed in the map.

So that meant whoever they were, they were high up; enough to get their hands on police vans and weaponry. But, I was still not privy to that information, I thought to myself bitterly. It was just something I had to accept I supposed. "Once we're in, and past security, chances are they'll try to evacuate the cabinet," I pointed out.

"That's why we need to act fast, get in, hit hard - track him down." As we both leant forward over the map, our foreheads touched and we stayed there for a second, leaning against one another; carefully not looking up. His hair tickled my face, and I could feel his steady breathing against my cheek. We broke apart and I pulled my eyes up.

*

Her sharp little teeth bit down on her rose stained bottom lip, nibbling on the skin there nervously. She had always done this when she was uneasy or anxious, ever since that first day when she had walked into my house. It seemed like forever passed as we sat, lost in each other, trying to figure out where it had all gone wrong for us. It was as though, for the first time in a long, long time, we understood one another. Everything was happening so fast, a runaway train gathering pace, and not one of us knew where it would end. Romany and I been finalising every little detail of our plan. It was a good plan, we both knew it, but we also knew that we couldn't prevent anything going wrong. We needed everything to prepare for every eventuality. I could feel a thumping in my head, the bright artificial light of the basement making it worse. There was something in her eyes as she watched me, a glittering of hope - she believed in me; that I could really do this. I wasn't so sure. She leant back with her feet up on the table, rubbing her eyes.

"You need to get home Romany," I said gently. "There's nothing more we can do tonight - and you need to be back by curfew."

She stretched, her top riding up; revealing her flat white stomach, her ribcage jutting out just a little. She tugged it back down as she stood to her feet, still yawning as she threw on her coat, pulling it tight, but not before I caught a glimpse of its scarlet satin lining. She pulled on her black leather sling back heels."I have to wear all this fancy stuff to work, and when I'm not there; I like to give my poor feet a chance to recover," she blushed.

"You don't have to explain." Although it was always a little disconcerting how noticeable the difference was between undercover Romany and Revolution Romany. Whenever I saw her heading to or from the office, she looked glamorous, and unattainable. But right now, with her slightly tussled hair and plain make up, shoes kicked off, she was my Romany again. I could see the teenager who had lain on my bed with me and smoked cigarettes, who had helped me up off the floor when I was too exhausted to train anymore. I preferred this girl, who was completely unaware of her own beauty. I realised I'd been gawping, and that Romany was stood awkwardly, frowning at me.

"Well, I had better get going," she smiled, that little anxious lopsided smile she'd done since she was a kid. It was another ghost of the person she'd been - before she'd become a heartless killer. Something had changed in Romany; that much was clear. I jumped to my feet and wrapped my arms around her, breathing in that familiar smell.

"Go careful, I'm going to need you." I could feel her body tense as she leant into me. "No way we're going to be able to win without you."

She leaned back, her eyes narrowed suspiciously. "You know, I can't make up my mind about you. Every time you're an arrogant asshole, you go and say something sweet," she grinned. It was as though we were just two normal people, chilling out on a Sunday afternoon together. As she turned away from me, with that self-confident swagger, she smiled over her shoulder at me. "Revise that plan Beckett; I know what your memory is like." She climbed up the basement stairs, and left me sat alone, staring at a map and trying to ignore the voice in my head that was screaming at me that I just blew an opportunity, again.

*

It was another cold afternoon, wet and miserable. The sunlight was faint behind the clouds, trying desperately to pierce through. I could feel the cameras on me, whirring and grinding. I passed an elderly couple holding hands. They glanced nervously at the cameras and scurried into their home. But as they shut the door, I could see the man planting a tender kiss on the top of his wife's head reassuringly. It brought a smile to my face. The Government posters on the wall had become torn and faded. 'Vote Bowman for a better Britain' one read, having been partially covered by another which read 'Bowman Is Britain." I resisted the urge to tear it from the brick, and set light to it in the street. When we were free again, I was going to be the first to rip a camera from the wall with my bare hands. I passed the guard without a word, and was relieved to see his obvious disappointment in my out-of-work outfit. Clearly, I was less attractive to him, which was marvellous. He handed me back my papers with a grunt and went back to the warmth of his van. He sat back in the driver's seat, stuffing a sandwich into his mouth, licking his greasy lips. Twelve days. Twelve days and everything we knew would change.

*

It was hard as hell to try and mask my excitement and fear. On the other hand, Christina deserved an award for the performance she was giving. She was quite the actress. Etienne seemed to be watching me more, and there was a palpable tension in the air. It fizzled like electric, and everyone seemed to be acting differently. The only person who seemed to be enjoying the atmosphere, who was always hovering and observing, was Harry. He had started to hang around one of the other girls in the office, one whose Daddy was high up in the government, Melissa, or Melody or something. I had made it my mission to avoid her, but even so, I felt a little sorry for her as she tried to look interested by another of Harry's self-promoting stories. He kept leaning in close to her, whispering in her ear and stroking her hair. I was amused to see him constantly glancing my way, probably hoping to see if I was getting jealous.

The sunlight was streaming through the glass, and I whirled around in my chair, staring out of the huge windows. The city should have been coming to life, bustling and busy. Instead it was dead, a ghost town. The odd person scurried down the streets, watching constantly over their shoulders. But as, just as my mood soured, a single bird fluttered by, and I began to pity the poor little thing, all alone. A second later, a whole flock flew by, enveloping the lone bird into the safety of its group. The clouds were clearing, the dull grey sky becoming impregnated with blue.

*

I walked into my house, tossing my coat on to the stairs. I went to lie down on my sofa but a knock on the door made me pause. I checked the dusty clock - still a few hours until curfew. I cautiously opened it and Etienne shifted nervously, thrusting a posy of flowers at me. His hand was shaking a little.

"May I come in?" His voice was high and squeaky, and I could see the flush of embarrassment spreading across his cheeks. I opened the door and watched as he strode into my living room, holding the rather sad looking flowers close to me as I followed. He sat on my sofa, leaping to his feet again, staring around awkwardly before flicking open a device and placing it on the table. That was never a good sign.

"You can sit," I offered.

"I'd sooner stand." His brow was glistening and my belly tightened. I sat myself in my tatty armchair, trying to mask my discomfort at having him in my home.

"Etienne," he turned back from my window, having pulled the curtains shut, "what on earth is wrong?" He paced back and forth, before throwing himself back down on the sofa.

"You know, I never wanted this job. It was my father who got it for me, after insisting that I follow in his footsteps. I wanted to be a doctor." His tone was sad, pricked by threatening tears. It made me uncomfortable.

"My mother and father didn't like me very much." I went to protest but he shook his head. "I know that because they told me - that I was a nobody, that I would never become anything." He wrung his hands, knotting them together. "The only day I ever saw anything than loathing in my father's eyes was when I told him I was going to be the senior head of our level."

He stood up, and came closer to me. His shoes squeaked as he moved. "I'm not proud of what I've done, or of the person I've become, but I'll be damned if I'm going to spend one more day being something I'm not."

He got down on one knee in front of me, and my heart was hammering, so fast I thought it might explode from my chest, a violent spray of blood and vessels.

"My father died a long time ago, and I have spent almost every day since then listening to his vile voice, wheedling into my brain, telling me that I'm a weak little boy, who'll never do anything because I'm scared of my own shadow. Well, I am a man and I do take risks."

He reached into his pocket and pulled out a ring box, flicking it open to reveal a beautiful diamond solitaire ring. "I love you. And I know, we hardly know one another out of work, and that this is crazy - but it's true." His eyes were watering with emotion. "The world won't always be like this Romany, and I promise you that one day I will take you somewhere amazing, anywhere you

217

want." He pushed the ring onto my limp hand. "I'll protect you."

I pulled my hand from his grip and stared at the ring, thinking of everything it could mean for me. The Revolution could fail, and if we did Etienne could protect me. He was a powerful man, with a seemingly greater wealth than even I could have anticipated. He was a kind man, even if he did work for the government - he was just doing the best he could to keep his head above the water while the rest of us drowned. Despite who he was, I did like him - he was attractive and he treated me like a real lady. But then, I remembered, he was falling for a lie. Gently, I removed the ring and handed it to him, and took a deep breath.

"I'm so sorry Etienne, but I can't marry you."

He looked at the floor, nodding sadly. "No, you're right... that was a mad idea; but we have something Romany, and I don't think we should..."

"No," I interrupted. "I can't be with you, at all." I took hold of his hand, pressing the ring into his palm firmly. "If we were in another place, another time, then I know I could really feel something for you, maybe even love you."

"But you can't now?" he asked pitifully, his eyes welling up as I shook my head.

"Love doesn't hold much sway in the world we live in Etienne - I mean, would you want to have children while we live like this? We can't even leave the city! It's too much for us to make a promise to one another to make each other happy, when everything around us wants to stop that from happening." Break his heart, my brain screamed at me, it'll mend in time.

He looked up at me, those big eyes staring at me, pleading. I leant forward, my hand on his cheek as he sobbed over the engagement ring he had hoped would change everything for him. He peered up at me, closing his eyes as my lips pressed against his. He smelt warm, like spices and leather - an expensive aftershave. Selfishly, I thought of my dreary little home and thought about what Etienne could offer me. I pulled away and tried to keep it together. "You'll never know how much I wish this world could be different, so you and I could have stood a fighting chance."

He stood up to his feet, sniffing and wiping his eyes on the back of his hand. "I'm not going to stop loving you Romany - and I'll wait every day if I have to. I know you'll change your mind," he said, only half believing it. "But for now, things will just..." He broke off, lost for words.

I wanted to spill everything, to tell him that very soon everything was going to be different. And that maybe then, he could find some peace - get that life he was dreaming of. "Carry on as they are." I said, defeated.

He walked away without a word, closing the door carefully on his way out. I remained seated, his pride had taken a blow and I knew he would want to be alone. I leant back with my arms over my head, fighting the urge to scream. Whatever he was, I cared for Etienne, and I felt as though I had deceived him; made him believe a fantasy. I could only hope that when the day came, he would understand why I had done it all, and why I had to say no.

I woke a few days later, my head thumping. I had spent every free moment that I wasn't at work, hurrying to Beckett's to go over the plan. I could tell he was nervous, from the tiny beads of sweat that lined the edge of his dark curls. Every so often he would reach for a pen, or a cigarette, and his hand would brush against mine, causing him to flinch. We hardly looked at one another until he finally asked me something, which I guessed he had been dying to get out.

"Why did you say no to him?" he asked me, nervously. I had stared at him, blinking ignorantly. "To Etienne," he embellished. "I was there, listening."

My jaw must have dropped as I searched for words, words that lay hidden in the fog of my mind. "What..." I dug my nails into the wooden table, "...the hell do you think you're doing spying on me? *Again*?"

He shook his head, trying to calm me down. "No, it wasn't like that." His cheeks had flushed a furious red, as though he'd been slapped. "I wanted to go over a few things; I was waiting in your kitchen. Once I'd heard everything, I didn't think it would be right to hang around."

"But it is perfectly acceptable to carry on breaking into peoples' homes," I'd retorted angrily. "You and Lexi need to learn a few manners." I'd taken a deep breath and chewed the edge of my nail, trying to regain a little perspective. Beckett was obviously embarrassed- as he should be, and I believed he genuinely wasn't trying to do anything malicious. "I said no, because I don't love *him*." I laughed to myself as I remembered how Beckett had stammered, trying to be cool.

"Oh right," he'd said, biting his lip. "Well, I'm glad to know that." I had changed the subject, leaving him to think about what had happened.

But, as wonderfully placid as things had become between Beckett and I, things with Etienne had taken a nosedive. I'd returned the necklace and the earrings, with an apologetic note, and he had responded by not speaking to me since - which Harry was absolutely relishing. I'd thought that I would feel nothing, that breaking his heart would be as easy as taking the life from someone, but instead I felt a sadness which made my stomach ache. In some alternate world, Etienne and I could've been so happy together, and seeing how carefully he avoided looking at me was painful.

I took two aspirins, an expensive luxury which, like a bottle of expensive contraband champagne, I only broke out for really dire situations. McLean had been patrolling the levels since the car bombing, and although I made sure to keep my focus completely on my case files, I could feel him watching me as he stepped out of the lift. On this particular morning, he stopped, lingering silently. I tore my eyes up to his and smiled brightly. "Good morning sir," I said merrily.

"What have you done to Etienne?" he asked bluntly.

"Sir?" I asked, trying to work out how much he knew.

"He's actually been producing reports at an alarming rate - knuckling down to some work. He's been shut in his office from the moment he gets here until he leaves, and that's not like him. He's usually to be found wherever you are. I take it you broke things off?" His face was blank, but I could tell from the pursing of his lips that he was trying not to smile.

"There was nothing to break off," I replied, a little anger slipping into my cheery tone.

"Oh, come now. Everyone could see how besotted with you he was." Now he was openly mocking Etienne, and it was one thing too many.

"Etienne and I have never been in a relationship. It is true that we share deep feelings for one another, but as we work together so closely, we felt the whole thing would be inappropriate. Of course, neither of us would want to do anything to upset the balance of this office and the important work we do." I had the satisfaction of watching his jaw drop. "And I don't think you have any right to ask me personal questions about my sex life, or who I choose to engage in that activity with."

His face turned violet. "You go too far Romany..." he warned, but I was too far in to care.

"No, sir, you have. You are my boss and I respect that, but it is none of your business if I am sleeping with every man I know, as long as it doesn't affect my work, or my status as a citizen."

His teeth were clamped down on his lip as he struggled to maintain a sense of propriety. "I can tell you've obviously had a hard week, with everything that has happened, so I am going to chalk this up as a serious mistake on your part, but I will not tolerate this happening again," he said in a lowered tone, leaning towards me so no one else could hear before striding away, his shoulder rigid with resentment.

I looked up, feeling triumphant and froze as Etienne folded his arms. It was clear he had heard the whole thing. I stared at him awkwardly, unsure of what to say. But as I searched for words he smiled, handing me back the box which contained the earrings.

"I thought about binning them," he explained, looking ashamed. "But they were a present, for a friend." As I went to pick it up, his hand clamped down on mine. "But I won't give up Romany. I promise you that." He walked away, chest puffed out as everyone in the level gawped at him. Harry was watching with those hawk-like eyes, the smallest of smiles on that stony face.

15

The next week flew past in a blur of covert meetings with Beckett, both of us drilling the plans into our heads over and over until we couldn't bear to think of it anymore. We'd smoke cigarettes until the embers burnt our fingers before lighting another. Lexi would be there, putting in her opinion every so often, usually after we'd discussed one point a hundred times; only for her to point out the clear mistake we'd completely missed. I loved the girl, but it took every fibre of my body not to gag her and tape her to the chair. And then there was that *energy* between Beckett and I, a glance here, a laugh shared over a silly joke. Perhaps it was nothing, I thought, but then again, perhaps it wasn't.

There was a tightening in my stomach, a nervousness; the time was growing close. It was the closing of one door, however it ended, and the opening of another, unexplored room. We could all die, and the Revolution, what remained of it, would have to start again. But if we survived, if we succeeded, anything could happen next. The world may have gone to shit, but we were the ones who could heave it back onto its feet. We could spread our message to Europe, America... We could start something massive. Or, just maybe, Beckett and I could settle down and live selfish lives filled with pleasure, just for ourselves. Anything could happen.

*

The office had gained a quiet, almost relaxed atmosphere - the calm before the storm, it felt like. Everyone seemed to be treading on glass, hoping it wouldn't crack beneath their feet. After the car bombing, the people had expected something to happen, right away. Our silence worried some more, and brought out the curiosity in others. We gained more members in that week than I can ever remember. Beckett was careful in what he told them, he didn't want anyone getting excitable and running off their mouth to the wrong person. But the sun really seemed to be breaking through the grey. I couldn't help but smile as I switched off the light at my desk and checked my watch. I had chosen to work late, perhaps out of some misplaced guilt for my colleagues. Soon, we'd all be out of a job; may as well at least pretend to give a shit for these last few days.

I packed up my purse and looked around the eerily empty level. Etienne had headed home just before, even offering to walk me back. I'd declined and he'd not argued. I had plenty of time to make it home before curfew, I thought, as I headed toward the washroom, making a stop before I left.

I scrubbed my hands, reapplied my lipstick and smiled to myself. Perhaps tomorrow, I would finally tell Beckett the truth - how I really felt. Maybe I would dare to kiss those lips and feel that stubble scratch against my skin. Yes, I decided. Tomorrow was perfect. Not too close to the event to seem rash, but enough time for us to maybe be together for a few days, if that's all we had. I wished I had done it sooner, had I known how quickly we'd be racing towards the final chapter - but tomorrow was as good a time as any.

Out the corner of my eye, I saw the door swing open as Harry stepped into the toilets. His eyes were focused on me and as he looked me up and down, a sneer spreading across his face.

"What the fuck do you think you're doing Harry?" I didn't turn around, choosing instead to reapply my scarlet lipstick. I wasn't frightened of him; I had nothing to fear anymore. His smile disappeared as he realised he would not intimidate me.

"Everyone's gone home Romany." He withdrew his hands from their pockets and folded his arms. "I don't suppose you know that the security guards on duty are extremely good friends of mine. I asked them to make sure we're not disturbed tonight. We're completely alone." His removed his leather gloves and threw them to the floor, along with his jacket. "I believe we have some… business to discuss."

I spun around to face him, meeting his eyes. "Don't tell me you're going to try and rape me Harry, because that would be a very fucking stupid thing to do." I half-expected him to look away, perhaps to be ashamed. Instead he rolled up his sleeves and stepped forward, grabbing my face in his hand. His ring cut into my cheek, and I felt my heart rate quicken. I couldn't let Harry get away with what he had in store for me, but if I fought back, my cover would be blown. My options were limited, and neither choice would end well.

"Harry," I purred seductively, my mouth tantalisingly close to his, "you really don't want to do this. I won't keep this quiet for you. Your career will be finished."

He leant closer, and I could smell the vile stench of stale alcohol on his breath. "I don't think so Romany, my

226

father is *very* good friends with the prime minister and they have both been very helpful in clearing up my little indiscretions. Why do you think I was transferred here so quickly? I needed to get away fast, before any questions were asked." I couldn't understand him; he was slurring and drifting off in his mind, rambling incoherently. "She was a little like you, but not nearly as clever. Stupid whore wanted to stay loyal to her fiancé, but that didn't stop her flirting with me did it? I knew that deep down, she wanted me." I felt sick as the stench of his breath hit me again, spit spraying my cheek. "But she wouldn't stop fucking screaming, and she kept saying she was going to tell everyone… I couldn't let her do that."

"You killed her," I said flatly.

He hardly nodded, but his eyes lit up. "Of course, her fiancé started to ask questions after she never made it home. I'm just lucky the P.M loves me as though I was his own son. He made it all go away, and brought me down here until matters were taken care of."

He placed his mouth close to my ear, whispering. "I am untouchable." He forced his mouth onto mine, biting my lip hard. My heart stopped, a wave of nausea swept over me. Harry was protected by the prime minister. If I fought back, they would know who I was. The guards would find Harry, they knew he was coming here to find me; they'd inform the police who I was. They'd search my home, hunt me down, it would jeopardize everything. I needed to stall for time, try and decide what to do next.

"Go fuck yourself Harry."

Harry pushed me away and hit me hard across the face with the back of his hand. I tried to ignore the fury that was flooding my brain. I wanted to rip his throat out. He punched me in the stomach, knocking the wind out of me and I crumpled to the floor. He removed his shirt and knelt beside me. To my horror, he began to stroke my hair.

"I'm not a monster you know. It's just, *annoying*, how women like you think you're better than me. I'm rich, handsome...I could give you everything you've ever dreamed of. What more could you possibly want?"

"Maybe a man who isn't fucked in the head for starters." As that smartass remark left my lips, he stood up. His foot came down hard on my face, breaking my nose. I knew I could kill him, without a second's hesitation, but I couldn't risk breaking cover. The sound of his fly being unzipped seemed deafening and as he straddled me, he put his mouth close to my ear.

"Don't worry, I'll be sure to be quick. If you keep your mouth shut, perhaps I won't persuade the prime minister to send the vans after you."

He began to pull up my skirt, and I was blinded by rage. I wasn't going to be another victim. Not like my mother, not like my poor Lexi. I punched Harry hard, and was satisfied to hear the noise of his cheekbone shattering. He screamed in pain and tried to hit me, his fist hitting the tiles with a crunch. I kicked him hard, both my feet hitting his stomach, sending him to the floor. As I turned to grab my purse, his hands came down on my shoulders. He pushed me into the wall, the mirror smashing as my head connected with it. My blood felt warm as it oozed down on my face. He grabbed the collar of my dress and tore it, and I heard him gasp as the top of my tattoo was revealed.

"What the hell..." he hissed, as he ripped it open more. "You sneaky little bitch. I knew there was something off about you. Well, at least I have a reason to let the P.M take you away. I'll be doing him a favour, handing him one of the Revolution's bitches. "

I reached down, my fingers grazing a shard of glass on the sink. He pushed himself against me, his bloody nose dripping down my neck. "I'm going to enjoy this...." My hand gripped the glass and I slammed my head back into his face. He stumbled backwards, and before he could come at me again, I spun around. The glass sliced his throat open neatly, splitting his skin apart like a soft peach. He fell to the floor, and gurgled as blood drained out, sprayed garishly across the white tiles.

The toilet door opened and McLean stepped in, his eyes scanning Harry and the glass in my hand. I dropped it and held my hands up, defeated. I tried to think furiously, think of a way to escape. His cold eyes crossed my face and suddenly, like a mask had been removed, they warmed. He pulled a gun from his holster and threw it to me. "You need to leave now."

I froze, confused and afraid. McLean bent down and picked up the glass. He placed his hands in Harry's warm blood and smeared it over his suit. He came towards me, and put his hands on my shoulders.

"Romany, please trust me. I can delay security but they will be here soon. You have to go. Run home as quickly as you can, grab whatever you need and get to Beckett. Don't wait for me."

Realisation dawned on me. McLean was Beckett's other Revolution mole in the building. He stroked my hair back, out of the bloody wounds on my face. "You know, I've always thought you were beautiful Romany. I was desperate to tell you who I was, so you wouldn't be so afraid of me. I am so sorry I didn't protect you." His face took on a new handsomeness I had never noticed before and he looked like a different person. "You have to go now."

"They're going to kill you," I breathed.

"I know," he replied, smiling sadly. I kissed him gently on the cheek, cupping his face with my hands. He sighed and rested his forehead against mine, his eyes shut.

"Thank you." I whispered as he hugged me hard.

"May God bless you and this country with more fortune than me," he whispered back as he let me go.

I ran out the door and hid around the corner as security thundered into the bathroom. I heard them scream at him to put down the glass, asking him where I was. "I let her go…" he shouted at them. "She left before I killed him… you have to listen to me... she didn't do anything wrong…" As I fled, my legs like jelly beneath me, I burst into tears as gun shots rang out.

*

I killed a man for the first time tonight. Beckett and I were out, after curfew, doing some recon for his father. He's too old to go out now, he does all his work from inside. We made it to the location, and we made it in. But, Beckett got distracted. This one asshole, he snuck up on him and managed to get hold of him before Beckett could reach for his gun. I hid in the darkness, barely able to move, - a coward. He hit Beckett so hard I could hear his cheekbone crunching. Beckett just fell to the floor, like a puppet with its strings cut. I could hear him choking Beckett, laughing at him; telling him that when he came to, he was going to find himself in a cell, naked and ready to be taught a lesson. I had my gun, but I couldn't draw attention to us; I couldn't risk more coming. I flicked open my knife and steadied myself. Beckett's legs were flailing, he wouldn't stay conscious. I took my run up, my feet barely making a sound on the floor. Matthew always said I should have been a ballet dancer, I was so light on my feet. He was knelt over Beckett, too engrossed in strangling him to notice me. Too busy to realise before I had slit open his throat. He didn't scream, just let out a choked mew as he slumped to the floor. His blood covered my hands. Beckett managed to stand.

I don't know how we made it home, but when we did, Matthew didn't even ask if Beckett was okay. He just hugged me. I couldn't move, I just kept staring at the blood on my hands. All the training hadn't prepared me for how it would feel. As Matthew held me tight and stroked my face, telling me how proud he was of me, Beckett just stood staring at us, rubbing the bruises on his neck; as though he could make them disappear.

I couldn't handle his eyes on me, looking at me with complete awe. He and I were one of a kind now, both murderers. And I couldn't bear to listen to Matthew's fevered excitable praise. He was crazy, I realised, what had I done that deserved approval? I had murdered someone. My head spun and I felt faint. I ran away from them both, up the stairs. I threw up violently, slumped on

231

the bathroom floor, cradling the toilet. I scrambled over to the sink, using it to get to my feet. I scrubbed my hands over and over, trying to remove his blood. After a few minutes, I realised, I would never be able to get rid of it. It would stain me forever.

*

I ran as fast as my legs would take me, out of the building and down the road. I froze for a moment in the fading light of the day. The vans would be out soon. The guard shouted at me, and I realised I was stood in the open, blood pouring down my face. I began to run again. Where could I go? They would be after me before I knew it. I moved as quickly as I could as I reached my road, trying not to arouse suspicion. I made it into my house, and grabbed the bag I'd packed for an occasion such as this. I grabbed my IPod and buried it at the bottom. My heart raced, my hand trembling. There was some money hidden away, in an empty cigarette packet. That came too, along with the gun and ammo hidden beneath my floorboards. I remembered at the last second, to grab two pieces of jewellery - my locket and the amber ring. Etienne's diamonds stayed in their box on my bedside cabinet. It didn't seem right to take them with me. I just made it downstairs when I heard the sirens. The vans were coming. There was no time - I had to get out. I ran out of the back door, leaving my house behind. I didn't look back.

*

"Is she here?" I burst into the house, pushing past Lexi and the others who had gathered for a meeting. She looked at me quizzically and, I grabbed her by the collar of her leather jacket, shaking her a little. "Has Romany come here?"

She pushed me away, grasping the height of my fear. "Why would she?" She grabbed my face, yanking it hard so I could see her. Her feline eyes were wide. "What's happened Beckett?"

"I was waiting for her, and she never came home - she must have worked late. I went to the office looking for her and all hell has broken loose, alarms are going off, it was swarming with vans. I heard their radios, they're looking for her."

Lexi's eyes grew wide and she began to shake. She didn't ask what I had been doing, waiting for her to come home, and I was glad I didn't have to explain how I'd sat at her table with a bunch of pathetic dying flowers, gained by unscrupulous means. "No..." she muttered over and over. Elise tried to calm her, but she pushed her away, her face screwed up in pain. "I have to find her." She stopped and whipped around to face me, defiant. I shrank back a little, Lexi's fury was on full display, and even I found her intimidating. She sprinted for the back door, and I reached to grab her, trying to stop her. She pushed me away with both hands, her full weight behind her. Her strength was surprising. "I'm not going to leave her out there for them to take. They'll know; they'll know she's part of the Revolution. They'll torture her, and then they'll kill her."

The image of Romany; her head shaved and her emaciated body covered in open wounds, tied to a chair, made my stomach heave. Lexi used my moment of shock to begin clambering out of the window.

"Lexi, she might come back," I grabbed her leg. "Romany's the best we have. She's not going to get caught, and she's going to be coming here."

She hesitated for a moment, weighing up the likely scenarios. She shook her head, kicking out at me. "I don't care; I won't make her fight to get here alone."

I followed her, pushing her against the walls of the alley. "Look, you have to listen to me, you're not only putting yourself in danger, you're putting Romany at risk. Nobody can avoid detection like Romany, but if you go charging out there, attracting attention, then you are going to put her at more risk than she already is."

"You know Beckett," she leant forward menacingly, "if you cared about Romany half as much as you pretend to, you'd already be ahead of me, trying to find her, whatever the consequences."

Reluctantly, I followed her down the alley, trying desperately to convince her to come back in. But, cunningly, she kept me talking, right up until we had made it to Romany's home. The vans were swarming around it, with scores of police officers tearing through her house. Her furniture was being thrown down the steps, they were searching every inch for any possible sign of her or where she may have gone. The only thing that was clear was that she was not in the house.

"Are you happy now?" I hissed. "She's not here Lexi; we need to get back now."

She nodded, her eyes fixed on the policemen. "What if they have her already?" She chewed the peeling skin of her lips.

"Then there is still nothing we can do to help her if they catch us now." I began to pull her down the road, trying to walk slowly and nonchalantly. I gripped her hand, wrapping my arm around her, trying to hold her steady whilst looking like nothing more than an enchanted boyfriend. We rounded the corner, out of sight and ready to run when we heard them shouting at us to stop. "Don't look behind you, just keep walking." I reached around to the inside of my jacket, where my gun was snugly tucked away. We walked a little quicker, still clutching one another. They shouted louder and as I glanced back, they began to sprint. I went to pull Lexi but she seemed to be frozen, her legs unable to move. She ripped my gun from my jacket and spun around, her eyes wild and frenzied.

"Where the fuck is she?" she screamed, firing blindly at them. I tried to stop her, to wrench the gun from her grip and force her to run. All but one of the policemen dove into cover, the bullets shooting past their heads. The remaining officer calmly removed his gun and aimed it at Lexi. With an easy squeeze of the trigger, he fired two shots. The first missed, I could feel it sailing gracefully past my ear, hitting a pedestrian who had peered out from behind a post box at the wrong second, neatly between the eyes. The second bullet did not miss. Lexi stumbled backwards, blood spreading across her white vest, a blooming rose of the darkest red. I ripped the weapon from her grasp and shot the officer dead. The others stayed in cover as I pulled Lexi away, helping her as she stumbled, losing blood quickly. How she managed to run, I don't know; the human body is a miraculous thing when it needs to be.

*

I sat in Beckett's house, waiting anxiously. The living room smelt of damp, and I had never liked to sit in there for long. You could almost hear the screams of those who had been dragged from their beds, and out of this house, anguished ghosts. The wallpaper was peeling from the walls, and the photographs were covered in a thick layer of dust, the occupants of them indistinguishable. Elise sat beside me, all reassuring smiles.

"I'm sure they're fine, look on the bright side; who else, other than you, always come out of everything smelling of roses?" The more she spoke, the more sick I felt. I wanted to tell her to shut up, but I couldn't bring myself to - she was only trying to be helpful. Suddenly, a crash came from the kitchen and before Elise could try and convince me to remain calm, I leapt to my feet. Beckett walked into the room, carrying Lexi.

Beckett's eyes locked onto mine, and I could see pity in them. He gently lay Lexi down on the battered sofa. She wailed as pain shot through her body. Her forehead was damp with sweat, her beautiful eyes barely open. I couldn't bear to step away from the door, to go closer to her. I wanted to run as far away as I could. As Beckett led me forward the smell of her blood became overpowering; the bullets had ripped open her stomach, and the gaping hole in her belly made my head swim. I would've fallen to my knees, had Beckett not been holding me up. "I'm so sorry," he whispered, as he turned away and left the room. I stepped closer to her, and knelt beside her. Her hand reached out to me, and its grasp was weak.

"Hi babe..." she whispered. "...pretty fucked up huh?"

"What happened?" My voice was a tiny squeak.

"They were already at yours, tearing up your house. I realised you weren't there but they spotted me, and I ran, I was outnumbered. I couldn't get a shot... and one of the bastards was good. Beckett had come to try and drag me back home... turns out he was actually right for once. I'm one lucky bitch huh?" She tried to smile and gulped as the pain hit her again. She began to cry. "I'm so scared." I could taste the salt of my tears, as they ran down my face. I'd seen death before; I'd taken lives without a moment's thought for my victims or their families. But now, as death came to take my friend from me, their faces came into my head. "I'm going to die aren't I?"

I stroked her shaved head, and wiped her tears away, though mine flowed freely. I didn't know what to say, I wanted to reassure her but as I shook my head Lexi shouted out at me.

"I've got a hole in my stomach Romany. A fucking *hole*. I've killed enough people to know that you can't just stitch this up."

"Why did you go looking for me?" I shook her, suddenly deeply angry at both myself and her. "You know the rules!"

"I had to..." she slurred.

"That's bullshit, Lexi. You didn't have to make sure I was safe."

"I did..."

237

Her eyelids fluttered shut and my heartbeat quickened. I had to keep her talking. "Why?"

Her eyes snapped open and her voice, strong and powerful, shouted out, "Because I love you!" She leant back on the pillow, and for a moment, she was my Lexi again. Fearless and hard. "I've *wanted* to kiss you, and hold you for forever. But you're *straight*, I know that." She spat the word like an insult, and gripped my hand tighter. She looked down at her stomach and shrugged, the fight draining from her. "I'd do this a hundred times over to know you were safe."

"Well..." I smiled weakly through my tears. "...I'd be a heartless bitch to reject you now." She laughed, and coughed, blood covering her lips. I leant forward, and placed my mouth on hers. I kissed her with every fibre of my body, and in that moment, I loved her in every way, I really did. Like a lover, a sister, a comrade and a friend. She kissed me back, sighing gently. I would have kissed her forever if it could have made her better. As I pulled away, I could hear her breathing becoming shallow. I rested my forehead on hers and cupped her cheek in my hand. "I fucking love you Lexi."

"I love you babe." She coughed again, and I wiped the blood away from her full, gorgeous lips. Her hand grew tighter and I closed my eyes, waiting for the inevitable to come. She began to ramble, barely audible; her eyes fluttering shut. "I can hear them...the seagulls..." I squeezed her tighter, and as her body went limp, I heard my sobs turn into screams of pain and heartbreak. I had lost my best friend. Beckett's arms closed around me and he cradled me, as I held Lexi's dead body against my chest.

As I lay her back down, I kissed her gently on the forehead before pulling a blanket over her. We would have to dispose of her body quickly, it was not going to be easy. Beckett was stood with his back to me in the corner, and his shoulders were shaking a little, I knew he was crying. Running his fingers through his hair, an insignificant gesture, made me even more furious at him. He should have stopped her, my brain screamed at me; he should never have let her leave. But, a little voice whispered, why didn't he go looking for you? He must have known you were in danger, but he didn't want to leave, he only went because Lexi had.

"Coward!" I spat out loud and froze as he whipped around to face me.

"What did you say?" he hissed, and unsteadily I stood to my feet.

"Why did you let her go? You're the *leader*; you're supposed to stop this from happening."

He shook his head, and wiped the tears from his face. "I *tried* Romany, I really did… but you know what Lexi is like…" At his use of the present tense he paused, and it made me lose control. My hand curled into a fist and, without a moment's hesitation, I hit him hard across the cheek.

"You didn't try hard enough." I turned my back on him. I wanted to walk away, but I knew he wasn't going to let me leave that easily.

"You were the one who said that in war, there must be sacrifices Romany. You have spent all your time preparing us for the time ahead, and you preached how we must be brave, unselfish…how we must be ready to lose some we love, but for the greater good. Are you telling me those words didn't apply to you?"

I spun around, my chest tight as I felt my heart beat race. "How dare you…"

"Shut up, Romany. I am the leader here, not you, although you have spent the last few months ensuring that you undermine my authority in every way. Lexi left because she loved you, because she wanted to help you… don't desecrate her memory by behaving like this. She did the honourable thing and died like a true martyr. You should be proud of her."

"Because she did the honourable thing?"

"Yes."

"Unlike you," I spat, and I had the satisfaction of seeing him reel in shock. "Yes, Lexi did love me, and do you know something? This whole Revolution was supposed to be about love, about saving the people and country we love. Yet, somewhere along the line it became about revenge. It's poisonous."

He grabbed my shoulders and shook me hard. "You think I didn't come after you because I don't love you? I didn't come because I have an army of people to care for, people that are relying on us to succeed. That is more important than you."

I pushed him away hard and tried not to cry again. "Well, maybe that's the problem. Maybe we've just forgotten how to be human; we've spent so long being soldiers of the Revolution." I stormed off down the corridor and could hear his footsteps behind me. I swung back around on the stair, his face inches from mine. "I am done hiding in the shadows, Beckett. I don't want to be an assassin anymore, or whatever the fuck we are. I want to be a person, I want a life. No matter how hard I try to spur us on, you hang back, you're not a leader, and deep down I don't think you want to finish this."

He shook his head but I was determined not to let him win, not to let him gain the upper hand. I realised some of the others had come out and were lurking in the dark, listening intently. "I am not waiting anymore Beckett. I don't give a shit if I am the only one storming Parliament in two days time; I am going to be there."

As I turned to leave, he grabbed my wrist. "I'll be there," he whispered, "but I am telling you now Romany, I will not lose you." His words seemed to punch the wind from within me, I almost doubled over. He backed away, and went back into the room where Lexi remained. I knew he was going to take her away, that he was going to take her somewhere dark and quiet where she could be in peace. Nobody could avoid the cameras like Beckett could, even when he was carrying a body.

As I walked into my room, I could see my reflection: pale, haggard, my cheeks stained by my tears. I didn't look like an assassin, I looked like a sad girl, lost and alone. My nose was broken, and as I moved it back into place, pain shot through my face. There were scratches across my face from the mirror in the washroom, but they would not need stitches. They would fade in a short space of time, unlike the pain in my heart at that moment. In a sudden blaze of anger my fist powered through the glass, and I watched numbly as the blood from my knuckles dripped onto the floorboards. I peered through the boards covering my windows at the other houses. I sank to my knees as I realised I was only experiencing what those poor bastards felt every day.

Grief. Loneliness. Fear. I had been trained not to think of the feelings of others, to work like a machine for the good of our country. But now I realised, we did have something to fight for; for them and for the hope that one day, maybe, we would all be able to live normally together. And for a moment, I realised that even if I did die trying to take the government down, at least I would die content that I was helping those who needed it. I crawled over to the bed and pulled myself into it, hoping that when sleep came, it would be silent.

16

I am a woman now, today is my eighteenth birthday. I pull the cover over my head, wanting to sleep just a while longer. For although today is my birthday, it is no different to any other day. There will be training and silence. There will be no celebrations. Since Rose passed, everything seems worse, if that were possible. Matthew never talks, except to bark orders at us during training. He is always out, meeting secretly with other members. Life has become so much more restricted. The police make regular checks, ensuring we aren't keeping any banned items from the list. They are desperate for a reason to arrest us, but they fear the backlash of the Revolution. I should be excited, I should be ready to have fun. But, as I always remember, nobody else is having any fun.

As I close my eyes, trying to drift back off, my bedroom door is noisily flung open. Lexi jumps on my bed, and thrusts a present at me. "Open it!"

Her demanding tone is not to be argued with. I rip open the packet and gasp at its contents. A brand new IPod, as I had whispered to Lexi I desperately wanted.

"How did you..."

"I stole it, of course." Her pride is evident. "Just don't get caught with it, that's all we need."

I threw my arms around her and squeezed her tight. I felt my eyes well up as I thought about how much she had risked to get me a blacklisted item, just because it was my birthday. I glimpsed Beckett in my doorway, smiling at me. He mouthed 'happy birthday' at me. Lexi shot him a look over her shoulder and rolled her eyes at me, clambering off the bed. She stomped out the door, leaving him stood uneasily. He came towards me and passed me an envelope and a small wrapped box.

"My father left me this to pass on to you. He said it was important and not to be opened until today." He walked away, and I watched him sadly. Before everything that had happened between us he would have given me a hug, wished me a happy birthday. "By the way," he paused for a moment, "the present is from me."

I opened the package first, and slowly removed the lid from the little box. Inside was a beautiful amber ring.

"How did you get this?"

"You don't need to know that, I just hope you like it." Before I could reply, he pulled the door closed behind him.

I looked down at his gift, and examined it closer. Trapped inside the amber was a little fly, frozen forever in time. I turned my attention to the envelope, and as I tore it open and removed the letter from inside, my heart stopped.

'To our beautiful daughter, today you are a woman. I do not know what will have happened by the time you read this, or where we will all be, but we wish you a very happy eighteenth birthday. I bought your present on my way home after you were born. You are the greatest gift we have ever had. All our love, Mum and Dad xx'

Hands shaking, I tipped the envelope upside down, carefully catching its contents. I traced the silver locket with my finger and stared at it. I turned it over and smiled at the engraving of my birth date. I was almost too scared to look inside. But curiosity had always been *my weakness. The picture inside made my heart stop. My parents smiled up at me. Nestled in my mother's arms, a baby smiled, chubby and happy. They radiated happiness and love. They had loved me so much, that they had sacrificed themselves for me. I fastened it around my neck, and sobbed into my pillow. I had never missed them more.*

*

Beckett was waiting in the basement when I woke, just before dawn. As I walked past the room where Lexi had passed away, I couldn't help but look at the sofa, still stained with her blood. A few members, a chosen few seconds, including Erin and Eve, were stood anxiously, waiting for our brief. Erin gasped at the sight of me, and ran forwards, checking I was okay. She examined my nose, and was impressed that I had set it back straight. Beckett didn't look at me; I could tell he was still furious.

"Tomorrow," he began, "we will bring down our fury on the Houses of Parliament. The prime minister is due to make his visit, ready to pass his latest law. He intends to bring all children under the age of 18 into training for his police force. We cannot allow this to happen, for it would be the ruin of the Revolution. Their numbers would be too great; he would brainwash these children against us." His gaze locked onto me, his jaw tight. "Romany will now tell you what the plan is." All eyes swivelled to me, and I knew that they wanted to see if my resolve had broken since Lexi's death.

"We will enter the building at midday. I have it under good authority that the police will be positioned in the street, and the security within the building will be relatively low. The prime minister likes to believe he is all powerful, that he does not need a huge swarm of protectors because his people would never harm him. We can use this to our advantage. With the power of the mob, we will storm Parliament. The citizens, I am sure, will fill the streets. Even if we do not have them all there, we will eventually. It only takes a few to capture the inspiration of many." I pointed to the map spread out before Beckett. "Beckett and our team will storm from the front. I know that one of our new supporters has been very helpful, planting Elise's explosive devices throughout. These are not powerful enough to bring the building down, but when we enter, it will hopefully be enough to disorientate them, and block most exits."

"So why don't we just blow the place up?" A tall black man, lean with a thin face, was leaning against the wall, smoking a cigarette. He asked the question with an air of incredulity.

"I want to kill Bowman myself, make sure he is dead. If we just blow it up, there's a chance he could survive and it is messy. This way, we are in control, and the risk of civilian casualties is far lower." He nodded, conceding my point.

I handed round piles of flyers. "These need to be posted through every letterbox in the city, or at least houses with people in them. It will tell the people where to be and what to do."

"Elise has ensured that the cameras will be off for the morning, allowing you a chance to do this without being spotted. Elise has worked incredibly hard to make this happen, and it has not been easy. As much of a genius she is, I don't doubt that they will find a way to fix it before the day is out.

"We will be moving our location today, whilst the cameras are out, to an apartment tower much closer to the House of Parliament. The rooftop is out of sight of all surveillance, and will allow us an excellent view of the Houses, and the streets below. The building is completely abandoned, so we will all be able to hide out there for one night."

Beckett dismissed the others, the meeting was over. He looked at me for a second, before turning his back on me and leaving, without a word.

*

I moved stealthily through the dark streets, aware that my face was now plastered across the wall of every police station in the country. I was wanted, and there wasn't much concern as to whether I was delivered to them dead or alive. I had to reach the apartment building before the sun came up, whilst the cameras were still down. God bless Elise, I thought, as I sprinted past a motionless security camera.

The apartment block was a bleak grey tomb of a building, generic and bland in every way. The doors and windows had been boarded up, but some rotting washing still remained, slung over the balconies. All apartment blocks had been evacuated by the government, the tops of them being out of the range of the audio scanners and heat sensors. They had remained as ghostly reminders of how the world had once been, slowly crumbling away. They were derelict. As a result, they were completely devoid of cameras. I carefully pulled open the boards of the main door, checking over my shoulder for the looming headlights of the vans. As I made it into the hallway, I stood still for a moment in the empty space, staring up at the endless staircases above me. The top floor seemed like an eternity away, with the lift out of service, and there was no guarantee I would find anyone else here. My footsteps echoed loudly, and every five seconds I found myself stopping, frozen by any slight noise that seemed deafening to me. As I passed door after door, I looked at each one, checking no one else was hiding out here. A child's bicycle lay abandoned on one landing, its rainbow coloured streamers now grey with dust. Police tape crossed each doorway, still intact but faded. I began to up my pace, desperate to reach the top, unable to look at the sad reminders of the buildings former occupants and consider their fates. At the top, I was relieved to see a small light in the hallway, and as I tapped twice, whispering the code word, 'Elysium'. Beckett let me in. Double locking the door behind me, he didn't speak, but wandered straight into the kitchen.

The top flat was a large space, with three bedrooms and a large lounge. The windows were all boarded and covered, preventing the lights from being seen outside. I followed the hallway, pausing to look at the faded photographs on the wall. A couple smiled joyfully at me, blissfully happy on their wedding day. In another, two freckled and mischievous children stuck their tongues out. This family had left in a hurry. I tried to shut out my thoughts of what may have happened to them, but surrounded by another families' personal belongings made that difficult. I pushed open one door, the name 'Lily' carved into a little sign hanging from it. Except for the mattress on the floor, the room remained much as I imagined it had when the little girl had slept there every night. My eyes adjusted to the darkness and I could see the stuffed toys, greying and grimy, sitting on a pink shelf. A small jewellery box sat beside them, and as I opened it, the haunting melody it played made my eyes sting with tears. The little trinkets inside remained, safely nestled in pink satin; a thimble, a little gold hat pin shaped like a koala, a shiny pound coin. The hidden treasures of a beloved daughter. Photos hung from the walls, and I gently wiped the dust from the glass with my sleeve. A pretty girl with large chocolate brown eyes and glistening auburn ringlets grinned at me. The cake in front of her had the candles blown out and a big number six in pink icing. In the frame beside it, a close up of her and her mother, and another of her with five other lovely little girls, all enjoying a hot summer's day, spraying each other with water guns. Another double tap on the door brought me back into the moment and I pulled the door shut on Lily's room.

Beckett had worked hard to prepare the flat for us. Every room had a mattress in it, and stacks of blankets. Even the worn sofa in the living room looked appealing in my worn state. I looked back as Elise and a shorter, blonde haired man entered the flat, shaking hands and embracing Beckett. Elise looked at the blonde man and I could see something in her eyes, a flash of love and fear. I was happy for her. I saw Elise look at the two doors, with their colourful name signs and shudder.

More and more Revolution members arrived, and joined us in the living room, all sat on mattresses, checking our weapons and ammo. McLean had served us well; we had a mass, in all shapes and sizes. Eve and Philip came in, and Beckett greeted them with open arms, introducing them to the others. After a while, Peter and Erin came in too. Erin looked fearless as ever, but I could sense the apprehension in Peter's tight shoulders and tired eyes. He was nervous, I could tell, but as Erin squeezed his hand, a little colour returned to his face. I opened the door to another knock and code word, and Christina smiled at me through the gap. She waved a little shyly and entered warily.

"It's okay," I reassured her, "you're with friends now." I led her into the kitchen and she placed her hands on my shoulders, shaking like a beaten dog.

"When I got into the office, all everyone was talking about was what you had done and about McLean. Etienne was in pieces, trying to convince everyone that they had to be mistaken."

"Did they take him?" I asked.

To my relief, she shook her head. "They sent him home, said he was exhausted, that he needed some time off. But they questioned all of us, and when no one was looking I slipped out, but I know the cameras would have seen me. I went straight to Beckett's house and he told me to come here if I wanted to help." She began to cry. "I thought they were going to find out who I was, that they were going to take me away in the vans."

"You're not going to have to worry about that after tomorrow."

Beckett came into the room, leaning on the door frame. "Christina, would you please go and guard the door. Double knock and code word, that's the only way anyone gets in." She scurried past him, still sniffing.

He pulled the kitchen door shut.

"I know you think that what happened with Lexi is somehow my fault."

"No, I don't." I turned away, resting my head against the boarded window, trying desperately to see the city lights. "I know it was my fault." His hand came down on the sideboard so hard it made me jump. I rested against the sink, leaning away from him, nervous.

"It wasn't your fucking fault Romany, none of this is. It's their fault, the government have done this to all of us!" He paced back and forth, tugging at his curls. "But tomorrow, we'll finally get to give them a taste of the pain they have caused."

"I don't care about revenge anymore Beckett, I don't care about getting even, all I want is a future." He stopped his pacing, finally listening. "Your dad was so focused on revenge, and that's all you believe in, it's all I believed in, too. He drilled it into our skulls day after day, that we were doing this for Rose, for my parents, for Eloise." He tensed at her name. "But that's not why we should be doing it; we should be doing it for ourselves."

I lit up a cigarette, relishing the burn in my throat. "Do you know what I want out of this? To be able to go on a holiday, to be able to get drunk in a fancy bar, maybe even have a family..." I trailed off, embarrassed with myself. Beckett looked away uncomfortably. "Tomorrow Beckett, I'll be focused. I am going to kill that bastard myself, or go down trying. But after that,

251

once it's done, I am going to live a normal life. I won't be an assassin anymore, I'll just be an ordinary person."

"You'll always be an assassin, Romany." Sadness stained his voice. "Our work won't be done just because Bowman is dead. If we don't finish what we start, then everyone we know will have died for nothing."

"Maybe I can't escape what I have done, who I've become, but I can damn well try. Yes, together we can all build a better country, and no, our work won't be done. But I want to enjoy life; I want to actually *live* for the first time since I was a child."

He pulled out his father's cigarette case, staring at it intensely. I stepped a little closer to him, and gently took it from him placing it to one side. "Your dad spent every day tortured by what happened to Rose, to Eloise, to every single other person he tried to save. He passed all that rage onto you, because he thought he was preparing you, so you would be able to prevent what he couldn't. You've gone so much further than him Beckett; you've brought us to the edge of this. Even if we fail tomorrow, you've given people something more than your father ever could, you gave them hope." I stroked his face, pulling it back to look at me when he tried to move. "But now you've bought the people this far, there's going to be a time when they don't need us, or need the Revolution. That won't be far away. Then what are you going to do?" We stared at one another, lost in anticipation and fear. He went to speak as the door flew open, Christina filling the doorway with her awkward frame.

"I'm sorry Beckett, but everyone wants to discuss tomorrow." I walked away and Beckett reached out for me.

"Where are you going?"

"It's my plan, remember? I don't need to be there." I couldn't look at him; I knew it would push me too far, to the point where I couldn't stop myself.

"What if you get seen?"

"I have a sudden urge to see the sun set - might be my last time. Besides, if tonight isn't the night to take a risk, when is?" As I walked away from the kitchen, my heart was thudding in my chest.

*

I pulled my leather jacket tighter around myself, shivering a little as the cold night air whipped across my cheek. From the rooftop, I could see far across the city. I found myself admiring the tiny glittering lights, beautiful beneath a starry sky. My heart pounded. What lay ahead of me? What was at stake if we failed? The people below me were why I was doing this, for their chance to have the life they deserved. They were what mattered. People like my parents, who deserved freedom, whatever the cost. In the midst of victory, there must be sacrifice; no one could afford to be selfish in war. That much, even now, remained true.

I knew the science behind a bullet entering a man's skull, but I'd never imagined how it would feel to be in their place. When it tore through my brain, would I know that I was going to die? I'd never feared death, but I was not ashamed to admit, that for the first time, I was terrified.

Suddenly, the hairs on the back of my neck stood on end. I could hear his footsteps coming up behind me. He had come to find me. He stood beside me silently, rubbing his hands together to warm them up. Beckett lit two cigarettes, passing one to me, which I took gladly.

"You know, you could die tomorrow." He didn't look at me, but I could tell from his voice that he was smiling.

I blew smoke from my lips. "So could you."

"How would you feel if that were to happen?"

I dropped my cigarette on the ground as my body went limp. The air suddenly seemed heavy, and I struggled to catch my breath. My palms were sweaty and my head swam. I desperately wanted to look him in the eye, but I just couldn't force myself to do it. No matter how many times I'd dreamt of telling Beckett my true feelings, deep down I'd always known I wasn't brave enough to go through with it. How could anybody put their heart on the line, just to risk having it crushed? A merciless killer I may be, but there isn't a woman alive who enjoys the prospect of being rejected by the one they love. I was no exception.

"I could live without you." The lie left my lips. I was daring him to break, to say I was bluffing. I crushed my abandoned cigarette beneath my boot. His eyes bored into mine relentlessly. I was forced to look away. Beckett's hand came close to my face, as though he was going to stroke my cheek.

"Say that again." His eyes were steely, staring into mine with a determined edge that made me blush.

"I said that I could live without you."

Beckett's face came down, an inch from mine. He drew me close to him, and gave a heavy sigh. A second later and the reality of what we were doing dawned on me. What if we were ambushed? We'd be here, kissing like teenagers, distracted and vulnerable. One of us had to be sensible. I pulled away, desperate to regain control. I started to turn from him and tried to walk away, but his hand, quick as a flash, gripped my wrist, stopping me from leaving. Truthfully, though it pains me to admit, it would have taken far less to make me stay. I had no control over myself anymore.

Beckett's voice, strong and passionate, rang out in the silence. "I couldn't live without you Romany, not now, not ever." He looked intense, a warrior claiming what was rightfully his. "Romany, we both have our reasons for doing this, and you think mine is revenge." The pause after his words seemed to last forever. "But my reason is you."

I processed what he had just told me. I slowly turned, utterly defeated."I've waited *years* Beckett, for those words to finally leave your mouth. I have spent every minute of every day, striving to prove myself to you. To prove I was enough for you. I've lived every moment for you." There was a split second where the world seemed to stand still. "I've always been yours."

He gathered me up in his arms, kissing me hard. Suddenly, I couldn't feel the cold; we could have been stood in the arctic and I still wouldn't feel anything other than my overwhelming need for him.

"If this is my last on day earth," he whispered in my ear as his hands began to unbutton my jacket, "then I can die a happy man." Breathless, I placed my finger on his lips and he paused for a moment, only one button left untouched.

"Tomorrow doesn't matter. Tonight, all I care about is us." His face broke into an enchanting smile as he lay me down on the rusty deckchair, slowly undressing me beneath the gaze of the universe.

Tension crackled like electricity through the air and adrenaline pumped through my veins, deliciously addictive. I purred with delight as Beckett kissed the back of my neck, following the line of my spine. His fingers delicately traced the outline of my Phoenix, cold against my damp skin. He lay back down on the mattress, his toned body brazenly displayed to me.

"Aren't you nervous?" I breathed, trying to prevent him from pulling me closer.

"Not even a little. Whatever happens, I'm ready for it." His lips brushed mine, his hand teasing my hair.

"What if we're all killed."

His teeth grazed my skin, and I pushed him away with both hands. "Then I can die knowing I tried." He sat up and stared me in the eye. "This is our life's work Romany, we've never been more ready; and you're ready to lead the people." He clamped his hand over my mouth, stifling my protests. "Everyone knows it, this was your plan for heaven's sake." He rubbed my shoulders and smiled. "Today, I am your second."

A bang on our door made us jump to our feet, pulling on our clothing hurriedly. Elise peered around the corner and grinned at us.

"It's beginning. I have hacked into the government's audio system, and they haven't got a clue what is going on. But the whole of London is talking about today, and from what I gather, the majority are preparing to meet us there." Her eyes scanned us both in our half-dressed states. "I'll give you two a minute."

As she closed the door, Beckett pulled his black top over his head and beamed. "I told you the people wouldn't let us down." A nervous smile swept across his face and he pulled out his cigarette case, taking out two - one for himself, one for me. "I'm so scared Romany." He sighed. "My father would've known what he was doing, he wouldn't be frightened."

*

I am not yet twenty and Matthew is dead. They came to take away his body today. My new employees at the Government Head Office have allowed me the day off to grieve for my 'father'. I came back to the old house, leaving my employee accommodation to meet with the police. They told us that Matthew had left the house to me and I could see Beckett biting down hard on his lip, stopping himself from beating the shit out of the police officer. And possibly me. They handed him what had been left to him and I could see the officers sneering at him as they did so.

"We checked it, made sure it's okay for you to have it, being as valuable as it is." They were humiliating him, and he had no choice than to take it. He took the parcel in his hands and unwrapped it. All that Matthew had left his son, the heir to his leadership, was a battered old cigarette case. But, as he placed it in his pocket, it didn't matter to him, it was insignificant. He was the leader now. And it was his chance to shine, to prove what he could do. And that left me, trailing in his wake, living in his shadow. I walked away from his father's house, determined never to go back.

*

I leaned forward and kissed him on the cheek, flinging my arms around his neck.

"You are a hundred times the man your father was Beckett," I whispered into his ear. "And I know you are going to lead us to victory, I know it."

He beamed at me, stroking my cheek with the palm of his hand. "It's your plan," he pointed out.

"I would never have thought of it if it wasn't for you." He pulled me to him and kissed me hard, holding me close; his hands tangled in my hair.

My Kevlar vest, fastened tight and hidden beneath my police uniform, made me struggle to breathe, as I stood waiting with the others, also kitted out in police garb. Elise was tapping away at her computer, trying desperately to maintain the audio scanner block. It was not yet four in the morning, we had time yet before the prime minister and the rest of his so-called government would be arriving for their meeting.

Beckett entered the room, and despite myself, I found his disguise rather attractive. In a normal world, Beckett would have made a rather wonderful police officer. I found my hands were shaking as he ushered me forward to review the plan again. The eyes on me made me feel dizzy, I tried to focus, but thoughts kept running through my head. Lexi dead. Bowman dead. Beckett dead. Things that had happened, things that would. It was time. We were ready, but I found myself wanting to run away, to just grab Beckett and run.

The walk down the flights of steps seemed endless. My feet dragged, but I was in front, the leader. I had to lead my team. They were as frightened as me, I could tell. We loaded up our white van, sat in the back, hidden out of sight as brave Elise took the wheel. The journey was short, but it had never felt longer to me. Beckett reached out and took my hand in his. If they caught us now, they'd slaughter us all. It would be a public execution. But the van wasn't stopped, and we moved through the streets. We sat, holding our breath, invisible inside the van. We knew that on the streets, people would be scattering, desperate to hide from the sight of the van.

At the Parliament checkpoint, on the historic bridge, Elise calmly passed the papers identifying us as part of the security team for the day to the guard. I held my breath as the policewoman checked them over, scrutinising every word. She handed them back, nodding at Elise to drive on. She looked over her shoulder, smiling through her anxiety. We each let out a sigh, able to breathe again. We pulled up and as she opened the doors, the sunlight burned my eyes.

We piled out, and calmly split up, heading off in separate directions. Another of our vans pulled into the lot but remained hidden from view, ready to disarm the guards on the checkpoint outside.

The atmosphere changed. The air felt heavy, almost suffocating. There was a rumble, faint and low. We could hear the shouts in the distance; the ground began to move beneath our feet. They were coming. They filled the streets, ignoring the protests at checkpoints, choosing just to continue. Perhaps the police were just in shock, or maybe they were in awe, but they just watched them walk by, their guns hanging from their hands. There were too many to shoot, the police would be overpowered by them if they tried. Men, women, children, they all poured into the streets, marching side by side. A mob, almost the whole population of the city, had come out to support us; to act as a distraction. They stood before the checkpoint, waiting patiently, ignoring the guards yells, waiting for something to happen. Now was our time, before their courage turned to disappointment and fear. I had only a second to look at Beckett, perhaps for the last time, before he gave his command.

We ran towards the building, shouting at the guards on the door that the people were turning, that we had to be allowed inside to warn the prime minister. They ran ahead of us and with my silenced gun, were both dispatched. The lobby was empty and two of my team began to set up the explosives. I stripped off my police uniform, glancing over at Beckett as he did the same. We all stood there for a moment, bracing ourselves. The whole building was crawling with police, and we had to get in and reach Bowman before they evacuated him. I checked my watch. The other half of our team would be at the other exits of the building, setting up their explosives. The hand clicked by and as it reached the twelve, I nodded to my team.

"For the Revolution." Beckett grabbed me and kissed me hard.

"Let freedom reign," he whispered into my hair. "Don't you dare get yourself killed," he said, as he kicked in the door.

I threw the smoke grenades, covering our entrance. Screams rang out and as they shouted to one another to protect Bowman, Beckett set off the explosions. The whole building shook as each entrance was blown to pieces, blocking the exits. Elise cut the power and in the darkness, the guards shot blindly at us, their shots useless as we hid behind the pillars. The smoke cleared and we ran at them, bullets flying through the air; some ours, some theirs. I took aim at a guard, and watched as the shot ripped through his neck, sending him crashing to the ground. Another explosion made me collapse to the floor, and I rolled to one side as a young policewoman ran at me, shooting wildly at the spot where I had fallen. I slid my knife swiftly out of its sheath, and buried it into the fleshy spot beneath her armpit, brushing against the sleeve of her bullet-proof vest. Her eyes widened as the life drained from her body, and she fell back onto the floor. I could hear Erin yelling at Peter as he swung out his foot, knocking over an officer about to take a shot at him. I felt the weight of someone plough into me, almost knocking me from my feet. The officer flung his fist out wildly, connecting with my shoulder. The brass knuckles covering his fingers connected and sent pain shooting through my arm. As he tried to swing again, I ducked, and threw myself into him, knocking him to the ground. Before he could think, before he could try to stand, I shot him. The bullet penetrated between his eyes, a great gush of grey brains and vermillion blood soaking my face. His eyes were glassy, and saw no more. I stumbled to my feet, inhaling deeply, trying to remain calm.

Another bang made the ground beneath my feet shake. I fell to my knees, ducking as smoke made me choke. Beckett hauled me to my feet.

"What the fuck was that?" I spluttered, struggling to breathe. "It's not time yet!" The second explosions had gone off too early. He looked around, and neatly fired a bullet between the eyes of a police officer sprinting towards us.

"A distraction." Another, smaller explosion caused my ears to ring, his speech muffled. "He's got a plan..." he yelled at me, his voice floating in and out. "...He's trying to escape..." Suddenly, the ornate ceiling crashed down, and with a violent strength, Beckett pushed me away from him. Dust fogged the air, and I screamed his name, over and over. Through the dust I could see him battling with a guard who had run to grab him whilst he was trying to protect me. I was trapped at the foot of the stairs by the burning remains of the ceiling. I had no choice but to proceed up the stairs. Beside me lay the body of one of the guards, her body crushed by the weight of the ceiling. I was lucky that Beckett had thought so swiftly. Bowman was bringing the building down around us, and we had only helped him in his endeavour. He was going to bury us under the Houses of Parliament, whilst he made his escape.

I clambered to my feet, and tried to breathe while the air filled with acrid smoke. I turned and there, at the stop of the stairs, was the man himself, flanked by bodyguards, staring down at me with a broad smile. The largest of his minions grabbed him, and began to drag him down the corridor, as the room they had emerged from exploded in a flash of flame, stunning me for a moment. Behind me, Beckett was helping a wounded Elise, trying to fend off more guards spilling in from outside. I could see Eve, her horrible scream making everyone stop in their tracks. Philip was at her feet, motionless. Blood trickled from his mouth, and his eyes stared outwards, unseeing. It felt like a hit to the stomach, as I saw her tears streaking a path down her face. She grabbed Philip's gun, pounding bullets into the onslaught of guards. I hesitated for a moment, knowing I should turn back and help, but I knew this was my chance, my moment. The guard crushed beneath the rubble still had a gun in hand. I gently prised it from her warm fingers, and began my pursuit.

*

The dust burnt my throat, made me struggle to catch my breath. I shot the guard who had grabbed me, and watched as he fell silent. Romany was stuck on the other side of the debris, but she was alive. Shakily she stood to her feet, and it was then I saw him, watching her from the top of the stairs. His cold eyes scanned her calmly, and as his bodyguards began to surround him, she turned and froze. They stood there for a moment, watching each other, neither of them daring to make the first move. Elise's screams made me snap to attention. A large officer was beating her, his gargantuan fists pounding her face. I hesitated. I wanted to run to Romany, but I couldn't leave Elise. It would have been easy before, to leave her behind and go after Bowman, but something had changed within me. I ran to Elise, and leapt on to the back of the giant, bringing my elbow down hard on the back of his head before slamming it against the wall. Elise smiled at me weakly, pulling the fallen officer's gun from his belt. She stumbled, leaning onto me gratefully as I grabbed her, stopping her from falling. I looked back at the rubble, and watched helplessly as Romany sprinted up the stairs after him. Bowman and his bodyguards armed and angry, against one fearless girl. She was the best we had, but she was still just a girl to me. My girl. Elise was steady and pushed me towards the stairs.

"Go!" she shouted as she began to head towards another corridor. "We'll flush the rest of them out, just go help her!" She disappeared, followed by the others who had yet to vanish into the rabbit warrens of the building.

*

The clock tower has 334 stairs. And as Bowman fled up them, with me in pursuit, I could feel every single one, turning my legs to jelly. He was quicker than me, dragged along by his henchmen. I could hear their voices echoing, as I tried to keep my footsteps light and silent.

A gruff voice, one I didn't recognise, was shouting to a crackling radio. "Helicopter in five minutes, blow the clock."

I braced myself, flattening myself against the wall as a blast nearly made me topple backwards down the 300 stairs I had climbed. Cold air hit my face, and I heard them begin to move again.

I found them at the top, shattered glass covering the floor, wind blowing through the destroyed clock face. I tiptoed behind them, holding my breath.

"Where the fuck are they?" screamed Bowman, shaking one of his bodyguards by the lapels of his jacket. There was no sign of a helicopter; the perfect sky was empty apart from a flock of birds and the odd cloud. He leant out of the clock face, looking down at the packed streets below. I could hear the shouts of the mob, their voices carrying up to us. Over and over they shouted the words 'Let freedom reign'.

"Oh god..." he gasped, brushing off the grasps of his guards, "...those bastards!" He whirled around and his face blanched as he saw me. He clicked his fingers, and shrank back as, before they could retrieve their guns, I dispatched his guards. Eyes wide, skin pale, he stared in disbelief at their bodies. I expected him to fall to his knees, to beg me to spare his life as Hardwicke had. But his eyes met mine, and they were empty. Not scared, not angry, but completely soulless.

"What is it you think you're going to achieve?" He stepped closer to me, and I aimed at his head. "There's a hundred men and women, just like me, ready to take my place. If you get rid of me, you'll have to rid yourself of whoever succeeds me, and the one who replaces them." My hands were shaking a little, I tried to steady them. "This won't be over for you, not even if I am dead and buried."

His arrogant eyes bored into me, and a smile crept over his face.

"Then I have a proposition for you..." His right eyebrow rose, as though it were pulled up by an invisible string. "As you clearly find me so laughable..." I placed the gun on the floor, placing the knives I had carefully hidden beside it. "...fight me like a man." I smiled

266

broadly, adrenaline working its magic. He removed his jacket, and the gun he too was wearing. He smiled back, but it was hollow and did not meet his eyes.

"You know, it really is going to pain me, to mess up a face as lovely as yours." He rolled up his sleeves.

"Fuck. You. Mr. Prime Minister." I took a run at him, but before I could land my punch, his fist swung into my stomach with enough force to send me backwards off my feet. I was stunned, struggling to breathe. I tried to stand to my feet, but my aching legs betrayed me.

"Did you really think I'd be stupid enough not to learn a thing or two?" He wiped the back of his hand on his mouth, before running his fingers through his hair. "Did you think I wouldn't prepare myself? And you'll never guess who trained me?" Names ran through my head, blinding me with confusion. "Matthew." The name hit me harder than his fist had. "You stupid girl," he said venomously, "he was the head of my security in the early days. He was all for showing me the ropes, in case I ever needed to defend myself." He watched as I tried to clamber to my feet, kicking me back to the floor. "Why do you think he worked so hard to bring me down? The man felt nothing but guilt for helping me become what I am today. He taught me how to fight, how to know my enemies - just like he taught you." Fuck. My brain screamed. He knows who you are. "Why do you think you managed to get that job in the first place? I'd been keeping tabs on you ever since Matthew took you in. When his son disappeared from my radar, well, I watched you even closer," he smiled. "I knew who you were as soon as I laid my eyes on you."

"Why didn't you arrest me?" I asked, back on my feet.

"It was much more fun to see what you'd do." He cracked his knuckles. "It was so amusing, hearing back from Harry about you. I put him as close to you as I could and he served me well. When he told me what he wanted in return, well, I had a feeling you'd be able to fend for yourself. I can't say I'm terribly sad about his death - he was a total prick." The taste of vomit made me swallow hard. "I thought killing your parents would've been a warning to Matthew that I was on to him and his little Revolution, but apparently he was more of a fool than I could have imagined."

My kick took out his legs, and I watched as he landed on his back, dangerously close to the edge of the gaping hole that had once been a clock face. He laughed as he pulled himself up, and I felt the rush of pain in my knuckles as my fist connected with his jaw. He spat blood on the floor and a shooting pain made my eyes water as his forehead cracked against mine. "You stupid little whore!" he screamed. "Matthew couldn't take me down, and he was the best fighter I've ever known. You don't stand a chance." He hit me again, before I had a chance to steady myself. I felt to the ground and curled in a ball as his feet kicked me, in the back, in the stomach. "*I'm the prime minister!*" he screamed, his face contorted with rage.

Fight back, my conscience yelled at me. Get up! But I couldn't, I couldn't find the energy in me to fight back. I wanted to, so much, but as his blows rained down on me, my body weakened. I could hear moans, my own mouth betraying me. To my horror, I was crying. I coughed, splattering blood across the floor. The morning sunlight made it glisten the colour of a ruby.

He crouched over me, rolling me onto my back by my hair. "Looks like Matthew put just a little more effort into training me," he said. "You're a pretty thing though, I wasn't lying when I told you that. It's a shame you know, you could have gone far working for me." He pushed his mouth onto mine and I relished his yelp as I bit down hard on his bottom lip. My brief moment of triumph vanished as the back of his hand struck me, making my ears ring. Blood poured out from somewhere on me, and I looked at it dreamily. A diminutive butterfly that had fluttered in on the breeze and made the dreadful decision to land beside me, crawled through the crimson ooze, its tiny wings stained by my blood.

Behind him, I could see the hazy outlines of two people, stepping towards us. A beautiful woman and a man, wearing little glasses. They were holding hands, their eyes full of warmth and love. The woman placed her hand over her heart and smiled sadly. They had come for me; they were ready to take me home. I thought of Beckett and felt sad - but perhaps this was the only way I could be free. Bowman was still yelling at me, speaking in nonsensical clichés. My father gripped my mother's shoulders and rubbed them gently. He whispered into her ear and together they mouthed an 'I love you' to me, before evaporating, leaving nothing behind but their memory.

"Let me show you what happens to my enemies, you little bitch," Bowman hissed, grabbing me by the collar.

*

He dragged her across the cold floor, and hauled her to her knees, forcing her to look out at the crowds in the street. Their shouts went silent as he screamed at them, demanding their attention. Blood seeped down her face, and she moaned as he ripped her head back, gripping her hair by the scalp. I could hear the crowd gasping, screaming in horror.

"Did you think the fucking Revolution could get rid of me? You belong to me!" he hollered, smoothing back his hair. He leant forward and whispered in her ear. "You stupid girl," he hissed. "Once I'm done with you, I'm going to go and find the rest of your friends, and I am going to watch the vans take them away. I'm going to stand outside their cells and listen to them scream and sob and beg me to let them go. Your boy is going to rot in one of my cells, if he isn't dead already." He forced her face up to his and spat in it. "Did you know this is how my dear old dad ended up? Couldn't stand what his little boy had become, so he threw himself out the window of his penthouse apartment -the apartment that *I'd* bought him. Ingrate." He pulled her closer to the ledge, ignoring her struggles. "Apparently he looked like a piece of road kill afterwards." Her hands gripped the sides as he stepped back, pulling out his gun. "I suppose you're going to look the same. Pity." He took aim at the back of her head, and his finger squeezed the trigger. The shot rang out in the silence.

*

Beckett stepped out from the shadows, Bowman screaming as the bullet passed through his knee. As he fell to the floor, I used every last vestige of strength left in my body to scramble to my feet, and pulled him backwards, until his head and shoulders were 96.3 metres from the ground; dangling in midair. His legs began to struggle and Beckett dashed forward, helping to hold him so he couldn't take me with him.

"You took everything from me," I began to sob, my hair tossed wildly around my face, which was warm and sticky with blood, "from all those people out there." His skin was sweating and pallid, his eyes panicked. He was strong, and I used all my energy as I forced his arms back down. "And do you know what we're going to do when you're gone?" He looked up at me, furious. "We're going to start taking back what is ours, and we are going to make sure nothing like this can ever happen again."

A calm, serene feeling came over me. I looked over at Beckett, at his bruised and bloody face. I was ready to end this. With one push, we together shoved Bowman backwards over the ledge, out of the gaping hole that had once been the face of our most famous landmark. I leaned over the precipice, watching as he fell through the air, his screams silenced as his body hit the concrete below. The crowd went quiet, and I could see Elise hobbling forward, kneeling beside his broken corpse, checking for his pulse. She stood to her feet, staring up at us. As the crowd broke out in a triumphant roar, Beckett pulled me to him, grabbing me in a fierce embrace.

"Don't you ever do that to me again; I thought he was going to kill you," he sobbed between kisses.

271

"Me too." I held him tight, and tried to focus for a moment. "The cabinet?" I asked, terrified I was celebrating too soon.

"Dead. The fire has taken care of them. He sacrificed them all to save himself." He kissed my forehead. "It's over Romany, we're free."

He pulled me to him again, his strong arms wrapped around my shoulders. I looked back at the pool of my blood, but the butterfly was gone. It had flown away, to another place, better or worse - but away from here. It too, was free.

We made our way back down the tower, and stood with the crowd, watching the Houses of Parliament burn up in a glorious funeral pyre. There was a sense of anticipation, the feeling that anything could happen. I looked around, at Peter and Erin who were kissing one another as though they would eat each other up. At Etienne and Christina, who were staring at each other as though they'd seen each other for the first time. Elise wrapped her arms around Eve, comforting her and celebrating all at the same time, torn between grief and joy. Everything had changed, and our lives were ours again. It was up to us all to make it count, I thought as Beckett gathered me up in his arms.

*

A girl ran through the field. Her little grass-stained legs stumbled as she hopped over the stile. She could smell the sea; she was close. Her dress snagged on a branch, making her eyebrows knit together and her tiny mouth press into a little pout. She was in a hurry; she didn't need silly things like that happening. She kicked off her shoes, and scurried over the sand, and there they were. Sat side by side on a blanket, cuddled up together. They were staring out across the sea, which seemed to sparkle like a sapphire. Her mother looked over her shoulder and waved, her smile as bright as the sun that day. Her dad pulled her mum up by the hand, and she laughed as her mummy squealed, struggling and kicking, as he dropped her into the shallow bit of the ocean- barely deep enough for paddling. Sometimes, she thought to herself, grownups could be silly.

One day though, she would be a grown up, and she would be able to do anything she liked. She could be a doctor, or a teacher - she could even be a superhero and save the world. Yes, she decided decisively, that was what she would do. And so that little girl strode down the beach and nestled close to her dad, inhaling her mother's perfume and squealing as she wrapped her cold, wet arms around her. She was a loved girl, who had a future in which she could do anything ahead of her. She closed her eyes and fell asleep on the beach, cuddled in the sun by her parents.

*

Four Years Later

The sharp tang of sea air filled my nostrils, the breeze teasing my hair. I stepped onto the sand, and felt the warmth of it between my toes. A black cloud hovered on the horizon, threatening to rain on our sunny day. As I reached the foam, I took a tentative step into the ocean. The water was cold, but beneath the heat of the sun it was refreshing. I pulled my sweater over my head and stood in my bathing suit, my arms flung open wide. I was exposed, covered only by flimsy pieces of fabric. The sun beat down on my back, and I stared out into the horizon. I could feel her standing beside me, but I didn't want to look around and break the spell.

"It really is as wonderful as you said babe." I turned my head, willing her to be there, but there was nothing but the vast expanse of coastline, beneath the crumbling cliffs. I could hear someone calling my name, and dreamily I turned to them. There he stood, bare-chested and beautiful. I waved to him, smiling to myself as he placed his hands on his hips.

A small child dashed across the sand, his steps unsteady and clumsy as he struggled to find his footing. His little face was screwed up in a scowl of concentration as he tried not to slip over. His mouth muttered words to an invisible audience as he tripped over, landing on his hands and knees. But, ever a brave, boisterous boy, he pulled himself up and resumed his course. Innocent to the horrors that had past, he had a bright future, his hands were clean of blood. My son peered up at me shyly, before flashing me a heartbreaking smile. His father's smile.

***

Danielle Carter